HI.
WICKED
GAMES

VIOLET E.C.

Contents

ASIN:
ISBN: 9798358305465
Imprint: Independently published
Cover art by Vivien Reis on Fiverr

Playlist

Hold Me Down – Halsey
Secrets – The Weeknd
Daylight – Harry Styles
Kiss & Tell – Mokita
Until The Sun Comes Up – Gabrielle Aplin
Die4U – Bring Me The Horizon
Drop Dead – Holly Humberstone
Could This Be Love – The Wanted
Chose To Stay (Acoustic) – April Jai
STAY (with Justin Bieber) – The Kid LAROI
I Need You To Hate Me – JC Stewart
Scene Four - Don't You Ever Forget About Me – Sleeping
With Sirens
Healing – FLETCHER

Listen to this playlist on Spotify® using the Spotify Code
below:

"The course of true love never did run smooth." —
William Shakespeare

To my Dad,
for your endless encouragement, your inspiration, and your
absolute joy of everything to do with literature.
I hope you can see from up there how proud I am of what
I'm achieving, because of you.

This book contains scenes of a mature nature that some readers might find distressing.
Please read at your own discretion.

PROLOGUE

eath.
The thought unwillingly invaded her mind and she tried to crush the despair that flooded her body as she glanced around the cold, dark cell.

The cramped space was lit only by the setting sun's orange glow trying to shine through the small sliver of a window. A wrist could perhaps fit through the narrow gap, nothing more.

The dungeon smelt like death mixed with rotting bodies and damp. The eerie dripping sound only added to the increasing fear pulsing through her veins. The low moans, shallow breathing, and occasional scream kept her on edge, her skin prickling at the back of her neck. She wrapped her arms around her knees, making herself as small as possible, and, pressing her forehead to them, she mumbled a quick prayer up to any of the Gods who would listen to her.

A deep, damning thought settled in her stomach,

turning it sour and making her blood run cold as she listened to the scraping of the metal lock and the heavy wooden door creak open. She was going to die here. And no one would hear her screams.

~

He paced the floor, anxiously awaiting her return. The room was silent, save for the flutter of his wings as he fidgeted, his small silver wings flapping softly in the air.

She should be home by now, his fingers drummed on the countertop as he stared out of the window. The cloudless sky was painted pink with streaks of orange, the sun setting and she still wasn't back.

Any second now he expected to hear the click of the latch on the door, feel the soft embrace of her arms around him, and smell her scent of baked goods and sunshine.

His stomach twisted, dread sitting like a stone in his gut. *They've got her.* He knew it, he felt it in his heart, in his bones.

Whatever magic they were doing at the palace, it wasn't the good kind and he'd told her to be careful. Begged her to come straight home after her shift had finished, and not go snooping.

When one of the other maids had disappeared, she'd been curious, felt that she owed it to her friend to go searching for her. He'd warned her, told her to mind her business, and yet she hadn't. It would cost her her life and now he was waiting in their empty home as the sun set on the horizon,

planning his payback.
He'd make them pay and he'd do it well.

CHAPTER ONE
A NIGHT AT CUCKOO

The delicious scent of freshly baked bread and sweet ambrosia cakes greeted me as I flew down the spiral stairs and into the busy kitchen. My mom was already up, flapping around the space as she baked delicious goods for the early risers in the Kingdom of Nissa.

The queue would be out of the door in half an hour or so, as it always was and I hurried to snag myself a cake before they all sold out. I subtly pocketed it, knowing it would be a sticky mess later. *It'll still taste good, though.* My stomach growled in response.

"Those pastries aren't going to bake themselves, Zinnia." My mom scolded me. We still had time before the shop opened, but my famous apricot and basil pastries were always a favorite. A weird mix to the ear, but they sold out in a matter of minutes, flying off the counter faster than we could keep up.

My mom, however, loved to be over-organized and so she'd prepped the mix as per my recipe and left me to roll them out, prep and spread the glaze on them, and put them in the oven.

"Good morning to you too," I grumbled. I was not a morning person *obviously*. "And it's Zia." I reinforced, trying to emphasize that I preferred my nickname over my birth name. It was a losing battle but one day, I hoped my mom would take it on board. It was no offense to her name picking, just my preference. The sun was barely up and she was bustling around like her ass was on fire.

I rubbed my eyes, still slightly crusty with sleepy dust and I heard her huff.

"Go and wash your face then come back. I don't need sleepy daughters burning my pastries." She pinned me with that look that said we'd been there before and of course, we had. I'd once slept late, staying up with Flora and woken early to bake. I'd fallen asleep while the pastries were cooking, resulting in a smokey room and a very red-faced Mom. Safe to say, she didn't let me stay up with Flora on working days anymore.

Speaking of my sister, she walked into the kitchen, limping slightly on her skinny legs. Her condition meant that she couldn't fly, her wings refused to flap. Fae's legs weren't meant for excessive use, hence why we had wings, and so her legs suffered.

My parents had taken her to every healer in the kingdom, offering all of our savings for help, but no one, not one single fae could understand why her wings wouldn't work. Flora was a mystery and one that wasn't getting better.

Her illness was worsening, though no one liked to say it out loud, Flora spent her days in bed more often than not, and she was always tired and weak. My heart constricted in my chest as she stumbled up the step that led into our kitchen, and I reached out to catch her delicate arm. It felt thin and so fragile in my hands. She was seventeen but looked about twelve and it broke my heart to see her like that.

"I'm okay." She whispered and I tried to give her a little of my magic, like a booster to help her through the day. I saw the glow between our skin- the transfer of magic, but nothing happened. Unfortunately, this wasn't the first time I'd tried to help her. It was like her body just couldn't accept magic. She didn't have any magic of her own either, which made everything all the more difficult when it came to thinking about her future.

"Flora, what are you doing up? You needn't be out of bed until the sun is up." My mom came to our side, cupping her youngest daughter's cheek. Her palm glowed too and I knew she was trying what I'd just failed to do too. Every day we tried, hoping one day, my sister's body would accept our magic and begin to heal.

She smiled brightly, but her hollow cheeks and dull skin spoke differently.

"I'm fine Mom, I came to help out." She said softly, but my mom's head was shaking back and forth before she'd even finished speaking.

"Absolutely not, remember what healer Aria said? She told you to conserve your energy. We don't need extra help today." My mom was lying, we did need extra help, just not from my sister. If she helped today, she'd be spending the rest of the week sleeping and making up for her one day of work.

"*Zia*," my mom rolled her eyes at me, saying my name slowly and I sighed. "Can you take your sister back to her room? Wash and then come down and make those pastries, please. It's market day today, so I need an extra batch." She fluttered about, flying over to the oven to check on her next batch of cakes, and I nodded.

Flora's body was light as I scooped her up and flew out of the kitchen, up the stairwell, and to our bedrooms. She didn't protest anymore but instead leaned her head against my chest as I carried her.

Our house was modest, with the bakery front attached. It wasn't fancy or even very big, but it was home and I loved it. I heard my dad flying around on the middle floor as I flapped my wings and landed at the top of the house. The spiral staircase was in the center and the house was almost like a ring around it.

I pushed open Flora's room with my foot, which was decorated in beautiful vines and flowers, courtesy of my magic. Lesser faes, a.k.a me, didn't have extensive magic, but we could do a few things and so I made Flora's room as homely as possible. We were not like the Royal line, who could- according to my friend Lilac- bind lesser faes into deals and even create magic from nothing.

The vines in Flora's room were from a tree outside our house, I didn't create them from scratch, they were just an extension of nature. I simply bent them to my will and made them evergreen so the flowers never wilted. An eternal summer for my sister.

I gently placed Flora back on her piles of soft cushions and brushed a strand of her dark auburn hair from her face, tucking it behind her pointed ear.

"I snagged something for you, while Mom wasn't looking," I whispered, grinning conspiratorially, and produced the ambrosia cake from my pocket. I knew they were her favorites and our mom forgot to save one extra for her. I was going to eat it myself, but Flora deserved it more. She smiled again, her cheeks pulling into the smallest of grins. It was worth it to see her smile.

"Sneaky sis, thank you." She whispered back and I pressed a kiss to her forehead, trying just one more time to push some magic into her. But it fizzled out as soon as it hit her skin and I sighed.

"Yell if you need me," I said as I flew out of her room, leaving her to eat the cake and I headed for the bathroom.

The steamy room was by far my favorite room in the house, the decor was green and leafy, vines intertwined and wrapped around the bathtub and the steam added an extra mist that made the room ethereal. I contemplated my family's problems whilst looking at myself in the mirror and brushing my long red hair. It was brighter than Flora's and made my green eyes stand out when the sun shone on it. My mom always said it matched my fiery personality, whatever that meant.

My mom and dad weren't poor but weren't exactly rich either. The bakery helped us scrape by, but the healers had cost so much and for nothing. My mom insisted they had helped, but I knew they were as confused as we were. No one had seen my sister's condition before. They had wanted to poke and prod her but we'd refused. She wasn't an experiment, she was a fae, a sweet one at that, and she didn't deserve to be dissected for the curiosity of healers.

Every month, the healers came by to collect their money and bring the potions for Flora, and every month, my parents lost a little more of their savings trying to keep us afloat. I knew Flora blamed herself, regardless of how much we told her she wasn't to blame. It wasn't her burden to bear alone and we loved her no matter what. But I worried one day, our savings just wouldn't be enough…

A bang downstairs interrupted my thoughts, I heard my mom yelling my name and I quickly scrubbed my face, brushed my teeth, and swooped back down to the kitchen, ready for a long day.

~

A familiar head popped through the back door as I just finished serving a customer.

"Zia!" He fake-whispered and I grinned.

I called my mom to the front of the shop, telling her that I'd be taking my break. I grabbed a paper bag for my lunch and stuffed some leftovers in there.

"Don't be too long, we've got more bread to bake." She pressed a kiss to my cheek as I flew by.

"I won't!"

One of my closest friends, Dillon, stood outside the kitchen, head tilted up to the sunlight. He turned to face me as I landed on my feet. His light blond hair almost glinted in the sun and he smiled at me.

The sun was crazy hot today, sitting high in the sky, and so we settled on a bench in the shade of the garden. We were surrounded by flowers and trees, creating a beautiful display of colors and aromas. I absentmindedly touched a pink flower, using my magic, and grew two more blooming peonies next to it. Their fragrance was beautiful, and I smiled contentedly.

I passed him a bun from my bag, stuffed with a tart crushed berry spread and honey and Dillon took a bite, sighing as he munched on it. Yep, my mom's bread was *the* best.

"How are you today?"

Dillon was younger than me, he and Flora had become friends as kids, spending lots of his days at our house and gradually, we'd become friends too. We spent more time outside the house together and he spent more time inside with Flora. It all worked out.

"Good, the bakery's busy as usual." I sighed, grateful to have a job, but aching for that taste of freedom.

"You could always sneak away…" He trailed off, knowing how much I craved to travel, to be free of the constraints my family put on me.

But our conversation was like a broken record, me complaining, Dillon suggesting, and yet, it never got further than that.

Dillon took a big bite of his bun, filling his mouth and I followed, essentially ending the repeated conversation yet again. There was no point in pining for something I couldn't achieve, I had no money, no experience, no purpose. It made sense to stay where I was, working in the bakery, but

Gods, did I want more.

"Did you hear? Another fae went missing yesterday, again from the Edge." I hadn't heard yet, but the missing faes were alarming. Though I wasn't sure, it seemed that it was mainly faes from the Edge- a part of the city where fae who had no money or homes tended to beg for food or housing for the night. The thought of one of them being snatched for whatever nefarious reasons sent a shiver down my spine.

"And I heard they arrested another one." Dillon spoke quietly, even though no one was around, I nodded, having heard the news of the arrest from a customer this morning.

The rebels had got worse, got more confident and a few had been caught trying to sneak into the palace dance last week. Everyone knew they were planning to take down the throne and unrest made the city feel tense. All the faes were on high alert and no one wanted to be caught sympathizing.

"I don't know what they think they'll achieve." I shrugged, munching on my bread. "But they seem to be willing to die trying."

The point of contention in the city was why the rebels opposed the throne so badly. No one could quite understand why they wanted to kill off the Royal bloodline. Their rule wasn't so bad, the latest King was stern but fair, not overtaxing the lesser faes or pretending we didn't exist.

"Wouldn't you die for what you believe in?" Dillon asked and I turned to him, wondering if I would put my life on the line like that.

"Depends on what I was believing in," I answered. I'd simply never felt passionately enough to want to die for something.

Dillon opened his mouth to say something but was cut off.

"There you are!" A high-pitched voice interrupted us and I saw my other best friend, Lilac, flying up the garden path.

"I told you I was having lunch here." Dillon shrugged and Lilac laughed.

"Not you silly, I was looking for Zia."

"Here I am." I smiled and she landed next to me, her wings folding into her back so that they lay flush against her.

"Scooch up, we have important things to discuss." She sat on the bench, wedging herself in between Dillon and me so that we both had to slide to the edges of the bench to fit three bodies on a two-person seat.

"Such as?" I enquired, watching as my purple-haired friend began to braid her long locks and gazed out into the garden.

"Your birthday of course!" Lilac grinned and I mentally slapped myself for forgetting my birthday was tomorrow, *how do you forget your own birthday?*

"Ah yes, about that," Dillon began. "I think we should lay low, perhaps throw a party here-"

"Hush, Dillon. We're celebrating her twentieth year, not some minor event. We're going out," Lilac interrupted him and turned to me, her purple eyes shimmering as she imagined our wild night out.

I wasn't opposed to the idea, I liked to go out sometimes, but with the rebel attacks, the city's nightlife had quieted down.

"So, I was thinking we could go to Cuckoo or there's a party happening down at the river, we could crash it." Her grin read mischief and mayhem, and I wondered how Lilac hadn't ended up being arrested for being a menace. Wherever this beautiful fae went chaos followed. You couldn't be fooled by her honeyed looks, she was a force to be reckoned with.

"I still think we should stay in-"

"I didn't ask you, Dillon," Lilac's tone was sharp and Dillon's mouth snapped shut. He was still getting used to my new friend's personality. Lilac and I had only become close recently and we were still figuring out our dynamic as a trio.

"I think going out could be nice-" I nodded.

"It's settled then." Did she ever not interrupt? "We'll go out tomorrow night." She clapped her hands in glee and rose from her seat, hovering over us.

"I'll come by tomorrow with some outfit options and we can pick one together! Ooh, this is going to be so much fun!" She grinned and flew off down the path, back into the bustling street.

"She really is something," Dillon blew out a breath and I laughed. She really was.

"Zia, are you sure it's a good idea to be going out? Especially at a time like this?" His concern was sweet and not uncalled for, but I felt trapped at home. We'd been busy, working harder than usual to meet our monthly payments and I wanted one night, just one night to relax. I knew having a party at home would only remind me of our problems, plus my mom would make us all be in bed at sundown like we were children.

"I think you should go out!" An airy voice called from above us and I glanced up to see Flora poking her head out of her circular window. Her hair was hanging down by her face, a smug smile painted on her lips. "I can distract Mom."

"Were you eavesdropping, little sister?" I teased and she grinned, her cheeks glowing red.

"It's not eavesdropping if you're talking right under my window!" She yelled back and I laughed.

"Well it's settled then, we're going out."

∼

Cuckoo was a bar, made out of a carved-out oak tree in the center of the city, packed with rich faes who liked the party on the weekend.

Although it was full of the upper faes, the venue itself wasn't fancy or even expensive. We hadn't paid to get in, just got there early and waited in the queue.

I instantly felt out of place, even dressed in Lilac's beautiful, magic-made dress. Her mother was a seamstress, and so Lilac had the most beautiful custom garments. She had used a little extra of her magic to make it fit just right for me. It was navy blue with silver thread through it, it complimented my hair and made me feel like I was wearing the midnight starry sky. Right after I'd told her it was too much, she'd announced it was her birthday present to me and I couldn't say anything except for how much I loved it.

Lilac's bright cream mini-dress looked divine against her dark skin and I was envious of my curvy, mischievous friend. She always turned heads wherever we went and she lapped up the attention.

The venue was packed, considering it was a Saturday night and the music was loud, with a live band in the corner. Dillon had put on his best shirt and gifted me two pretty silver hair clips to match my dress. They glittered in the party lights as I caught my reflection in a mirror on one of the walls. I looked sophisticated, more grown-up, and mysterious than my twenty years of age, but for tonight, I was someone else. Someone different.

Dillon yelled to us that he'd grab some drinks and made his way over to the bar, swerving and ducking as he flew through the packed crowd of fae partygoers. Lilac began to swing her hips to the beat of the music and I joined in, letting myself get lost in the rhythm. My wings flapped to the beat as we danced. Some faes hovered above us, others sat on ledges carved out of the tree. Cuckoo was so different from anything I'd seen before and I loved it.

Dillon brought back three cups of sweet mead and we toasted to my birthday, celebrating another year around the moons.

The music was loud and intoxicating, Dillon didn't dance, but he stayed close, perusing the crowd like he was looking for someone, as Lilac and I danced like no one was watching.

The night became a blur, one song merging into another. At one point, Dillon brought us water and we gulped it greedily like we'd been thirsty for days, our mouths as dry as the desert. He yelled something about the music being enchanted, but we laughed, caught in a daze of music and joy.

It was one of the first times I really felt free for a long time. No weight on my shoulders, no thinking about my family's debts, my desire for freedom, or Flora's problems. Just me, my friends, and the sweet music.

As Lilac danced to a sexy tune with a fellow fae who looked far too drunk and all too interested in what was under her dress, a tap on my shoulder interrupted my reverie.

A tall, stern-looking fae in a dark outfit beckoned

me with a finger. I glanced at Dillon and Lilac, unsure of what to do and the former was at my side in an instant.

"Not him. Only the females." The fae's voice was low and his tone told me that he didn't ask twice. But before I could even think about asking Dillon what to do, Lilac grabbed my arm and dragged me across the dancefloor, following the guard, a mischievous grin played on her lips.

I threw a fleeting and apologetic glance at Dillon who looked clueless and lost, standing in the middle of the dancefloor. He'd probably go home, which was for the best considering I knew he didn't really like to dance. Lilac would take care of me, she'd make sure I got home okay. I was in safe hands. Or so I thought.

The guard led us up a set of wooden curved staircases, through an intricately carved door, and into a room that was dark and overlooked the dancefloor we were just on.

The music was quieter in here, muted, and allowed the partygoers inside to talk. There were velvet sofas, where people lounged and held their drinks. It looked fancy and I immediately began to back away, aware that we were out of our league here. I didn't want to be owing someone something for even being in the room.

I hurriedly glanced around, looking for the guard who led us up here, but he was nowhere in sight. Instead, a gorgeous, if not slightly drunk fae swaggered up to us. Even in the dark light, I could see his large golden wings, flapping boldly on his back.

Lesser faes had small, silver wings, while higher faes had huge, golden wings that covered the expanse of their backs. They always wore them proudly, knowing they held rank over us. A spike of jealousy ran through me at how just by birth, these faes had an easier life, were blessed with beautiful wings, and were destined for great things.

The fae gave us a once over, his features even and sharp. His white-blond hair curled around his pointed ears, giving him a sweet, good-boy look that I was sure was a pretense. A hint of a smile appeared on his face as he took in Lilac, her gorgeous, goddess-like figure with curves in all the right places. She was insanely beautiful and males dropped to their knees for her regularly. But she didn't want anyone, she wanted a higher fae or even better; a Royal.

I, for one, did not care about the status of a fae. But ever since my mom got wind that Lilac had her eye on a higher fae to marry, she'd got it into her head that I could do the same. Really, I think she wanted me out of the house and married off so she had one less mouth to feed, and less financial strain, and wow, did that hurt to think about.

Lilac giggled and the fae took her hand from her

side, brushing his lips over her knuckles in a kiss. It was intimate and I felt a blush crawl up my cheeks. Gods, to be touched like that by a fae male was something of my dreams.

Let's be real here, I was not in any way a prude but I'd just never met my match. Someone who really got me, didn't placate me, and certainly didn't hold me down.

After my mom's attempted matches- and yes, there had been many. I'd decided that finding my own partner would be more successful than her pathetic attempts at playing cupid. Don't get me wrong, I loved my mother, but she didn't get me and my courting preferences at all.

Lilac fluttered away, following the enticing fae male and I was left on my own. I glanced around the room again, trying to look inconspicuous as I watched the higher faes interact. I wondered if this was a normal night for them, not a treat to celebrate their birthday.

Just as I considered how much one of their outfits would cost, a waiter flew to me with a tray carrying a flute of golden, bubbling liquid.

"From the gentleman in the corner." He said and I took the glass, my eyes shooting over to the corner where a large, burly fae who looked like he liked too many cakes was waving at me. *Ugh, just my luck.*

I held the cool glass in my hand but didn't take a sip as I watched him fly over. His wings looked as if they struggled under the weight of his body and

I stifled an inappropriate laugh at the ridiculous sight in front of me.

He landed a few steps away, and boy, he was even uglier up close. His features were flat and almost concave as he grinned, his thin lips spread over his teeth like he was planning on devouring me. I stepped back as he stepped forward and suddenly we were in a game of cat and mouse.

I slid to the left and he followed, his grin getting wider as he delighted in the game. *This is all I need, some idiot getting off on the fact that I want to avoid him.* My heart began to race in my chest as no one else paid us any heed in this ridiculous dance. I faked right and went left, his hand snaked out and grabbed a handful of my ass. I gasped, shocked by his audacity. No one and I mean *no one* had touched me like that. It took me so much by surprise that I lost my footing and stumbled over my dress, crashing into a shoulder next to me.

I spun around, all thoughts of the game forgotten as I went to apologize profusely. *This is exactly why I don't socialize with the higher part of society, I'm such a clutz.*

Furious, dark eyes met mine and I cowered as the fae I knocked into seethed. His beautifully embroidered shirt was covered in both my untouched drink and his very expensive drink, the dark liquid stained the luxurious fabric. I bit my lip, knowing that would be another cost if this fae decided to charge me for it. Which I didn't doubt, considering the fuming look on his face.

"I am so sorry, I wasn't looking-" I blabbed, panicking about what this fae might do if I didn't start groveling. He was fuming, staring me down with those intense eyes. As he stared down at me, I took inventory of his features; angular nose, shoulder-length dark hair which was tied into a loose ponytail at the nape of his neck. Strong cheekbones paired with intimidating eyes, which in the dim light of the room, I couldn't tell if they were black naturally or just because he was staring at me like he was wishing I was dead.

The room felt too small and even though about three people had noticed our collision, it felt as if the whole party was watching us.

Without saying a word, he grabbed my upper arm, dragging me into a side room that I hadn't even noticed was there, slamming the door shut behind us.

"You." He seethed and I swallowed thickly, panic bubbling in my gut. Oh Gods, was he going to hit me? Or worse, use his magic on me? We were forbidden from using magic on others unless it was for good, like healing, or in defense if you were being attacked. But I was sure that wouldn't stop a higher fae like him. Especially with that look on his face.

"You owe me big time."

Chapter Two
The Deal

"I'm sorry, I didn't-"

He waved his hand in front of us, dismissing my pathetic attempts to resolve the situation. "Do you know how much this shirt cost?"

I opened my mouth to answer "fucking expensive", but then thought better of it and snapped it shut, shaking my head. *Best not to poke the troll.*

"Yeah well you wouldn't, you wouldn't even be able to comprehend such luxurious clothes." I frowned, catching onto his insinuation as I glanced down at my dress. No, it wasn't luxurious, but it was beautiful and a heartfelt gift.

"And this was my favorite shirt." He added. I highly doubted it was, but I didn't want to get myself into any more trouble than I was already in. He was being contrarian and it was winding me up. I wanted nothing more than to speak exactly what was on my mind but I kept my lips sealed, trying to dampen down my raging temper.

He watched me with calculating eyes and I felt nervous for some reason; my hands fidgeted with the fabric of my dress and my skin warmed just a little too much. Gods, I was a weak, anxious wreck around rich, cruel males.

I could tell he was cocky and arrogant, and I hated it. But I couldn't lie, he was devastatingly handsome. My heart did a strange thump as I ran my eyes over his face for the second time tonight. He was tall, towering over me, broad but slim on the hips. I felt a flutter in my stomach as I took in every aspect of this arrogant stranger.

"When you're done gawking, we'll discuss the matter at hand. Or am I just too hard to resist?"

The arrogance of this male! I wanted to slap him right there and then and tell him to go to the fiery depths of the Abyss but again, I kept my mouth shut, grinding down my teeth. I'd already caused enough trouble tonight.

"I have half a mind to charge the cost of mending this shirt to you, but I know I'd probably never be able to wear it again, knowing you wouldn't be able to afford it in your lifetime."

The insults just kept rolling off his tongue and I bit mine, so very tempted to say exactly how I felt. It was dancing on the edge of my tongue, the temptation to say the worst words I knew.

I glanced at the dark stain on his shirt and I felt a tiny trickle of guilt before I stomped on it in my mind. This male did not deserve any of my guilt, he probably had thousands more shirts just waiting for him at home, all hanging up neatly in a little row. Gods, even the thought of *that* angered me and I really didn't know why.

"So, I have a different proposition." My gaze snapped to his face and his eyes wandered down my gown again, he gave me a once over and I felt irritated by the look in his eye like he was teasing me, acting like he was interested when I knew he *certainly* wasn't.

"This stays between us." He motioned between us and pinned me with such a glare that any other fae would have flown off, running for the hills, screaming. And yet, somehow I was still glued to the spot.

The stranger glared at me and I nodded dumbly. My mind raced, *what kind of proposition*? Would it involve something I didn't like? There wasn't much I could do about that anyway considering I'd ruined his favorite shirt. Gods, I wanted to slap the living daylights out of that stupid fae who was chasing me. *If I ever see him again, I swear...*

"I need to court someone, look respectable, and not like I spend most of my time in the arms of every female who crosses my path." He rolled his eyes, obviously annoyed to be spoken about like that. "So, you will pretend to be my partner until I consider your debt paid off."

Wait, what?

Was he out of his mind?

His *actual* mind?!

There was no way, no way in the deep, dark, and fiery depths of the Abyss that I'd fake-court this male. Nope, never. Not in a million years, not even for his annoyingly handsome face.

I shook my head firmly and fumbled around my body for my small coin purse, perhaps I could pay him what little money I had and then leave this whole mess behind.

"If you don't agree," he interrupted my search, and using his index finger, he tilted my chin up to face him. "I'll have to put you in a binding spell and you'll owe me until you've paid off your debt to fix my shirt."

All of this over a shirt? This was ridiculous.

"No."

He quirked an eyebrow, looking surprised at my audacity. I wondered if it was the first time he'd been told 'no', or even denied anything. *That'll teach you to walk all over me, expecting me to fall at your feet.*

"No." I reinforced myself. I would not be pretending to court this arrogant, cocky, beautiful male. *No way.*

"So you'd prefer a binding spell? Prefer to owe me for a long, *long* time, and trust me, I can make it as long as I deem necessary." His voice lowered at the end and the threat was clear.

Exasperated, I ran a hand through my hair. My options were pretty slim here. Not to mention, he was blackmailing me. I didn't have the money nor magic to fix his shirt cheaply, which would mean asking my family for help. I stopped myself mid-thought. No, my parents could never know I'd fucked up this badly. *Gods, why me?*

"Why?"

"The whys are not important, what's important is you making the right decision. I'm sure you don't want to be owing the crown for the next however many years I decide."

The crown?! Wait, hold up a second, was this… *Holy shit.*

It hit me like a kick to my chest, like a fucking boulder in my face.

Prince Asher.

I'd only seen him once, at the Royal Parade, more than a few years ago when we'd attended because Flora had begged me to take her. She'd gone on and on about it, about how much she'd wanted to see the princes in real life, and me being the dutiful sister, had accompanied her. She hadn't been disappointed as she'd gawked at their excessive wealth and dashing good looks, but I'd been thoroughly bored. Asher was grown up now, not the gangly teenage prince I'd seen on the carriage, lapping up the attention.

Flora. My heart clenched at the thought of another debt for my family, for my parents who were already weighed down by the constant need to work to meet the next payment.

Fuck. My mind was a mess, I did *not* want to be fake-courting one of the princes of Nissa. But at

the same time, the debt and the binding spell…
They were pretty serious and something told me
that Asher wouldn't go kindly on me if I rejected his
offer.

He was leaning against the wall by the door, arms
across his broad chest as he watched me.

"Why me?" I asked, blowing out a long breath
after deliberating for a moment.

"Because you owe me, and because I need someone
for a short while who can make me look good, then
you can go back to your sad existence in the outer
city like nothing ever happened."

Ouch, I pretended his callous words didn't sting.

"So let me get this straight, you want me to fake-
court you."

"No, *I'd* be fake-courting *you*. We'd be seen at
events, dinners, and dances together. Showing a
united front and all of that." He waved his hand like
he didn't care for all the semantics.

"And just until my debt is paid off?"

His smug grin told me that this was not going to
be easy. "And not a moment longer."

"But you don't even know me, or my name."

"Not important, all I need is a pretty face and
yours will do, given the situation."

Gods, was it so hard for him to give someone a
compliment without slapping them across the face
at the same time? Metaphorically, of course.

"But you have hundreds of girls at your beck and
call, why me?"

"Because you're here and you owe me. Now, are

you done with the stupid questions? I have a party to get back to."

"But I don't know anything about the Royal family," I begged, desperate to make him change his mind.

"Then you better start reading."

"I have bad breath."

"I don't care."

"I'll make up stupid lies about myself to your family, make it look like you picked an idiot."

"True, but no one will really care. It's only a temporary arrangement between us after all."

"I haven't even said yes yet." I was at my wit's end, desperate not to go through with this deal, to make him change his mind.

"From where I stand, you don't really have another choice. I'll send a guard to collect you in the morning."

"You don't even know my name!" He made no effort to look like he'd heard my final plea and he turned on his heel and without a second glance, threw open the door and rejoined the party.

As the door clicked shut again, I sighed, flopping down onto a chair next to me and putting my head in my hands. *Gods, what have I done?*

~

The morning sunlight burned my eyes as I rolled over, vaguely aware of the pounding in the back of my mind.

"Zia?"

I cracked an eye open to see Flora standing in my doorway, her halo of auburn hair scrunched up on top of her head and tied up with a vine.

"Yep, I'm awake."

"Mom told me there's a palace guard waiting for you in the bakery."

Fuck, so that wasn't a dream.

One night, all I'd wanted was just one, single night to be normal and celebrate my birthday, and instead I'd got myself caught in some elaborate lie with the Prince of the whole kingdom!

"What's going on? What happened last night? Dillon told me you went off to some private room with Lilac and they wouldn't let him in."

"Flora, what I'm about to tell you cannot leave this room, you understand?"

Her eyes widened and she stepped into my room, perching on the end of my bed. She nodded seriously. I cast a small hearing spell, creating a bubble so Flora and I could talk in private. I did it quite often, so we could talk openly without our parents listening in. The sound from the outside world dampened, my ears popped slightly and Flora leaned in closer, her eager eyes sparkling.

"Last night, I met Prince Asher and after I fucked up and spilled a drink on him, he told me I'd have to do a deal with him or else he'd put me in a binding spell forever." It rushed out of me in one breath and I watched my sister's expression change.

"Holy sh-"

"Don't swear, Flora." I scolded her, but she shrugged.

"You do it all the time."

"Yeah, well I'm older than you."

"By three years."

"And those three years count, so watch your mouth."

She rolled her eyes, obviously annoyed with my logic.

"So what's the deal Prince Asher gave you?"

I cringed, knowing she'd probably lap this up like a cat with milk. She loved the princes and anything to do with the palace.

"He told me he'd be fake-courting me for pretenses. Something about wanting to look respectable." I sighed, thinking about the whole crazy night. Straight after Asher left me with no options, I hadn't even bothered looking for Lilac. I'd gone straight home and dived into bed, not caring to change out of my dress. I'd fretted the whole flight home and got a few hours of shut-eye where my dreams were plagued by Asher and his dark eyes.

"Woah, this is insane Zia, like crazy." Flora's eyes were like moons and I knew she was in awe of this whole thing, of course, she was. "But *so* awesome." She was obsessed with the crown.

"I know, and exactly what I don't need." I threw my head back on the pillows, staring up at the domed ceiling of my room. "And it's *not* awesome," I added, but she was ignoring me. I really was screwed either way, I'd had no other choice.

"Just think- living with a prince!" Flora pretended to fan herself and I sat bolt upright.

"Live? No one said anything about living."

Her face fell, she looked a little guilty, she bit her lip and glanced at me.

"Mom said the guard told her to pack a bag for you, I assumed-"

"What?!" I interrupted her, furious that Asher was making plans without me. I leaped up off the bed, breaking the hearing spell, and flew downstairs.

I swooped into the kitchen and spotted my mom making hot tea for the palace guard who was sitting at the table, happily digging into an ambrosia cake.

He was tall and broad, dressed in the typical uniform. He looked anything but menacing though, with a big grin on his face as he sipped tea from a dainty leaf-shaped cup that looked about five times too small for his large hands. His helmet rested on the table, exposing his cropped dark blue hair. His almond-shaped eyes crinkled as he took a bite of the cake. Yep, he was a fan.

"Oh, Zinnia, good you're up. This lovely guard was just telling me that he's come to collect you to live at the palace-"

"I'm not living there." I stood firm, arms crossed,

probably looking like a walking disaster with unbrushed hair and a crumpled dress. I was tempted to cast a quick fixing spell for my hair but resisted. If I wanted to prove a point, I couldn't be looking like I was ready to go.

"But don't all kitchen staff live at the palace?" My mom asked the guard who was munching on a particularly large mouthful of cake. My eyebrows rose and I blinked a couple of times.

Kitchen staff? But I wasn't a member of the Royal Kitchen.

Unless…

My mind was working slowly this morning. Asher had obviously wanted to cover up our secret little fake affair thing, so he told everyone I was working in the kitchens.

Made sense, I guessed.

"Yes, they do if they live further away in the outer city as you do. And can I just say how amazing this cake is?" The guard mumbled through his mouthful, spraying crumbs on the table as he spoke and I huffed.

"Oh you're too kind, let me give you a couple to take back and eat on the way." My mom busied herself with packing three cakes into a bag and I gently grabbed her elbow, casting another hearing spell.

"Aren't you the slightest bit weirded out by all this?"

"Oh Zinnia, the guard told me about last night."

I went stock still, wondering if he was in on the charade.

"What exactly did he tell you?" I asked carefully, my heart thumping in my chest at the thought of her knowing how much I'd fucked up.

"He said that you had met one of the kitchen staff while you were out last night and mentioned you worked at a bakery. They said they were in need of a pair of hands and the rest is history. Why didn't you tell me such great news? A paid job for you and freedom! Just what you wanted."

My mom's pure elation at the situation grated on my nerves. On the one hand, yes she was right. I did want a paid job and to get out of the house. Although I worked at the bakery, I never took any pay because of Flora's bills, so all the money went to pay off our debt.

But on the other hand, I hated lying to her and my dad. Not to mention, her excitement at having me out of the house kind of hurt. I always thought I'd move out when I was ready, not be pushed out because of some deal with a prince.

I just *hated* the whole stupid situation.

But instead of being honest, because really who would it have helped anyway? I grinned, plastering on the fakest smile I'd ever given in my life, and broke the spell.

"I just wanted you to be surprised this morning, it really is great news."

My dad flew into the kitchen before stopping and surveying the scene. His face molded from surprise to a frown.

"Oh, Will, isn't it just the best news?" And my mom proceeded to tell my dad the whole giant web of lies that Asher had spun while I finally cast a fixing spell and excused myself to change into something more appropriate.

Back upstairs, Flora was frowning as I landed.

"What does he mean, 'kitchen staff'? You're dating-" I cut her off, pressing my hand to her mouth and indicating for her to be quiet as I brought a finger to my lips.

Casting yet another spell, yep I'd be pretty tired this evening after using all this magic, I began to get changed as I spoke.

"It seems Prince Asher has given me a cover story, so if anyone asks what I'm doing there, you guys can cover for me."

"How does that work? Does the guard know?"

I grabbed clothes from my wardrobe, peeled off last night's very crumpled dress, and slipped on a loose linen dress which was light blue, and super comfortable.

"I'm not sure, but I'll try and keep you updated. I'll see if I can visit you."

I felt Flora's arms incircle my waist, resting her head on my shoulder. She smiled at me through our reflections in the mirror in my bedroom and I sighed.

"I'm going to miss you." She sounded sad and I bit back the wave of emotions that threatened to spill in the form of tears. Yeah, I was going to miss her too. "But you're dating Prince Asher!"

I rolled my eyes and laughed.

～

The palace was nothing like how I'd pictured it in my head. After rushing to pack a bag of my belongings, I grabbed a batch of freshly baked pastries from my mom to give to the staff at the palace because everyone deserved a little pick-me-up. Everyone *apart* from Prince Asher.

The flight was long and I was tired after flying for an hour to get to the palace. My wings weren't used to such prolonged journeys, we usually stayed in our area of the outer city.

We landed at the palace gates and I stared up at the huge building. It was beautiful, huge with pillars and stone carvings of previous kings' faces. It was surrounded by grass and trees, overlooking the forest at the back of the kingdom. The flowers were in bloom and the scent was heavenly. I brushed my hand over one and my magic grew an extra flower of its own accord, adding to the beautiful bush. Other guards opened the gates. I thanked them as they let us through, smiling politely, but they watched back with blank expressions. I guessed they didn't speak to the kitchen staff then.

I'd come to learn that the guard who escorted me was Henrick and he was so lovely, if not a little overly talkative. He'd told me a lot about the Royals as we flew, keeping it professional even when I'd asked less-than-polite questions back. I'd remembered that Asher was the middle prince, between Prince Finn and Prince Cain who was the youngest and wildest. Henrick told me Cain and Asher were a force to be reckoned with, but Finn was more mature, taking his duty as future king very seriously. Gods, why hadn't I made a deal with him instead?

We flew up the steps, landing at the palace doors. I was relieved to use my legs for a while as my wings ached and felt like lead. I'd need to train them if I wanted to go back and visit my family a few times a week.

Perhaps they'd have some fancy training room where you could lift heavy objects to build wing strength. As ridiculous as it sounded, I knew the palace would be the one place that had crazy stuff like that. I glanced back at my small, silver wings and shook my head. *Perhaps not.*

My thoughts were interrupted by another guard opening the large door to reveal a female fae on the other side.

She rushed over to me, smiling widely and I instantly warmed to her.

"You must be Zinnia. I'm Laurel, I'll be helping you get settled in and will be assisting you where

I can."

"It's just Zia, actually." I corrected her and she nodded.

Henrick leaned down, whispering to me.

"If you ever need anything, don't hesitate to ask." He gave me an encouraging smile and flew off, back the way we came.

I wasn't sure if he knew about Prince Asher and my deal, considering he didn't drop me off at the servant's quarters, but I thought it was best to keep it quiet for now.

"Welcome to the palace." Laurel smiled warmly, she was probably in her middle life with a dumpy build- perfect for hugs- and beautiful blue eyes that reminded me of my mom's. I felt a pang of sadness realizing I wouldn't be seeing them every day anymore. Even though this was what I wanted- freedom, I couldn't help but feel lost and child-like without her holding my hand every step of the way.

But I was twenty, not a child anymore and I needed to take this in my stride or else we'd be homeless if we had any more debt.

No, I wouldn't let myself ruin anything for my family, so I'd suck it up and fake a romance with the prince if that was what he wanted. Didn't mean I had to *enjoy* it.

Laurel insisted on carrying my heavy bag, but I insisted on carrying my pastries so we were somewhat even. She'd laughed as I'd less-than-graciously tugged the paper bag from her iron grip.

As she weaved her way through the palace, my eyes were wide as I marveled at the decorated gilding and beautiful carvings. Flying on my back, I almost bumped into Laurel as I gaped at the gorgeous painted ceiling. It told a story of Nissa's history, of a battle but which one, I didn't know. Soon, we arrived at a long corridor, with about ten doors lining each side of it.

We flew past a couple before we came to a stop. I landed softly to my feet, hoping not much more flying was involved because my wings were in desperate need of a rest. She knocked on one and waited silently. I stayed quiet, glancing at her from the corner of my eye just as the door swung open.

And there he was.

Prince Asher was in no way unappealing to look at, and in the broad daylight, he was even more striking. His dark hair was rich and thick, it was loose this time, hanging around his face in soft waves. His pointed ears were a stark contrast against his raven-colored tresses and under his heavy brow, his dark green eyes almost glowed as they raked over me.

I'd kind of hoped he'd got uglier overnight because I didn't like the way my stomach fluttered at the mere sight of him.

He said nothing but pulled the door open wider and turned away, flying back to his desk on the other side of the room. Laurel led the way and I followed, taking in the sight of the ornate room. His four-poster bed, carved of dark wood was at one side, unmade and like he'd just rolled out of it. His dark green velvet curtains were thrown open and the morning breeze ruffled them through the open window.

His room was full of rich colors and screamed wealth- well, he was a prince after all. I felt so out of place in my plain linen dress and slip-on shoes.

Asher was dressed in a loose white shirt, not as fancy as the one he wore last night and plain leather pants. His feet were bare and I averted my gaze as soon as I noticed. A flush slowly crawled up my neck, it felt too intimate, seeing him in his space, in his casual clothes, far too much too soon. The way he dressed made him look more like an everyday fae than a part of the Royal family. The silver crown glinting upon his midnight locks was the one thing that set him apart.

He sat at his desk, writing something with a quill as Laurel and I stood there, in the center of his messy room. I put down the paper bag of pastries I was carrying on a nearby table so I could smooth down my dress. I didn't know why I felt the need to look presentable, but the look in Asher's eyes told me I needed to do a quick once over. I really just wanted to sit down and relax after that long flight. I threw Laurel a questioning glance but she continued to watch the prince.

He spun around from his chair, his arms draped over the armrests, and kicked his feet out.

"So you didn't flake out."

If that was supposed to be "good morning, hope you had a good sleep and journey" then my stay here was going to be just as I expected: horrific.

"No, um-" I glanced at Laurel again and she nodded encouragingly.

"Laurel knows of our arrangement. You don't need to be a prude around her. Now, tell me exactly why you decided to wear *that* dress to the palace."

My mouth fell open as I looked down at myself again, okay so the dress wasn't unflattering, but also wasn't form-fitting or delicately embroidered like I imagined most of the Royal clothes were. Gods, their undergarments probably had their initials stitched onto them too.

"I'm waiting." Asher's gaze bore into mine. Again, why was he so attractive? If he'd looked like a troll, then his personality would have matched perfectly.

"Well, your Highness, I wanted something that really showed off how much of a noblewoman I am for you to be courting." The sarcasm dripped off my tongue and I heard Laurel inhale a sharp breath next to me. She'd probably never heard anyone speak to any of the princes like that. Well just because I was here, didn't mean I had to be polite.

"Excuse me?" He growled- yes, *growled*. His face was like thunder as he shot up from his chair.

"You're excused," I replied before I could stop myself. Gods, what was I doing to myself? I was about to get executed at this rate.

"You better drop that tone, Zinnia. Or else you

and I won't be having a smooth journey here." Hearing my name slip off his tongue had my stomach doing all kinds of twists and turns. The way his mouth shaped to each syllable made me want him to say it again.

Gods, I *hated* my full name, named after an orange flower- yes, because of my hair- my mom loved the name. I, however, hated it, and so shortening it to Zia made it slightly more bearable.

"It's Zia," I told him and he made no indication of hearing me or taking what I said on board.

"As if we were going to anyway," I muttered, mainly to myself but also making sure Prince Asher was in earshot. Just so he knew how much I anticipated the clash of our personalities.

"Are you always like this?" He stepped closer.

"Charming and sweet? An absolute delight to be around? Yep, every single day." I said it in the most upbeat and sing-songy voice I could muster. I grinned and Asher's face hardened at my words, his nostrils flaring with distaste.

"Laurel will fetch you when it's dinner. This will be our first public appearance together, so try and look more put together than that. I know it'll be difficult." His tone hit me right in the chest. He knew how to get under my skin. "And if I see you wearing that ugly dress again, I'll personally burn it."

"You're so fucking rude, learn some manners!" I yelled and without looking to see what his expression was at my less-than-elegant mouth,

I spun on my heel, threw open the door, and stormed out of his room.

I heard the door softly click behind me and I sighed, slumping down on the wall beside it until my butt hit the floor. My wings ached, I was tired and honestly, overwhelmed by this whole situation. The weight of pretending to be someone I wasn't settled on my shoulders like a boulder, threatening to drag me under with the current and drown me.

I tried to hold back the tears that threatened to spill, the burn in my eyes and the lump in my throat made it hurt to swallow. No, I wouldn't cry, I'd got myself into this mess and I'd get myself out. I just need to be strong and not let the Brat Prince get to me.

The door opened next to me and I saw Laurel's feet shuffle out. I stood up, brushing a stray tear from my cheek before it had a chance to fully escape and she smiled sympathetically.

"It's a big change," she said softly, not judging me for my very un-lady-like outburst. She linked her arm with mine, looping hers through my elbow, and encouraged me forward. "Let's get you to your room and you can have a nice hot bath."

She walked four paces and stopped in front of the door opposite His Royal Highness's room. *Ugh, we have to be neighbors now too? Could this day get any worse?* Laurel pushed open the carved wood door and hesitated, before following her in.

The room was beautiful and thankfully, not as dark as Asher's. It had huge windows with sheer curtains that let in all the light. Beyond the windows was the beautiful expanse of woods and a garden. It was gorgeous and overgrown, but in a tamed kind of way, with wildflowers and trees everywhere. I found myself peering out of the open window before I'd even acknowledged my tired wings were taking me there.

"It's stunning, isn't it?" Laurel smiled next to me, looking out too. The sun washed the grass in a beautiful golden light and the trees looked so luscious I just wanted to climb up into them and sleep there, bathed in dappled light through the leaves.

"Even though it's very different from where you imagined yourself to be, Zia. Don't lose sight of who you are. You may not fit in straight away, but I know one thing for sure; the prince has never met his match before and I think he may have in you."

And with that, she flitted through to the joined bathroom and I heard the sound of running water splashing into the empty tub.

I pondered her words as I inhaled the fresh air. I'd spoken to a prince in the same tone I'd use for my friends like Dillon, only with a little more sharpness and sarcasm. He just brought out the absolute worst in me without me even acknowledging it. In my opinion, he needed to come down a peg or two if no one had spoken to him like that before, but he was a prince after all, even if he was an asshole.

"Your bath's ready!" She called, flying out of the bathroom and drying her hands on a towel. "I'll come and help you dress for dinner in a few hours. In the meantime, relax and try to enjoy yourself."

I liked Laurel, she didn't try to make me like the Brat Prince or convince me how lovely the palace was, or how lucky I was to be there. She just was a sweet fae who I needed at my side.

"Thank you." I smiled gratefully and she left the room.

Today was going to be a long one.

$\sim$

After spending far too long in the bath- my fingers were like prunes- I emerged feeling more like myself. Laurel had added some flower petals to the water, making the room smell sweet and floral. She'd also left oils to wash my hair with, which I'd greedily used leaving it silky and shiny.

I'd paced my bedroom, thinking about going out to the garden, but then not wanting to run into Asher or any of his friends or even his brothers. I'd heard Prince Finn wasn't as vile as his brother, but I couldn't take any more prince encounters than necessary right now, and I had to focus all my energy on tonight.

Even thinking about it gave me a surge of nerves mixed with anger. Prince Asher had blackmailed me into this situation all because of that stupid, horny fae who couldn't keep his hands to himself. If he'd never sent over the damn drink and we'd never had followed that guard to the room, I wouldn't even be in this stupid predicament.

Obviously, I'd spent the *whole* day thinking about my debacle.

The bath oils were a perk though, and I felt better in myself, I probably smelled the best I'd ever smelled in my life. The thought made me smile a little, better enjoy the perks while I was here. Who knew how long Asher intended to keep me around?

I decided it was time to write to Flora, even if I couldn't talk about our deal. I could tell her about the palace, what my room was like, and how sweet Laurel was. I settled down at the vanity, grabbing a piece of parchment and a quill from the desk. The ink was enchanted so I didn't need to refill it, which I guessed was yet another perk of living in the palace. We'd never had enough magic to waste at home on such trivial things.

I didn't know whose eyes passed over the letter before it was delivered, so I kept it short and sweet, not criticizing the crown or the Brat Prince. Even though I wanted to tear him apart, limb from limb in the letter, I didn't bother mentioning him. Flora would be disappointed, but if she met him, she'd see how dislikable he really was and understand why he wasn't worth mentioning. (Also maybe because I didn't want to be held accountable for treason? But that was a minor point.)

Laurel came to find me in the early evening as I

was lounging on the velvet couch by the window, watching the birds twitter about in the trees. Nature made me feel so comfortable, it lured me in and made me feel safe but also sad at the same time. I longed to be out there, frolicking about the gardens, not stuck up in the palace mentally preparing for a dinner with the King and Queen of the whole kingdom.

And for the hundredth time today, I wondered: *what had I got myself into?*

"Wipe away those tears girl, it's time."

I brushed away a stray tear on my cheek, not even realizing I was crying. I guessed my emotions had got the best of me, but I needed to steel myself for this dinner. It wasn't going to be easy.

She ushered me to the vanity, sitting me down in front of the mirror. My reflection stared back at me; curly auburn hair, fair, freckled skin, and light green eyes. Who was I?

Apparently tonight I was the girl who had captured the Brat Prince's playboy heart. *We'll see about that.*

She began brushing my hair, it was smooth and soft as she braided it onto my head. Laurel chatted away, talking about mindless gossip the staff had spread. She said one of the kitchen staff just didn't turn up for work one day last week and no one knows where she went. There's speculation that she eloped or ran off with some prince from another kingdom. Laurel told me she didn't believe in any of it, but it didn't stop her from telling me about it.

Then she applied a little crushed pigment to my eyelids, making my eyes pop and as she pulled out a dress from the wardrobe, I gasped. It was a gorgeous silver color, flowy and fitted. It was full-sleeved, made from a beautiful mesh-type material that hinted at showing off the bare skin of my arms, and it came down to just above my ankles, so I wouldn't trip over it if I needed to run away from something, or *someone.*

Laurel helped me step into it, the soft, silky fabric brushed against my skin, creating goosebumps, and suddenly the nerves came back full force. This was *real.* Like real as real can be. I was going to deceive the crown all because I'd spilled a drink on Prince Asher's supposedly favorite shirt. *Gods above, I'm in such a tangled mess.*

I glanced in the mirror and noticed my wings poking out of the back of the dress. They looked lost in the large slits in the fabric that was made for them, reminding me that this dress was made for a higher fae. My anxiousness made me jittery, but Laurel's firm hands on my shoulders grounded me back to reality as she looked at me through our reflections in the mirror.

"We can't change who we are, only show others the best side of ourselves and hope they'll accept it."

Her words offered no comfort, I stood tense as a fishing rod while she began to button up the rest of my dress from the back.

Suddenly the door crashed open and Asher flew in, face unreadable. Laurel excused herself, leaving me half buttoned up as she hastily fluttered out of the room, gently closing the door after her.

Gods, what does he want now? Ridicule me some more?

He stopped a few feet away from me and landed gracefully on his feet, his big wings folding on his back. He gave me a once over, it was hard to know what he was thinking and I itched to smooth down my skirt for some irrational reason.

"Are you done with your tantrum? Because we have a dinner to prepare for."

I opened my mouth to say something rude, but snapped it shut, opting to nod my head. I'd pick my battles and this was not one I needed to fight. Hopefully, it would be only a couple of weeks, and Asher would grow bored of me and I'd be out of there, back home with my family, baking bread, and sipping hot tea in our kitchen like nothing ever happened. I just needed to hold onto that.

"Well?" He prompted and I refused to rise to his bait. "How did we meet?"

"You tell me, you're the one whose bright idea got me into this mess," I mumbled, crossing my arms over my chest.

"I think you're forgetting that *your* clumsy feet and wings got you into this mess."

I unfolded my arms, balling my fists in anger. He just got under my damn skin so quickly. We'd barely been together for five seconds and I already wanted to strangle him.

"You're the one who blackmailed me to be in your fake courtship!" I yelled, struggling to keep my voice down as he tried to pin this whole debacle on me.

"And who's fault was it that my favorite shirt got ruined?" He arched an eyebrow, challenging me. Gods, I wanted to rip him a new one.

"It wasn't your favorite," I growled. " It was damn ugly, you brat." I could barely hold back my seething anger, it was bubbling under the surface, and I knew my face was probably red and blotchy from just getting so fucking annoyed with him in the first place. He'd goaded me into this stupid game.

Within a flash, Asher was grabbing my neck with his hand and pushing me against the vanity. The wood from the furniture dug into my lower back painfully and his dark green eyes bore into mine. Although we both had the same color- it was common among faes- his were darker, like a sinister, mysterious forest while mine were lighter like sunbathed grass.

"Watch your tone, Zinnia. I won't tell you again, we need to get through this dinner unscathed, or else no one will believe this pretense, and you'll be owing me for the rest of your miserable life." The way the prince's hand was wrapped around my throat and the way my pulse raced under his touch, completely conflicted with how I felt. I wanted to smack him, kick him, spit in his face, but when his thumb gently rubbed the pulsing vein on my neck, something else trickled into the mix of emotions.

His eyes dropped to my mouth for a split second and a single, delicious, and very forbidden thought filtered through my chaotic mind.

Kiss me.

I shook my head, willing the devious thought away as quickly as it came. I did *not* want him to kiss me. Or did I? I refused to entertain the idea and I struggled against his grip but he held me firmly, not hurting me, but not letting me go either.

"You better pray my family doesn't ask you too many questions for your fragile little head." He condescendingly patted the top of my head and without another word, flew out of the room, leaving the door wide open as I slumped against the vanity, trying to catch my breath and calm my racing heart.

Laurel poked her head in and sighed, seeing my flushed cheeks and messy hair.

"Let's get you finished here and off to dinner." She said and I nodded wordlessly, unsure of whether I could trust my voice.

Asher had shaken me up and Gods help me, this dinner was going to be a test of my strength.

We quickly re-styled my hair after that damn

prince had messed it up, and she finished buttoning up my dress. I fidgeted with the material, my wings flapping with excess nervous energy. I saw Laurel shake her head in the mirror as she tried to clasp a necklace around my neck.

"Your wings keep whipping me in the face, just stand still. Not much you can do now." Her tone was a little irritable and I felt guilty. She'd been nothing but kind to me.

"Sorry," I mumbled and she gave me a reassuring pat on the shoulder.

She was right, I was fretting unnecessarily. It was out of my hands now if the King and Queen liked me.

I spun to face her, making sure not to hit her with my wings. There was only so much this fae could take in one day and an extra wing in her face might just have pushed her over the edge.

"Can you deliver a letter for me, please?"

Her face softened and she nodded. I took my letter out of the vanity drawer and handed it over. She smiled before pocketing it.

"I'll make sure Henrick delivers it himself." She winked and I felt lighter in my chest, knowing I had a few friends in the palace.

The flight between the bedrooms and the dining hall was short and I panicked the whole way. I thought my fake partner would stop by and escort me, or at the very least give me a hint of what our backstory was. We hadn't even got onto that because he'd got under my skin and I'd flown off the handle, yet again.

I needed to keep my temper in check because now I'd just created another rod for my own back. I was going in blind, not knowing what in the Abyss was waiting for me on the other side of those oak carved doors.

The doors creaked open as I landed and Laurel gave my hand a comforting squeeze before flying off and leaving me to face the dragons on my own. I only hoped I had enough courage to make it through the meal.

CHAPTER THREE
DRESS UP &
PLAY PRETEND

The dining hall was as grand as I expected it to be and it matched the palace's decor. Large dark wood paneling with intricately carved leaves, flowers, and vines covered the walls. The ceiling depicted yet another story, but from just a glance, I knew I'd need a closer look to figure out which tale it told. The dining table itself was huge, the King sat at the far end, upon his carved wooden throne and to his left was the Queen.

The King was middle-aged for a fae's lifespan, with dark hair that showed some dustings of white around his huge crown. His heavy-set brow made him look menacing, not someone I'd want to get into a fight with. *Ever.*

His dark blue robes made him look regal and every part King of Nissa. I'd never seen him in real life before, but he was better looking than I thought he'd be. I saw where the Brat Prince got his looks from.

And then my gaze moved to his wife; the Queen. She was gorgeous, willowy, and the complete opposite of the King. With her milky skin, her white-blonde hair, and light, delicate features, she practically glowed and while the King was dark, she was light.

My eyes caught on Asher, again, his silver crown lay upon his dark curls, and the weight of him being an actual prince along with the gravity of this situation hit me like a gale-force wind.

Here I was, standing in front of the Royal family, pretending to be in a fake courtship with Asher. I was lying to the crown. I was well and truly in too deep.

I bowed into a deep curtsey, my skirts brushing against the stone floors before the King nodded his head and I stood back up.

Before I could analyze who else was in the room, a guard next to the door gestured for me to sit.

The room was silent, the only sound was the servants' wings buzzing as they flapped around in the corner, pouring drinks and preparing the food.

Everyone was watching me and as I turned to take my seat next to my supposed partner, I heard the whispers:

"Lesser fae."

"Look at her wings."

"What does Prince Asher see in someone like her?"

I swallowed the nasty words threatening to fall off my tongue, I didn't need my big mouth to get me into more trouble than necessary. I just had to get through this meal, that was all.

"Ms. Greenstem, lovely of you to join us, we're keen to know who's stolen our son's heart." The Queen smiled sweetly and I forced one back. At least she hadn't said anything about my wings. *Yet*.

"Thank you, Your Majesty, it's an honor."

The same guard who gestured to me pulled out my chair and I sat down gracefully, avoiding eye contact with everyone at the table. He pushed it in, not too gently either and as his hand wrapped around the back of the chair, he caught the edge of my wing with his fingers and pressed it into the hardwood cruelly.

I flinched, the nerves in a fae's wings were very sensitive and private too, not just *anyone* touched your wings. My stomach rolled sourly and I sat forward, pulling my sore wing out of his grasp. I didn't want to make a scene out of it as I caught a sneer on his face.

I bit my tongue, not letting my temper get the better of me, although it was tough, the anger rising inside of me was slowly getting too much to control. I ignored his behavior, smiling shyly at everyone around me.

The King stood once I was seated and every eye turned to him. I mentally counted ten others at the table. Obviously the King, Queen and their princes but also five others I didn't know. They looked important, perhaps nobles. Their large wings showed me that they weren't lesser faes at all. Gods, I was *so* out of my depth.

"I'm so glad to have you all here tonight, some old and some new faces." I looked down as the King's voice boomed out across the hall. I fiddled with my hands, with the excessive amount of jewelry Laurel had adorned me with. Honestly, you'd have thought I was getting married at the size of the stones in rings on my fingers, the jewels wrapped around my throat and hanging from my ears.

"Tonight, we feast as family and friends, as one. So begin and be merry!" He grabbed his silver goblet from the table and thrust it into the air. Everyone followed suit and I scrambled to grab the drink in front of me. I cheered weakly before sipping the sweet mead and surveying the table.

To my left sat Prince Cain, the youngest and supposedly best-looking prince. He had Asher's dark hair and looked the most like his father. He leaned in close, his breath smelling sickly sweet. I automatically leaned the opposite way, my gut told me to get away from him.

He laughed, his eyes were gray up close, washed out and haunting, not the beautiful green color of his brother's. His face was similar to Asher's though, with a heavy brow and high cheekbones. He was like a less handsome version of his older brother, not that there was anything wrong with him per se. But something in his eyes made my stomach roll sourly, threatening to bring up the few sips of mead I'd had.

"Are you afraid, little fae?" His sinister smile made me lose whatever was left of my appetite as he laughed again and whispered closely in my ear, his hot breath making me nauseous. "You should be."

I swallowed thickly, reaching for my water with slightly shaky hands. I didn't know what to expect with Prince Cain but that was not it. His threat made me shake all over, my body rigid with fear.

I turned to check if Asher had been paying attention, but of course, the Brat Prince paid no attention to me, engaging in a conversation with his mother and older brother; Prince Finn.

The eldest prince was the only one who resembled the Queen; tall, blond, and regal-looking. His long hair was smoothed back in a low ponytail, exposing his amazing bone structure, with a long nose and full lips. He was reserved, speaking politely with his parents and his father laughed heartily at a joke while Prince Finn simply smiled, his lips turning up at the corner reservedly.

I suddenly wished I'd been set up with the older prince, he seemed nicer and so much less of an asshole than Asher.

"Ms. Greenstem, tell us about your family." The

Queen smiled encouragingly from across the table and I sighed internally, wondering whether to lie or tell the truth. I was sure no one there came from the same modest background as me, but I knew that lying would end up leaving me tangled up in my own web.

I briefly glanced at Asher who was looking away from me. I knew he'd be no help, he hadn't been any so far so why would now be any different?

"My family are bakers," I spoke quietly. The conversations around the room slowly ground to a halt and I felt my skin heat under everyone's judging gaze. The whole room wanted to know who their playboy prince had picked. This was my chance not to fuck up. However much he'd pissed me off, I needed to hold it together, for both of our sakes.

"They run a place in the outer city, everyone loves my mom's bread and my dad's cakes. There's always a long line on market day when the traders come into Nissa for my family's goods. They stock up for their journey home." I smiled wistfully, remembering the traders queuing for hours just to get a delicious ambrosia cake. I wondered how my family was fairing without me. I didn't want to admit to myself that they were probably fine while I was feeling lost and without a purpose.

"Perhaps they could bake for one of our events." She smiled softly and I returned a genuine one.

It would be a dream for them, and Flora's face when she saw the palace would be worth its weight in gold.

"Thank you. They'd love that," I said quietly, thinking about how proud my parents would be baking for the Royals.

A snicker from the other end of the table indicated that not everyone liked my vision of my family baking at the palace.

I turned my head to where the noise was coming from and frowned at a noble female fae giggling with a male, who I assumed was her partner. I refrained from rolling my eyes as she looked at me, and then fluttered her hands like tiny wings. Her partner-in-crime laughed and I clenched my fists around my cutlery, the metal biting into my palms.

These fucking snooty faes and their stupid big wings.

If Asher noticed my change in demeanor, he didn't do anything about it as he kicked back in his chair and drank a long glug of his mead. *Guess I'm left to fend for myself out here then.*

The focus shifted off me as the Queen made small talk with Asher and I sighed, grabbing my cup and taking a sip.

"Run along home to your bakery, little fae, you're not wanted here." Prince Cain's dark voice made my skin crawl and I licked my dry lips, trying to force myself to look like I was enjoying myself while a fucking prince bullied me.

I straightened my shoulders and turned slightly to Prince Cain.

"I think I'll stay right here. Asher chose me after all." I smiled at him too sweetly and his eyes darkened. He was going to make my life in the palace awful, I could already tell.

As if contending with Asher's attitude wasn't already bad enough, Prince Cain's dark stare promised me a different kind of torture. The way his eyes narrowed and he ground his teeth, I realized, similarly to Asher, he didn't like being stood up to. *Well, guess what brother, dear? There's a lot more nerve where that came from.* I was probably biting off more than I could chew by acting like that, and I was more talk than action, but I refused to be bullied.

Turning away from Prince Cain while he glowered at me, I caught Prince Finn's eye. He smiled ever so slightly and I thought I saw a hint of admiration. Thankfully the dinner wasn't a total disaster then, at least one out of the three princes liked me enough not to treat me like dirt. Yet.

I settled back in my chair, still feeling nervous but not as petrified as I had been earlier, as the food was brought through from the kitchens. It smelled absolutely divine and my mouth watered at the different meats, fruits, sweet, and savory dishes that lay before me.

Honestly, I'd never seen so much food in one place. Of course, I hadn't grown up poor, but this was a different type of luxury. There was more food here than all of us could eat at the table. I felt slightly guilty, admiring all the food while lesser faes slaved away in the outer sides of the city, scraping by with barely enough food for one meal.

The twinge of guilt was only emphasized by a memory of Flora giving out stale bread to the poorer faes at the end of the day. My mother used to tell her to throw it away or else we'll get beggars all the time, but Flora always divided it up and gave it to them. She had the sweetest heart, unlike the spoilt faes before me.

Gods, I missed her so much and I'd only left her this morning.

Swallowing the sudden flood of tears that threatened to overflow, I took a sip of my mead and smiled at the fae serving us different dishes. None of them met my eye, out of fear or something else, I didn't know. Instead, I watched the food pile up on my plate. I hadn't eaten anything all day and my stomach growled like a feral creature.

Smaller conversations started between the guests and I lapsed into silence, savoring the delicious food. Every morsel was mouthwateringly tasty and I had to force myself to slow down otherwise I'd be sick. Didn't want that to happen in front of the Royal family. *Gods above, I'd never live that down.*

"Asher, tell us how you and Zinnia met, we're all *dying* to know." Prince Cain drawled next to me and I felt the Brat Prince stiffen. This was a sore subject and one we still hadn't discussed. *Guess we're going in blind here*, I just hoped he didn't make up some elaborate lie that I'd get caught up in. I wouldn't be able to remember all of the details, I was sure of that.

I wanted to correct Prince Cain on my name, but decided now was not the time.

"Zinnia loves to tell the story, and she tells it better. Why don't you enlighten my family on how we fell into each other's arms?" He smiled too sweetly and I knew he was testing me. *Well, two can play this game, your Highness.*

"Sweet Asher, he was so lovely and he rescued me when I clumsily fell over at Cuckoo one night. He was so kind and considerate, asking me if I was alright and when I looked in his eyes, I knew it was love at first sight." I cooed, making my voice all gooey and romantic.

"Apparently it was for him too, though he'd never tell you that." I overacted the role, pretending to be coy and stupid because according to my Mom, no one loved a partner who thought too much for themselves.

Without even looking, I knew the Brat Prince was angry. Well if he hadn't been such a grumpy guts earlier, we'd have got our story straight and I wouldn't have had to use my terrible improvisation acting skills to keep his family at bay.

I grabbed his hand, holding his palm in my own, ignoring the little spark I felt from his touch, and I pressed a kiss to the back of it. I glanced up into his eyes, pretending to be absolutely loved up, and saw the anger rolling off him in waves. Yep, he was pissed alright. My work here was done. I bit back the smug smile that threatened to break through and ruin my performance.

Taking my hand away from his unresponsive one, I glanced around the room. The Queen looked positively ecstatic- a submissive and adoring wife for her prince, what more could she possibly want?

Except I was none of those. I was foul-mouthed, didn't take no for an answer, and certainly not from someone as spoiled and pushy as Prince Asher. A shame really, because I was sure I'd have made a lovely daughter-in-law for her.

"That's not exactly correct now, is it my love, Zinnia?" He spoke through gritted teeth and my stomach dropped as my mind raced, thinking about what he might say. Okay, I'd really put myself in the firing range this time.

"Don't forget your babbling about how good-looking I am, and how I'm a prince, and especially about how much you'd *love* to live in a palace. It was really so quaint." His condescending tone made my blood boil. Gods above, I was about to commit treason and strangle him blue for what he'd just said. Making me look like a golddigger- the cheek of this prince!

I'd played my role as dumb fae nicely, perhaps a little too nicely but being insulted by Asher at the dinner table with his family just didn't go down well at all.

To the Abyss with Asher's stupid games, I am not going to sit here and be made a fool of. As I opened my mouth to throw something worse back, the King interrupted.

"Well as lovely as that sounds. I'd have hoped for someone with a little more than a mere bakery." He watched our little display as he spoke. "A kingdom perhaps."

The King's words were like a blow to my heart. The room was silent, tension thick and heavy as everyone looked between Asher and me. So the King wanted wealth, power, and marriage to secure deals with other kingdoms. And what did I have? Nothing except the clothes on my back and they weren't even mine.

I didn't even care about Asher's thoughts, didn't care if the King didn't like me, but somehow his words had hit a sore spot, had highlighted how little I was worth, how insignificant I was. And, *fuck that hurt.*

Somehow I needed validation and approval, deep down I wanted to be accepted, even if it was all pretend.

Despair crept into my heart and I swallowed back another wave of tears. My eyes burned and the lump in my throat hurt as I went to drink some water. My hand shook again and I willed myself not to spill my water. This whole meal was a tidal wave, from one emotion to the next.

I wanted to escape, flee to the safety of my chambers and possibly cry my heart out at tonight's humiliation. My appetite had vanished for the second time tonight and a sour feeling twisted in my stomach.

"Well, I'm sorry to disappoint you, Father. But Zinnia is who I've chosen to court."

My mouth nearly popped open in shock. Asher came to my defense? What was happening, was the world tipping upside down? Admiration swelled in my chest for a millisecond before I stomped it away. I was a pawn in his games, nothing more. No point getting soppy over someone who couldn't care less about me.

"Shame about her puny wings though." Prince Cain sneered from beside me and I ignored his comment, no matter how deep his words cut. I was already in pieces, what was another insult at this point?

The Brat Prince didn't respond and I sat for the rest of the meal in silence, not looking up from my plate as I pushed food around, not really eating it. No one else asked me anything, or even said anything remotely close to the courtship. It was a topic to stay clear of.

As the dinner came to a close and the plates were cleared away. The King announced he'd be retiring for the night and the Queen quickly followed. I glanced at Asher, but he ignored me and Prince Cain said they'd be playing games in a different room.

I wondered if anyone would notice if I snuck out, so I decided to chance it. No one would care, and after tonight's ridicule, I doubted anyone would blame me for leaving.

As a guard pulled open the dining hall door, Laurel's round face came into view.

Her sweet blue eyes made the tears that had threatened to spill all night come back in full force. I sobbed, barely making it out of the hall and she took me in her arms. We quickly flew together back to my room, me trying to weave my way through the palace with my blurry vision. Laurel was gripping my hand with such strength that I thought she might yank my whole arm off as we whizzed through corridors.

Soon enough we were back in my room and she seated me down at the vanity and sighed.

"I knew it wouldn't be pretty, but the worst of it is over. Sleep now and tomorrow will be better." She unpicked her fine work in my hair and brushed it out, untangling the curls and gently running her fingers through the soft strands. The rhythm of it made me think about when my mom used to do the same and tears still ran down my cheeks, darkening the fabric on my chest as they dripped off my chin. She pulled a soft nightdress out from the wardrobe and brought it over.

"Here, let's get you changed, and then you'll feel better in the morning." Laurel's sweet disposition made me wonder how she survived at the palace. She was so kind and caring, how had she not been eaten alive and spat back out again by those vile higher faes?

"Laurel, it was awful." I sighed, sniffing and wiping my eyes as she finished unbuttoning my dress. I stood up and the fabric slid down my arms and pooled on the floor. She turned away as I slipped out of my underthings and pulled the soft nightdress over my head.

I sat back down and Laurel pulled my hair into a loose braid down my back. She got a washcloth and wiped away the rest of the makeup left on my face, the stuff that hadn't been washed away by my flood of tears. She spun me around to face her and cupped my cheeks. A stray tear trickled down my face and her thumb brushed it away.

"You can do this, sweet girl."

I nodded, not feeling strong enough to argue and she bid me goodnight before closing the door softly behind her.

The moonlight shone through the open curtains and I wandered over to the couch by the window, looking out into the moon-bathed garden. I stared at the sky, looking at the three moons that lit up the darkness, and thought about my family, wondering what they were doing right now. Was Flora looking at the same sky? Were they worried about me?

I guessed they were happy I was out of their hair and Flora, well, she'd miss me of course. I wished I could tell her all about how awful dinner was. She'd know what to say to make me laugh, to put a smile back on my face. A deep sigh escaped me and I rested my head on the window sill, gazing at the stars.

Just as I was finally finding some inner peace, the door suddenly burst open, bouncing against the wall behind with a bang, and the one person I really didn't want to see stumbled in.

I jumped, my heart beating twice as fast when I noticed the bottle in his hand. He looked around the room, at the bed and the vanity, his face confused before his eyes found me. He grinned like a dragon who'd just found gold and I internally groaned.

"Well, dinner went successfully, don't you think?" He swaggered over, his expensive boots clacking against the stone floor.

I turned away from him, not in the mood for his games.

"If that's what you want to call it," I mumbled, gazing back out into the garden.

"Oh, come on Zinnia, you didn't expect them to actually like you, did you?" I gritted my teeth at the use of my full name yet again.

"It's *Zia*." I ground out, turning back to the window.

My heart clenched painfully at his words. In truth, I hadn't expected them to *like* me, but I also hadn't expected such public humiliation. I thought the King was nicer than that, but then again, you need only look at Princes Asher and Cain. Their sparkling personalities weren't much to go by. I guessed I'd thought wrong. I was naive to believe the palace was the stuff of fairy tales where princes charmed you and everyone was nice. I was a fool.

"Just get out," I said wearily. I was tired of this game, tired of this day, and tired of the Brat Prince.

"Make me."

His words sent a strange jolt through me, making my skin prickle and flush. Gods, what was wrong with me? I turned to face him, trying to ignore the weird wave of emotions swirling inside me.

"You've humiliated me, made me look like a fool, and ignored me for the whole of dinner. You're a spoiled, rich, little prince who dragged me into his stupid, fucking games and I want to be left alone, so GET OUT!" I yelled, fed up with him and his infuriating personality. His green eyes sparkled like he was amused by my outburst, which only annoyed me even more.

The prince's face watched mine before he stepped closer to me. But his alcohol consumption made his actions clumsy so he stumbled over the leg of a chair and went flying to the floor, the bottle of booze rolling out of reach. So much for his big wings being of use.

"You know, Zinnia, you're not what I expected." He said from the floor, rolling over to look up at me, he rested his face in his hands.

"No shit, Your Highness. If you wanted some sweet female who likes to curtsey and play nice, then you've got the wrong fae."

Asher studied me again and I flew to the door, yanking it open, and gestured for him to get out. He sat propped up on his elbows, watching me.

"The exit's this way."

"I know."

"Then use it."

He heaved himself up before walking over to me and gazing down at me, even drunk, he looked more put together than I'd ever be. His dark hair was unruly and his crown slightly lopsided. It'd only add to his handsome features if I wasn't so fed up with the day and with him.

"Your pastries were the most delicious food I've ever eaten." He said it thoughtfully, quietly and for a second, I almost laughed in his face.

Did he really have no limits? I'd had enough of him treating me like shit.

"I'm done with your mocking for today. Get out."

He walked through the door and just as I pushed it shut, he said:

"I meant it."

～

Monday.

Usually one of the busiest days of the week at the bakery and yet today, I sat bored as anything, gazing out of my window, watching the birds in the trees. I'd chosen a soft dress, with simple embroidery around the cuffs and neckline, tiny red roses against the light green fabric, nothing too fancy but I knew better than to test Asher with my wardrobe choices today. There were bigger battles to fight.

Laurel had woken me up, bringing me breakfast as she said that the Royals were busy this morning, otherwise usually they'd be eating breakfast together and I'd be expected to be there. *Yay, another painful meal with my pretend family-in-law to look forward to.*

She sat with me as I ate, telling me fun facts about the palace, how many rooms there were, how often they held fancy balls and how much she loved to gaze at the beautiful gowns the faes from far away kingdoms wore.

But then she'd left to attend to her duties and I was alone again.

I'd stayed up half of the night, my mind reeling from dinner and Asher's confession. He'd said he liked my pastries. And not as a joke. Was that his version of an olive branch between us? Or was he just messing with me? Trying to gain my trust, then throw me to the dragons and laugh at my naivety?

Fed up with my own thoughts and the confiding space (even though the room was triple the size of my bedroom at home), I decided to wander the palace to take my mind off the swirling hurricane of thoughts bottled up inside my head.

The hallways were quiet, and the Brat Prince's door was shut, as were the others along the corridor, but I'd heard movement in the hallway at sunrise this morning, so I knew everyone was out or busy, and so I was alone.

I took a left out of the hallway and flew down a stairwell. The landscape of the palace changed dramatically and I knew I was in the lower quarters with no paintings, only plain stone walls, and threadbare rugs. The delicious smell of fresh bread lured me to an open door as my heart gave a sad jolt. I missed the bakery.

The kitchen was huge and my first thought was how much my mom would love this place. Their ovens- yes, in the plural- were bigger than our whole kitchen and I gaped at the amount of bread and cakes stacked up in the room.

A kitchen maid noticed me and was startled, fumbling into a curtsey. The others turned, following suit and I flushed, embarrassed by the display.

"You don't have to do that."

They remained silent, watching me with wide eyes and I cleared my throat.

"I'm Zia, nice to meet you all. I'd love to help if I can?" I asked hopefully, my idle hands were of no use to anyone and frankly, I needed to do something or else I'd go insane in this place.

The three maids watched me closely, their expressions guarded. They looked around my age, but it was hard to tell with their hair covered and their plain gray and navy uniforms. An older woman turned around from the stove, she looked to be middle-aged, and she smiled warmly.

"We'd usually love help, but we're busy and we don't have time to teach anyone today." She spoke softly, not scolding me for being there, but when she turned back to her work, it was obvious she was busy. Her words said as much, but I still wanted to help.

"But you wouldn't have to teach-"

"There you are!" Laurel bustled into the kitchen, flapping her wings in a flurry before setting herself down on the stone floors.

"I was looking for you."

"I wanted to help, make myself useful." I gestured at the busy kitchen, suddenly envious that they had a purpose while I lacked any reason to be here, other than pretend to be in love with Asher.

Laurel watched me for a second before turning back to the kitchen.

"Elsa, would it be okay if Zia worked in the kitchen on the lower floor?"

The middle-aged woman, who I now knew was Elsa, turned to face Laurel.

"She can do as she pleases, just not in here today. We're too busy."

"Of course. I'll get her out of your hair."

Laurel ushered me out of the door and flew in front of me as we navigated another corridor and stairwell. Why this palace had so many stairwells when faes flew nearly everywhere, I'd never know.

We arrived at a darker, quieter kitchen and I looked around the room curiously.

"This is the second kitchen, it was built a while ago but was never used properly, only if we had huge parties but even then, the upstairs kitchen is always enough. If you can get the oven working, then it's yours."

It looked to have been in disuse for a long time, cobwebs and dust covered every corner and usually, I'd have wilted at the amount of cleaning, but instead, I rolled up my sleeves and turned to Laurel.

"Do you have a broom, a bucket, and a mop?"

She grinned, obviously pleased that I was applying myself and not moping around in my bedroom, and flew out of the room as I surveyed the space. It was smaller than the other kitchen but still bigger than our one at home. It would be perfect. Well, once I cleaned it up.

A blood-curdling scream from down the hall tore me away from my happy thoughts and I spun around, my heart beating double-time. My skin prickled uncomfortably as I tried to find the source of the horrific sound.

Looking in the direction of where the scream came from, I tentatively flitted closer to the dimly lit corridor that led down more stone steps and into darkness. I leaned over the banister, curious about what lay down there.

The air was colder here, it smelled like death.

I could hear moans, yells and the occasional slamming of metal which I presumed was a door. Another scream came, this time it was weaker and it made my hair stand on end. A sinister shiver rolled down my spine.

Something was wrong.

Someone needed help.

Just as I was about to call out, a hand clamped down on my shoulder making me jump out of my skin.

"Don't go wandering off again, Zia."

Laurel steered me back by my shoulders to the safety of the kitchen and I tried to turn to look back at the dark corridor.

"What's down there?"

"The dungeons. I wouldn't recommend a trip down there. You might not come back."

My heart felt icy cold and my blood froze in my veins.

"What do you mean?"

Laurel spun me around, bringing me to face her and I looked into her serious blue eyes.

"I mean, people who go down there aren't usually seen again. You'd do best to stay away." Her voice was stern and there was no room for negotiation.

"But I heard-"

She put her hand up to silence me.

"No more buts. Heed my warning, sweet girl. The dungeons are not a place for the likes of you."

I nodded, giving the dark corridor one fleeting

glance before turning back to the neglected kitchen.

Laurel had brought a mop and bucket as requested and she'd filled it with some water. She'd found a broom too and she offered me a handful of material.

"What's this?" I asked, accepting it and holding it out in front of me to examine it. It was like a jacket but back to front as it tied at the back.

"It's to keep your clothes clean while you're working. You know how Prince Asher is about presentation."

Didn't I know, it was what had got me into this position in the first place. How could I forget?

"Thank you." I smiled gratefully and she helped tie it around my back, it was more practical than the simple apron my mom used to make me wear to clean our kitchen. I rolled up my sleeves and prepared to tackle the forgotten room.

Two hours later and I was covered head to toe in dust, cobwebs, grime, and general dirt. I'd scrubbed the counters and cleaned the floors, the kitchen was starting to look more like somewhere you could cook and not die after consuming the food.

My arms ached like they had lead weights in them and sweat dripped off my brow as I scrubbed the front of the huge oven. I hadn't done hard labor like this for so long that I'd forgotten how much elbow grease it actually took.

But I was determined to get this kitchen up and running, and not waste my time in the palace.

I could have used magic, but mine wasn't that good and I'd probably be more tired using up all of my magic on cleaning than I would be if I'd just cleaned by hand.

I sat back after scrubbing the final door of the huge oven and rested my arms on my knees as I glanced around at my hard work.

The room was looking pretty good and I smiled, proud of my achievement.

All that was left was to stoke the fire in the oven.

And that was the part I hadn't thought about yet. Perhaps someone in the kitchen had some flint and some firewood to light it. I'd need some bellows and twigs to stoke it too. Fire was a tricky one and getting one this big, this hot, would take time.

I sighed, standing up and stretching out my back, it cracked satisfyingly and I almost groaned out loud.

"There you are."

Asher's voice made me jump and I spun around.

"Gods, you scared me. Can't you announce yourself or something?"

He smirked before looking around the room.

"I never knew this place existed."

"Yeah well, you've probably never even ventured out of the comfort of your own room and the dining hall." I rolled my eyes and watched him as he looked around.

"And I've never seen so many staff either."

"And I assume you think this palace is run off dreams and wishes, Your Highness."

His eyes focused on me and I bit my lip, wondering if I'd fucked it up again.

He suddenly laughed, rolling his head back. It was a beautiful sound and I smiled. I wanted to make him laugh again, I ached to hear the sound and I tried to squash down that feeling in my chest.

Thankfully, I hadn't fucked up too much. He was in a good mood, something I had yet to see from him.

"I'd like to think I'm not as naive as that."

As he circled the room, I took a moment to take in his appearance. His dark hair was tied up at the nape of his neck. A few curls escaped and framed his face. His cream collarless shirt was loose, showing the top of his chiseled chest.

I averted my eyes quickly, although seeing a bit of his toned skin had me blushing like a rose. His cream shirt was tucked into his brown leather pants that lead down to his shiny boots. The shirt was embroidered with little green ivy leaves along the neckline and cuffs. It was so delicate and pretty and it looked similar to the design of my dress. *Huh, must be a popular design with higher faes and Royals.*

"Do you need it to be lit?" He pointed at the oven and I blinked out of my trance. He watched me with one eyebrow raised, a slight smirk on his lips.

"Yeah, but I need to find some wood to burn."

"No need, I have magic, Zinnia. I'll light it."

I stared at him, brow furrowed.

"Did you just offer to help me?" I put my hands on my hips. "What's in it for you?"

"Pastries, of course." He said simply. He flicked a finger at the oven and the fire roared to life. I stumbled back, mouth agape, utterly shocked by the sheer strength of his magic. I'd never seen anyone do anything like that before. Usually lesser faes' magic was minimal and for small things like healing wounds or turning on a light.

"You can pick your jaw up off the floor now."

And then he was back; arrogant Prince Asher. For a second there, I thought I'd seen the hint of someone else underneath all his bravado, someone likable.

I snapped my mouth shut and pursed my lips. He stepped closer, his body crowding my space, but somehow I didn't want to take a step back, even though he'd been rude and crass.

His right hand snaked up to my waist, tugging me close to him so that our bodies were inches apart, and my breath hitched. I stared into his eyes, unsure of his actions and yet, somehow trusting him at the same time.

His hand inched up further, brushing the swell of my breast and I nearly moaned at the briefest of contact. He leaned in, looking like he was ready to kiss me and I licked my lips, mentally preparing myself for the feel of his mouth on mine.

Yes, I was desperate and Gods, forgive me because Asher had me on a string, dancing to his tune, and I didn't want it any other way.

"It won't kill you to say 'thank you', you know." He breathed, breaking the spell and I pushed him away roughly, running a hand through my hair.

I needed to clear my head, and get myself out of the gutter. What was I thinking, kissing the enemy? Asher was the whole reason I was here in the first place. I needed to remember that and not get caught up in the sheer intensity of it all.

I gritted my teeth, instantly annoyed by the tone in his voice. I would not be giving him any form of thanks. *Ever.*

"You can leave now." I dismissed him, turning away from him and preparing to peel off my dirtied apron and finish up in here for the day.

"You look awful." He ran his eyes down me and I realized I was still wearing the grubby gown Laurel had given me to cover my dress.

"That's what happens when you do hard labor and don't sit on your ass all day, Your Highness."

He ignored my remark and dragged his eyes up to my face. I resisted the urge to run a hand through my hair again. *I don't care what he thinks about me. His opinion is irrelevant.*

"There's a dinner and dance tonight at one of the noble houses and we'll be attending."

Ugh, another dinner. I crossed my arms over my chest and pursed my lips again.

"Don't look so overjoyed." He said sarcastically and I sneered at him.

"Oh don't mind me, barely containing my joy because the last one went so fucking well." I rolled my eyes and he stepped closer to me.

"Zinnia, what have I said about watching your tone? And your words too. This is no place to be using that language."

"And where is that?" I threw back, annoyed that I got picked on for every little thing. What I wore, how I spoke. Was nothing in me good enough for him? "Your bedroom?"

Gods, *why* had I said that? My brain-to-mouth filter needed work. Asher's eyes darkened, his jaw clenched and I knew I'd fucked up.

"Take this as your last warning about your tone." His voice was low and I bit back my next remark.

Without another word, he turned on his heel and stalked out of the room.

"Wait," I said, cursing myself as I did. The last thing I wanted was to owe him, but I needed this.

He froze, slowly spinning back to face me. His expression was unreadable, but his balled fists at his side told me he was pissed.

"I need you to put a glamor on my wings tonight," I said quietly, dropping my gaze to the floor.

"Why?" His tone was sharp and I clenched my teeth. I hated admitting weakness but I needed his help.

So I swallowed my pride and tilted my head up to look him straight in the eyes.

"Because I don't want to be the laughing stock of the party, that's why!" I snapped, fed up with his attitude.

"What do I get in return?" He raised an eyebrow and I wanted to slap that stupid feature of his stupid face.

"What do you want, Your Highness?" I was exasperated. He was so demanding and rude, but also for a moment, he was softer around the edges and that just confused me even more.

"Pastries. And lots of them."

I almost laughed in his face. This prince, this big, bad, moody, arrogant prince wanted pastries? And not just any pastries, but mine, baked by me; Zia Greenstem.

"Really?"

"I meant what I said."

And with that, he left, leaving me open-mouthed and surprised.

～

Back in my room, I bathed and made sure to scrub every part of my body, getting rid of all the grime and sweat from today's work. Even if it made my arms ache, it was a good use of my time in the palace and it gave me purpose. I wasn't going to just sit around and do nothing while I was trapped here.

A knock on the door interrupted my vigorous scrubbing.

"Who is it?" I wasn't sure why I even asked, both times the Brat Prince had come in, he'd stormed my room like he owned the place. Well, he did. Kind of.

"Laurel."

I smiled as I dipped my head back into the water to wash my hair.

"Come in," I called and heard the door click shut. Laurel appeared in the doorway of the bathroom carrying fresh towels.

"I'll wait out here for you." She put the towels down and left me to bathe. Although I wanted to stay in the soapy water all day, I knew I had yet another dinner to attend. So I hauled myself out of the tub and wrapped the towel around me. My wings popped up over the top of the towel and I fluttered them softly to disperse the excess water. They looked pretty and iridescent in the golden sunlight streaming through the window. I couldn't help but sigh at how they kept me apart from the others in the palace. Not that I wanted to be a Royal or even a higher fae, but the way we were treated simply because of our wings was unfair.

I wondered if Asher would stick to his word and glamor them so I didn't have to be subjected to any more humiliation than necessary.

I wanted to believe he had a shred of kindness in him, one that I'd perhaps seem a sliver of. But I didn't want to hold my breath either. If he was anything like Cain then his kindness was just a mirage, something to lure me in before he hurt me.

Wandering through into the bedroom, I saw Laurel sitting on a chair by the vanity. She smiled as I flew through the room. She gestured to the chair and picked up the hairbrush, ready to brush out my wet curls.

"Do you know where the dinner is tonight?" I asked as I sat down in my towel in front of the mirror.

Laurel picked up a bottle off the vanity and began applying floral-smelling oil onto my hair. It was delicious and smelled like lavender mixed with roses- the scent suited me.

"No idea, sweet girl, but best to be prepared and looking your best regardless of where it is."

I nodded and watched her brush my hair in the mirror. I sighed, thinking about making small talk and having to socialize with higher faes who sneered down on the lesser faes. It was an act, pretending to be one of them, and one I didn't enjoy one bit. It felt like betrayal.

"I have a surprise for you." She reached into her pocket and produced folded parchment. I saw my name scribbled on top of it and I practically ripped it out of her hand.

"A very handsome blond fellow dropped it off at the kitchens today. How he got into the palace I don't know, but Henrick escorted him off the grounds nicely after he said he was delivering it to you." Her eyes twinkled and I knew she meant Dillon. I was excited to see what he had to say. She passed it to me and I began to unfold it.

"Not now though. Save it for later when we aren't pressed for time."

My fingers itched to unfold the pages and greedily drink in my best friend's words, but Laurel was right. I needed to focus and be prepared for tonight's trials. I opened the top drawer of the dresser and tucked it away for later.

After she'd braided my hair in an elaborate style that involved lots of pins and flowers, she pulled out a beautiful emerald green dress. It was similar to the one I'd worn at the previous dinner. Obviously, this was a popular style, but it had tiny white camellias embroidered around the waist like a belt and on cuffs. It was beautiful and reminded me of Asher's shirt earlier.

"Who makes these clothes?" I asked Laurel as she helped me slip into my underthings and then the dress. She pulled it on from the bottom up, it had a lace-up back and was cut lower than the last one, showing off my cleavage a little more. I guessed modesty had gone out of the window for this dinner.

"I believe Prince Asher made this one and the

one you wore yesterday evening too."

I just about stopped my mouth from falling agape as I marveled at the material. It was heavier, almost velvety and it hugged my curves. I loved it. I had to admit, the Brat Prince had taste.

But more importantly, if he made his own clothes, was that why he had been so pissed that I'd spilled a drink on his shirt? Or was his magic so disposable that he just blackmailed a foolish fae who knew nothing about Royal magic into believing she'd actually ruined his favorite shirt?

Thoughts to tuck away for later.

"It's gorgeous." I breathed, turning to face myself in the mirror as Laurel laced the back.

I barely recognized her, the fae who stood before me, who mirrored me, was a beautiful, regal looking one, who looked as if she belonged in huge dining halls with expensive wines and elaborate dishes.

I wished I felt like her, she was an image, a façade and I turned away from her, suddenly feeling less confident than I looked.

"It is, isn't it?" She grinned, her blue eyes sparkling as we both looked at me in the mirror. I slipped on some soft, heeled slippers and did a twirl in the mirror. Playing dress-up had never really been my thing when I was younger, but looking at myself now, dressed in this expensive gown, adorned with jewels, made me wish I'd been born into this life, if only for a second.

"Good luck," Laurel whispered, squeezing my hand gently and she guided me to the door.

Asher was waiting on the other side for a change. He was in a formal shirt, his jacket was golden, which matched his wings and when I looked closely, I could see the same camellias embroidered on the lapels of his jacket.

We matched and looked like a couple, I didn't know how to process that.

His crown sat upon his dark curls, making him look as regal as ever and I felt as if I should curtsey even though I knew it was beyond ridiculous. We were way past formalities at this point. The things I'd said to him over the course of the last few days definitely warranted a spot in the dungeons and yet, he still put up with me. Well, I supposed it was for his benefit.

"Your Highness." Laurel bowed to her Prince and gave me one last smile before leaving me alone with him.

His eyes leisurely ran over my body, and I looked away, not wanting to see how they halted at my cleavage. I didn't want to be used by Asher anymore than I felt I was already.

"Your wings." He said and I hesitated for a moment before nodding. I saw his hand extend and he pressed his palm to the soft, delicate membrane. It felt intimate and too much for me, but I needed this. I couldn't face any more humiliation at the moment. My cheeks burned as he caressed my delicate wings. I looked away, staring at the shiny stone floor.

I felt the warm magic like a caress over my wings for only a few seconds and then it was gone, leaving behind an empty feeling.

I glanced back, seeing magnificent golden wings adorning my back. I gasped, knowing it wasn't real, but it still shocked me to see my little silver wings transformed into these huge, beautiful ones.

I flapped them gently, testing them out and they blew the air around them. *Wow, okay I'm more than a little jealous that Royals get to have these every day.*

I offered Asher a small smile and he, in turn, offered me his elbow wordlessly. *No snide words or comments?* I took it gingerly, trying not to hold onto him too much. I didn't want him getting ideas as we flew through the palace to the main entrance I'd come through only a few days ago.

We landed and I saw a carriage awaiting us at the bottom of the steps. It was gorgeous, shaped like a dome and covered in green and gold vines. It was big enough to fit at least six people with space between the seats and wasn't exactly inconspicuous. Two guards stood on either side of it. I couldn't tell if one of them was Henrick as they all wore the same armor and helmets, I hoped he was there though, I needed a friend tonight.

Asher turned to me, holding onto my upper

arm as his dark eyes caught mine.

"Let's try and get through this evening unscathed. So here are a few ground rules, Zinnia. Only speak when spoken to. Don't dance with anyone but me unless we switch partners in the dance, and don't go anywhere on your own. Not all nobles are to be trusted."

My mind flitted back to the horny, stupid fae who'd pursued me at Cuckoo. Yep, he was not someone I'd like to meet in a dark hallway on my own, I did not trust him one bit.

"Yes, sir." I mock-saluted the prince and his eyes darkened. *Oops*, perhaps 'unscathed' was an overly optimistic word. He turned away from me and began to walk to the top of the steps.

"And my brothers are accompanying us tonight." He spoke coldly and I nodded, dreading each second as we flew down the steps and landed at the foot of the carriage.

Asher didn't offer me a hand as we got in and I wondered why he acted differently around his brothers and me. I'd have thought it'd be the opposite way around, trying to prove to his brothers that he was actually interested in me, and treated me like a fae he'd court, and not just another addition to his long list of lovers.

"Oh good Asher, I see you brought your pet. I hoped we'd have some entertainment tonight." Prince Cain laughed and I sat down opposite him, next to his brother. *Great, now I have to stare at his face for the whole journey.*

The carriage was as luxurious inside as it was out, with red velvet seats and gold vines tangling on the ceiling in some elaborate design.

I tried to sit comfortably, folding my wings behind me, but they didn't sit gracefully. They were too bulky and wide for me to have them flat against my back. I fidgeted and Prince Cain's eyebrows rose as he stared at me.

"Gods, Asher, did you really glamor her wings like it would make a difference? I'm sure half the kingdom knows she's a lesser fae by now."

He was starting to get on my nerves. I turned to see Asher flexing his jaw, perhaps I wasn't the only one who didn't like Cain The Pain. Yep, I was a big fan of that nickname I'd made up for him.

"For tonight, she's one of us."

That was all he said and Prince Cain sat back sulkily. The eldest prince offered me a small, perhaps apologetic, smile before turning his attention out of the window and I felt the carriage fall into motion as we rolled out of the palace and into the city.

The journey was painfully slow through the city. No one said a word and I didn't bother trying to engage in conversation, I knew the Brat Prince wouldn't care and I didn't want to give Cain any more of my time or energy.

We came to a halt outside a beautiful house and I looked up at the trees that connected each section of the house. It was amazing, beautiful, and huge. Even from the outside, the sheer volume of windows indicated that it had many, many rooms.

The carriage door opened and one of the palace guards offered me his hand. Before I could take it, Prince Cain rudely pushed in front of me and out of the carriage. Something told me he didn't like being put in his place. The guard stepped out of the spoilt prince's way before giving me his hand once more. I thanked him and gathered up my dress as I descended the steps out of the carriage.

The air was balmy, warm, and light for the evening and I could see the sun setting in the East, it painted the sky in a beautiful pink and orange hue.

The house was noisy, the party had obviously already begun and faes stopped to bow at us as we flew in the front door.

Asher took my elbow without asking, not that I expected him to, and flew with me through the entrance and into the great party.

People stopped and stared, I heard whispers about us, about Asher and me. I wanted to yell at them to say it to my face because I *hated* people talking behind my back.

The party was already underway by the time we made it through the front door, and the large room was stuffed full of nobles and higher faes, all dressed up in expensive and bright fabrics.

Acrobatic faes swung from the high ceilings, swirling around in rich colored ribbons, while a band played a merry tune on the other side of the room. Some faes were perched high up on ledges, watching down at the crowd below. Others danced and laughed, chatting away. It was loud, saturated, and enough to knock any lesser fae off their feet. Everything was so overwhelming, over stimulating, my heart hammered in my chest at the vast room, filled with everyone below us.

"This way." Asher all but grunted at me and he pulled me towards a group of upper faes.

They bowed to him and the females curtsied. I stood, holding onto his elbow, marveling at the surreal experience. So this is what it would be like to actually court a prince. One who didn't hate your guts preferably.

I glanced around the room while Prince Asher made small talk. I didn't feel comfortable enough to introduce myself, but he made sure that I was known.

"This is Zinnia Greenstem, we're courting." He said it like it was the most obvious thing ever, but little flutters filled my stomach and I tried to squash down the feelings. *It's fake, a.k.a not real, Zia, get a grip.*

Some of the female faes looked at me with a mix of jealousy and curiosity, as if they had anything to be envious about. I was a lesser fae with fake wings in a fake relationship with a prince who didn't even like me. There was nothing to be envious of.

"How did the two of you meet?" A fae with pink hair asked and I was about to open my mouth to reply when a familiar lilac head crossed my peripheral vision.

"Excuse me for a moment," I said politely, Asher sent me an unreadable look. I ignored his dark eyes and flew over to the one person who I recognized in this crazy party.

"Lilac." I breathed, snagging her arm and she spun around. Her eyes ran down me and then back up to my face. She grinned, her bright white teeth sparkling against her dark skin and I was sure a lot of males turned their heads to admire her beauty.

"Zia?" She gasped before pulling me into a hug. I embraced her and noticed her glamored wings too. I guessed we both had the same idea about wanting to blend in.

"I've missed you, what's this about you and Prince Asher? I stopped by your house and your mom said you were working in the kitchens, but then I saw you come in with the princes-"

Before she could even finish her sentence, Asher swept in and grabbed my arm, pulling me into a dance. The band was playing a slower song, so he wrapped one arm around my torso and pulled me close, my heart thudded in my chest. Our bodies were a breath away, I could feel the heat radiating off his body and I struggled to think straight as he twirled us around.

"You interrupted me," I grumbled, annoyed I'd barely been able to speak to Lilac.

"I told you not to speak unless spoken to. What part of that concept do you not understand?"

"I'm not a child!" I whisper-hissed.

"Then stop acting like one!" Asher bit back and I wanted to stomp on his foot. But our heated conversation was drawing us too many curious looks so I plastered on a fake smile and looked up at his dark eyes, pretending to be all dopey and love-struck.

"Isn't the music just amazing?"

Luckily, Asher wasn't stupid and caught on quickly to my charade.

"Beautiful." He smiled tightly before spinning me out, holding my hand as my dress flowed around me. The song blended into a more upbeat one and I recognized the tune. It was a partner's dance where you switched between the people beside you. Of course, they'd play something like this at a dance, but my stomach squirmed at the thought of having to dance with a judgmental higher fae.

Asher made no move to leave the dance so we continued into the next song. Faes began to line up with their partners and we fell into step. Asher spun me out and our palms met, flat against one another as we stepped around each other.

The dance was a love song, traditionally a song for courtship parties and I felt the blush crawl up my chest and into my cheeks as Asher's forest-green eyes bore into mine. He watched my every move as we switched hands and our palms pressed together once more. The tingles in my hands caused goosebumps to erupt on my skin,

I tried to squash down the feelings and thoughts that flooded my mind every time we touched. It wasn't healthy to obsess over something false, it was a pretense. *Not real, Zia.*

As we spun out and prepared to switch partners, I noticed Cain The Pain with Lilac, dancing together. I suppressed a groan, knowing Prince Cain was nothing but bad news for Lilac, even if she was a little minx herself. She grinned up at him and he returned her smile, his sinister smirk made my skin crawl.

I twirled away and Asher's younger and much-less-friendly brother nipped in, catching my arm and smirking as I tried to pull away.

"Now, now little fae, let's not cause a scene, shall we?" His hot breath felt like a snake slithering down my neck as he spoke. His grip on my hand tightened uncomfortably and I swallowed thickly.

I glanced at Asher whose face was unreadable as he watched his brother spin me out. I avoided Cain The Pain's stare like it was the plague and I felt his creepy gaze on me as he danced behind me.

"For a lesser, you're still alluring, I'd take you to my bed, show you how to keep that mouth of yours shut."

Gods, I was about to scream, Cain's lewd and threatening comments made my stomach roll with disgust. Asher's intense gaze watched me and he completely ignored Lilac's attempts to get his attention while they danced together. She was trying her hardest, because to Lilac, all higher faes were fair game unless married and even then, I was sure she'd still try her luck.

And just when I thought this evening couldn't get any worse, the horny fae from Cuckoo stepped across the room two dancers, down from me.

And that was exactly when I panicked.

Cain's hand gripped my waist so hard I thought it would bruise. His fingers squeezed my flesh through the fabric of the dress as if he couldn't feel how much he was hurting me. I gritted my teeth, determined not to let him get a rise out of me.

"Play nice, little fae, we have an audience after all." His lips ghosted my neck and I wanted to vomit there and then. *Gods, get me out of here!*

As he spun me out, he kept a death grip on my hand and I threw Asher a pleading glance. His eyebrow quirked, but he did nothing to help. Cain's grip was suffocating me, making me feel claustrophobic.

I needed to get out.

I needed fresh air.

Now.

It was suffocating, my chest was heaving, hot air clogging my desperate lungs. My chest felt like it wouldn't expand, Cain's cruel hands stopping it from doing its primary function.

The heat of his hands on me and the tang of his scent in my nose had my heart hammering in my chest in panic.

Without another thought, I yanked my hand from Cain's grip and he stumbled forward, not expecting me to tug so hard. He let go to catch his balance and I darted to the left, just in time to see the horny fae turn right and grin as he made his way towards me.

I spun around to face the other way, looking for a escape route. My only option was to fly higher, up and out. Just as I considered that the only viable option- even if Asher was going to hate me even more for it, I flapped my wings and lifted off my feet, someone's hand wrapped my ankle and harshly yanked me down, knocking the breath out of me just as a loud eruption flung me sideways. My body slammed against the nearest wall, my mind was scrambled and stars spotted my vision. My head throbbed and I tumbled down the wall as the screams filled my ears.

Chapter Four

Chaos and Black Arrows

The first thing I noticed was the taste of blood in my mouth. I realized with a start that I'd bitten my tongue on impact and I almost gagged as I tried to swallow the iron-tasting liquid in my mouth. I spat it out, staining the floor red and I focused on trying to settle my cramping stomach, it was threatening to bring up everything I'd eaten today at the most inopportune time. I heaved myself up to a sitting position, my head spinning, and I assessed the room.

All around me was chaos.

Faes were screaming, yelling, being knocked down. Smoke began to fill the large space and I couldn't see anything past my hands. I coughed, my lungs heaving and burning as I inhaled the smoke, it clogged up my airways, filling my throat and chest. I test-flapped my wings as I sat on the floor, feeling weak, but knowing I needed to escape, even if my vision was obscured. I didn't even know what was happening, was it an attack from another kingdom? Was this some struggle for power?

A yell came from my left and I saw shapes moving in the thick haze. My ears rang from the explosion and just as I was about to heave myself off the floor and make an attempted run for it, a hand grabbed mine.

"Zinnia."

Asher's hand wrapped around my shaking one, he seemed unharmed though a little dirty. His thick hair was loose and fell around his face and shoulders as his eyes ran over me, assessing for damage I guessed.

"What's happening?" I croaked out, gripping his hand as he pulled me to my feet.

"Rebels." He shook his head. "We need to get out of here now."

I nodded as he pulled me along the wall, keeping low and hidden as screams and crashes went off all around us. He kept one hand on the wall, brushing his fingers along it and I saw the fog thinning as we moved. I assumed we were close to the entrance.

Asher turned to speak to me, his mouth opening as he gripped my hand when suddenly a thin, dark shape shot out of the fog, and his face contorted in pain as it lodged itself in his back.

A scream ripped from my throat as he fell forward and grunted. I stumbled to catch him as he sank to his knees.

"Fuck, Asher!"

He grabbed my hand and tried to heave himself up, but he fell down to the floor, his eyes fluttering shut. It was then that I noticed the dark, wooden arrow protruding from his back, between his wings, buried in his flesh. Blood was seeping out and staining his beautiful jacket a dark red color.

Shit.

I glanced around, aware that more arrows could come from any angle, so I knew what I had to do. I sank to my knees and heaved Asher's limp body up. We needed to get to safety.

Fuck, he's heavy.

He was dead weight in my arms, knocked unconscious and I began to worry even more. What if the arrow had hit his heart, what if he was bleeding out internally? *What if I accidentally drop him and that only wedges the arrow in further?! I'd then be responsible for a dead prince!*

I calmed my panicky thoughts, knowing they'd be of no use now when I needed a level head. Heaving Asher up, I slipped my arms under his arms and half-carried, half-dragged his body across the floor. I could feel his hot breath against the top of my bare chest as I pulled him up the steps, his face was basically pressed into my chest, my arms looped under his and gripping his shoulders with all my strength.

My wings flapped furiously, trying to assist in any way to help even out the load, but both of us were too heavy for my wings alone. My muscles screamed and my chest heaved for fresh air as I yanked us up the stairs.

Down below us, the fog had begun to dissipate and the chaos was revealed. Faes were scattered around, running in all directions, or trying to carry others to safety. Many were bleeding, limping as they held their wounds. I couldn't believe the rebels would attack innocent faes at a party. It made no sense whatsoever, then again, neither did the rebellion.

A guard dressed in the Royal uniform lay on the floor, an arrow protruding out of his chest. Red blood dripped off his torso and onto the stone steps below. His face was blank, eyes wide, and empty as he stared up at the ceiling, unseeing. His helmet had been knocked off, revealing his cropped green hair. He looked close to my age and I swallowed thickly as I heaved up Asher's limp body once more.

Sweat dripped down my brow and my breath came out in quick pants. I kept turning my head back to check behind me in case any rebels decided to take advantage of a female fae dragging an unconscious prince to safety.

"Asher, you're so fucking heavy." Yep, I cursed a lot under pressure and it was a very high-pressure situation.

I prayed to every God under the three moons that someone hadn't destroyed or stolen the Royal carriage because dragging Asher back to the palace would be the death of both of us.

Once out in the fresh air, I felt the delicious wind on my sweaty, overheated skin. I glanced down at Asher and noticed his olive skin was flushed a pasty white color. *Uh, oh.*

Looking around, I craned my neck to see any kind of transportation. Anything we could use to escape this nightmare. But nothing was there.

"Fuck!" I stomped my foot, angry tears blurred my vision and I decided staying out in the open wasn't the smartest idea. Heaving Asher up once again, I gripped his torso, careful not to touch his wings or the arrow embedded between them, and dragged him to a nearby tree. I lay him down on his front, twisting his head to the side so he could breathe and I couldn't help but brush his hair out of his face.

Unconscious, his face held no contempt or arrogance, he was just a fae prince who looked as if he was sleeping. Minus his pasty skin and the blood-stained jacket. A stupid thought filtered through my panicked mind and I wondered if Asher would get mad about his jacket being ruined.

Okay, now is not the time for dumb thoughts, Zia.

I wondered how far we were from my parents'

home. *Perhaps I could try and drag Asher to the bakery, get some help from my family and alert the palace guard that he's safe.*

I thought back to when we were in the carriage and remembered that we'd turned left out of the palace, instead of right and so we were on the opposite side of the city to my family.

Fuck, fuck, and fuck.

Desperation crept into my veins as I stared at Asher, as I racked my brains on what to do. Another crash and screams came from inside the house and I automatically crouched lower to the ground. I wondered about the other two princes, whether they'd escaped. And Lilac, I hoped she was okay.

Gods, what had happened? One minute was escaping that horny fae and the next, a full-blown attack ensued.

Footsteps pulled me from my thoughts and I peeked around the tree to see two Royal guards approaching the entrance, swords drawn.

Without thinking twice, I stepped out of my hiding spot and screamed.

"Help! I need help!"

They both jolted and stopped in their tracks and I thought for a horrible moment that they weren't real guards, that perhaps they'd been killed and the rebels had stolen their clothes and were pretending to help.

But when one of them turned to face me, I knew we were in safe hands.

Henrick flew over, looking over my shoulder to see his prince unconscious and laying in the grass. I stepped aside, feeling myself crumble from the events of the day.

"It's okay, you're safe. We need to get back to the palace."

Relief washed through me as I nodded and tears flowed from my eyes. Henrick scooped me up, while the other guard slipped his arms under Asher's body and picked him up with ease. I noticed how dirty and ripped his clothes were from all the dragging I'd done. *Well, at least he's alive for now.*

Henrick flapped his wings and I watched the chaos behind me get smaller and smaller in the distance.

We were safe.

～

I paced back and forth outside the closed door, chewing my nails down to the wicks and repeatedly running my hands through my hair. I stopped ever so often, straining to hear the hushed voices inside.

Once we'd got back to the palace, all the staff had taken Asher off in a flurry of clean linens, warm water, and on a stretcher of some sorts. They'd just left me in the entrance hall, in my blood-stained, dirty gown, with Asher's blood and my own smeared on my sweaty skin.

I'd flown to his room and patiently waited

outside his door ever since. The Royal healer had been inside, along with many maids. Every time the door opened, I'd tried to get a peek inside, but it had slammed in my face.

No one would tell me anything, no one even spoke to me and I was getting increasingly frustrated. I had just saved his fucking life, hadn't I? If I hadn't dragged him out, he'd probably be lying dead on the cold floor of that enormous house. I couldn't believe that I was treated like that, like I didn't matter when I'd *saved* him. Or at least, I'd hoped I had.

Both of the other princes were fine. Apparently, Finn had been close to the entrance, and so he had made a quick escape and Cain had managed to fly up and out when the first explosion had happened. Finn had sent guards back once he realized their brother wasn't home.

They'd been locked up in the throne room discussing the events of tonight with the King while Asher was being tended to.

Just as I was biting down my final nail and was pulling out my hair, a familiar head popped out of the room and I finally stopped my pacing.

"He's healing, he just needs rest. He's incredibly lucky the arrow missed his wings." Laurel said and I let out a cry of relief.

"Best to get cleaned up and get some sleep. You can see him in the morning."

I wanted to protest, to see him straight away and

know that he wasn't dead or hurt. But something in Laurel's eyes told me it could wait. At least someone had finally told me something.

I nodded, throwing one more glance at the closed door. I walked across the hall and opened my own door.

Laurel flew into the bathroom, and the sound of running water filtered through my thoughts.

I followed her in, dragging my tired body through the door and she undressed me in silence. She peeled off my dirty and blood-stained clothes. I didn't even know whose blood it was at this point. I didn't care about modesty, my body was numb as the events of tonight came crashing down on me. This game had taken a dangerous turn.

Once the bath was full, she let me be and I sank into the hot water, feeling the warmth envelop me like a hug.

I scrubbed my body until my skin was raw, my mind replaying the events of tonight over and over again. Asher's face as the arrow hit him, the dead guard with the unseeing eyes, the screams, the blood. It all haunted me, replaying over and over.

After a long soak, and draining and refilling the bath twice to wash away the remains of the night, I heaved myself out of the tub and wrapped a towel around my body before heading into the bedroom. The lump on my head throbbed and I cast a small healing spell to take away the pain. The relief was much needed.

I rummaged around in the wardrobe, sure that my favorite clothes had been destroyed by Asher's command. When my hand hit the soft fabric of my pants, I sighed and pulled them on, pairing them with a plain shirt. I knew sleep would evade me and judging by the position of the moons in the sky, it would be early morning soon and so I set to work.

Flying my way down the many stairwells, I landed at the lower kitchen and was surprised to see the fire still burning as bright as when Asher lit it. I guessed magic fire didn't need stoking. The oven was hot and perfect for baking.

I popped back up to the main kitchens and was greeted with the same curtseys as yesterday. *When will they understand I'm like them and not a Royal?*

"I was wondering if I could have some ingredients to bake," I asked politely. The staff looked at each other, their expressions a mix of confusion and curiosity. None of them moved an inch and I wondered if I'd been heard at all.

"You heard her, she wants ingredients, so let's get about helping Ms. Zia." Elsa's voice came from behind me and I smiled warmly at her.

"Thanks, Elsa."

"What exactly do you need? I'll get it delivered down to the lower kitchen. I'll make sure it gets properly stocked so you have your supply of ingredients when you want to use them."

I listed off supplies gratefully and Elsa set some of the staff on putting ingredients out for me to take to my kitchen.

As I was loading flour and butter into a bag, a couple of maids walked past and knocked my shoulder purposefully, pushing me backward and sending me stumbling. They giggled as they went by.

Luckily the bag didn't fall from my grip and I clenched my teeth, counting to ten in my head before letting out a breath.

"Ignore them," Elsa said as she placed the last of the ingredients I needed on the counter beside me. "They're just jealous."

I blinked, surprised at her honesty.

"Of me?"

"Of course, you've got Prince Asher wrapped around your little finger." She said bluntly and I was silent, wondering what the right response was.

"In all the twenty-five years that prince has been alive in this palace, he's never once come down to the kitchens, and yet, within a day of you being here, he's down here, helping you light a fire."

I knew Asher was spoiled and he'd never ventured down to the kitchens, so it didn't surprise me to hear that, but that he'd come here for me? That was something I didn't want to think about just now.

"And that's why they're jealous. Because you've had his attention for more than five minutes."

She laughed to herself before putting the eggs and honey pot in a box and flying out of the kitchen.

I followed her and thought about what she

said. Obviously, she didn't know about our deal, everyone thought Asher was smitten with me, which meant we were doing something right in the charade. But that was all it was; a charade.

Elsa left me with my ingredients and I began to prepare the pastries. I needed something to occupy my mind so I didn't overthink everything that was threatening to burst inside my head.

The routine of making the mixture, chilling it, and then rolling it out and folding it into pretty patterns kept my mind busy, and soon it was well past dawn. The delicious smell of apricot and basil made my stomach grumble and I tried a freshly baked pastry from my batch. It was mouth-wateringly good and I was content with them. Baking came naturally to me so I would have been surprised if it tasted terrible. However, with my luck recently, I didn't want to leave anything up to chance.

I gathered the still-warm pastries and put them into a box before flying up to Asher's room and landing at the door.

I knocked gently and held my breath as the door creaked open. Laurel's sweet face popped up on the other side and I smiled.

"He's awake." She whispered and pulled the door open for me to slip in.

The room was dark, curtains drawn, and just as messy as the last time I'd been in here.

"I'm just going to fetch some fresh water." And

with that, Laurel left us and I took in a deep
breath before turning to face Asher.

He was propped up by approximately a hundred
pillows, his bedsheets were drawn up to his waist
and he was shirtless.

Yep, *shirtless.*

My heart skipped a beat, actually more like
a hundred beats as I stepped closer. A white
bandage was wrapped around his chest and
shoulder, contrasting with his skin, and Gods, he
was *so* attractive.

There I said it. Prince Asher was insanely
gorgeous and equally infuriating.

His dark hair was hanging around his shoulders,
dangling like vines down his collarbones and he
smirked as he noticed the box in my hand.

"Is this a 'thank you for glamoring my wings' or
a 'get better soon' gift?"

"It's an 'I just saved your ass, you're welcome
and you look like shit, by the way' gift." I grinned
sweetly as I put the box on his bed and stood
beside him. He was even more attractive up close
and I had to stop my eyes from wandering down
his body. He obviously kept physically fit and it
paid off.

"What did I say about your clothes?"

I resisted the urge to roll my eyes. He always had
something to pick on with me.

"That they're stylish and I look great in them."

"You look like a farmer's daughter."

"That's exactly the look I was going for, how'd you guess?" I pretended to be surprised and Asher's mouth pressed into a hard line.

"Zinnia, you're a fae of the court now, you need to look the part. It's bad enough that you spend time in the kitchens, you don't need to look like one of them too."

Gritting my teeth, I pushed down the simmering anger that threatened to spill.

"One of them?" I said, calmly. Almost too calmly.

"Yes." He opened the box and pastries and plucked one from inside. It looked and smelled delicious, that was my pride and he was criticizing me over the way I dressed? I'd just worked hard and baked fresh pastries for him.

"And what exactly is that, Your Highness?" I mocked him and Asher's brows drew together.

"A lesser fae."

"That's because I am! You fucking brat!" I exploded, fed up with Asher's attitude.

He said nothing, his mouth pressed into a hard line and I spun on my heel, keen to have him out of my sight.

"Oh, and by the way," I turned back around to face him and proceeded to do the worst curtesy ever. So bad I was sure it was offensive. "You're welcome, you know. For saving your life."

And with that I flew to the door and slammed it shut behind me, leaving Asher and all his gorgeous expanse of bare skin to think about what I said.

Why did I bother doing nice things for someone who wouldn't even think about doing the same back?

~

Back in my room, I seethed, pacing the floor as anger boiled in my veins, before feeling exhaustion settle into my bones. I'd been running on adrenaline for the last ten hours and I needed to sleep before I crashed.

I ran myself a bath- yes, another one- it was my favorite place to escape to in the palace and rummaged through my wardrobe for some other clothes.

As I found my blue linen dress, the one I'd worn the day I arrived in this place, I remembered Dillon's letter and sprang up, flying to the dresser and digging it out.

Back in the bathroom, I stripped off, slipped into the hot water, and opened the envelope.

His familiar, spidery handwriting sent a little pang of sadness to my heart. I really missed my old life.

Zia,

I hope this letter finds you well and you're settling into palace life. Your family told me that you're working in the Royal kitchens, what an honor, and I'm very proud of you.

I smiled, glad that he was proud before my smile fell. I wanted to confide in him, and explain all the problems I was facing and I couldn't. I probably wasn't even allowed to have guests. I continued reading.

I wish I could write to you with warmth in my heart, telling you of all the great things that are happening here, but instead, I have to tell you some bad news.

My heart began to sink, my stomach twisted and I quickly read the next line.

Flora's taken a turn for the worse, she fell down the stairs yesterday morning and she's been in bed ever since. Your parents took turns looking after her last night, but they're both worried about her more than ever.

Zia, I want to help, but I don't know how to. She might have to stay with one of the healers and I know your parents can't afford it. I'm worried for them and your sister. I wanted to stay with her, but my duties took me away last night. I'll go back tonight to help.

I couldn't read anymore. This wasn't Dillon's burden to bear, he couldn't afford to take time off his work or even contribute to a healer's cost. I was in the richest place in the whole kingdom, someone had to be of help.

Without thinking, I jumped out of the bath, wrapped a towel around me, flew out of my room, and straight into Asher's. I didn't bother knocking, on account of this being an emergency and although he was an asshole, I thought maybe he'd be more inclined to help if I reasoned with him.

As I burst into the room, I took note of two things:

1.   A female scent lingered.
2.   A pile of pink tulle and mesh lay in a heap on the floor next to the bed.

My eyes snapped to Asher and his expression was smug as he lazily ran his eyes down the length of my towel-clad body. He was still shirtless, lying with his arms folded behind his head as he watched me.

"Can I help you?" He goaded me and then I noticed the gorgeous blonde fae who lay next to Asher, sleeping soundly and unaware of the rage that burned through me at the mere sight of her.

My heart was in my mouth, jealousy like I've never felt before flooded my veins and my hands shook as I gripped Dillon's letter.

I opened my mouth to yell, to rage, but nothing came out. I was in no position to yell or complain when everything between us was a devious game.

"Excuse me." I barely gritted out through clenched teeth and flew back out of the room. I didn't even look at Asher as I yanked the door shut behind me, too embarrassed to even consider that others might be around.

"Ms. Greenstem."

I spun to my left and saw Prince Finn standing in front of my door. The tips of his ears were tinted pink and he cleared his throat, keeping his eyes trained on my face.

Oh, he's modest, how sweet.

"Your Highness." I bowed my head and began to

make my way to my room, trying to side-step around the prince.

"I was wondering if you'd like to get some fresh air out in the gardens." I arched my brow and he stammered. "When you're fully dressed, of course."

I smiled, a dose of the shy, eldest prince was exactly what I needed to scrub out that image of Asher in bed with a female fae. One that wasn't me. I mentally shook myself for thinking such stupid thoughts.

"I'd love to."

~

I hurriedly changed into a soft gown, half-taking on board what Asher said about my clothes. I guessed he was right, I was part of the court and so should dress appropriately. The stubborn side of me wanted to rebel, but I reminded myself that I needed to pick which battles I actually wanted to fight. This one probably wasn't worth it. Even if I liked riling up Asher sometimes.

Finn was waiting for me outside my room and I smiled apologetically.

"I'm sorry you had to see that. I don't know what I was thinking."

Just as Finn was going to reply, Asher's door creaked open and the blonde fae popped out, giggling before flapping down the hallway, dressed in nothing but Asher's loose shirt and carrying her bunched-up dress.

The anger I'd felt a few minutes ago reignited like a flame and I spun away from her, flying in the opposite direction.

"Let's go this way." I angrily gestured to the double doors that led out to the garden, already five paces ahead and Finn silently followed me out.

The gorgeous smell hit me first. The flowers were in full bloom and I flew over, touching them gently. My magic worked of its own accord and soon there were dozens more flowers in the hedge. I blushed as Finn looked at them, his eyes studying the new growth.

"You're a Bloom Fae."

"A what?" I asked, watching his face. He smiled and reached out to touch the flower.

"Some faes have certain affinities, so they specialize in one area of magic. Your magic seems to be at one with nature, like when you touched that flower, you didn't even have to think about creating more, did you?"

I shook my head, watching his face as he softly stroked the petals.

"You're a Bloom, probably why you have an affinity for baking with plants or fruits too."

I quirked a brow, wondering how he knew that. Finn grinned sheepishly.

"Asher told me about your infamous pastries, I'd love to try them someday. He swears by them."

I laughed lightly, trying to picture Asher swearing by anything, and then the image of Asher in bed with that fae popped up into my head, *such an unwanted thought.*

I blinked a few times, pushing the thought away,

and wondered about my family. Were they Blooms too? Why had I never heard of this before?

"There are other magic affinities?"

Finn nodded, watching the flowers on the bush.

"Many. We studied all the types of magic growing up."

The Royals were lucky, they'd had such a good education, armed with a wealth of knowledge about the world around them while we, lesser faes, were taught by our parents and learned as we worked.

I thought about my parents, wondering if they had the same magic as me? I knew they had general magic, but did they specialize?

"Does it run in a family?"

Finn shrugged, eyes still on the fresh flower I'd made on the bush.

"Sometimes, and sometimes it just shows up in one person. It's like eye color, sometimes it shows up generations later. As Royals, we don't have an affinity for one type because our magic comes in many shapes and forms."

He touched the vines and they extended, intertwining with my fingers like a hand holding mine. I smiled up at him.

"Is that how Asher could make a fire so easily?" I thought back to how easy it was for him to light the oven's fire. He didn't even have to think about it.

"Ah, Asher. He's full of many, many emotions and our magic can reflect that. His magic calls to the anger in his veins, and so destructive magic such as fire comes to him naturally. He's a strong fighter too, but his healing and mending magic, that's what takes time for him. He's still learning."

I was surprised Asher hadn't mastered all the magic. With his arrogance, I'd have thought he'd have everything under his belt and at the tip of his fingers when we needed it.

The vines holding my hand slithered away and Finn smiled.

"How are you liking the palace?" Finn changed the topic and I was grateful, my thoughts were swirling around my mind about magic and I didn't really fancy a headache today. "Minus yesterday's incident."

Ah yes, that minor incident yesterday where we got attacked and nearly taken out by rebels wanting to destroy the crown.

I sighed, wondering whether to tell Finn the truth; that I really didn't fit in, that I was constantly worrying about my family and then there was Dillon's letter. Flora's health. My parent's debt. Gods, there were so many problems and I had no idea how to even start fixing them.

"It's different." I settled on a neutral statement, not wanting to piss off everyone in the palace.

Finn surprised me by laughing. He grinned as we flew away from the flowers and began to explore the gardens. We flew leisurely, flapping our wings in slow strokes as we wandered the perimeter of the walled gardens.

"It's an acquired taste, living like a Royal."

"You can say that again," I mumbled and he

chuckled again, smiling softly.

"Asher can be a force to be reckoned with and he'll never say thank you, so I'll say it on his behalf. Zia, what you did yesterday, saving Asher's life was beyond noble and we're all incredibly grateful for it." Finn gently touched my arm and I blinked, surprised that one of the princes could be so kind and caring when the other two were the exact opposite.

"Thanks," I said quietly, thinking about how I actually did save Asher's life and he can't even say one nice thing to me? Okay, apart from the pastries.

"I have to admit, there's a reason I asked for your company." He landed on the grass and I followed, we both sat on a bench at the end of the garden, looking at the palace in all its glory. It was stunning with the flower beds, trees, and perfectly manicured lawns. I wanted to simply stay here all day.

"There's someone I like," Finn said hesitantly, he was fiddling with his fingers, not looking at me. "A female, but I'm not sure how to approach her."

I grinned, for once it felt normal, him asking me for advice about a female like friends would. It filled me with warmth that Finn wanted to ask such simple questions and trusted my advice.

Staring at the palace, I wondered who'd caught the attention of the next King. Was she a beautiful fae from a faraway kingdom? Or a sweet noble's daughter who loved to dance? Wow, my imagination ran away with me and I shook myself. It wasn't my business who she was.

"Well, what do you think she'd like?"

Finn looked at me with confusion and I blew out a laugh. Gods, he was so hopeless, I wanted to help him.

"Perhaps invite her for tea? Get to know her, if you like her from afar, then you need to see if you still like her when she's up close." I smiled encouragingly, patting Finn's clasped hands in his lap. He looked worried like he was nervous and I desperately wanted to know the details.

"Okay." He said quietly and I wondered whether that was the answer he was looking for. "It's just that-"

He was interrupted by an angry yell from across the lawn.

I spun my head around to see Asher flying directly to us, at full speed, his face like thunder. *What's new?*

"What are you doing?!" He demanded incredulously, landing with both feet on the ground and towering over us. Finn laughed lightly, grinning up at the Brat Prince.

"Relax, Ash, there's nothing to see here."

"Your hand holding suggests differently. Don't forget she's mine." He snarled.

Before I could even think about taking my hand off Finn's, Asher grabbed my arm and yanked me up.

"Stay away from her." He all but growled at Finn and I threw an apologetic glance over my shoulder as he pulled me away from his brother. Why I was apologizing for the brute that was dragging me back through the gardens and manhandling me like I was a child, I really didn't know.

Finn's laughter faded into the distance as we flew into the palace. At least he was lighthearted about Asher acting like I was his favorite toy that Finn had stolen.

As soon as we landed in Asher's room, I wrenched my arm out of his grip and made a point of rubbing it, pretending he'd hurt me just so he'd feel something other than his selfish, ridiculous, and intense emotions.

"What the fuck just happened?" I demanded, majorly pissed off with his behavior.

"You and Finn were all over each other. You don't have to like me, but at least act like it in public because gossip spreads fast in this palace, and don't forget, we have a deal, Zinnia."

I threw my hands up incredulously, baffled by Asher's stupid and moronic behavior.

"All over each other? He asked me for a walk, not for my hand in marriage! And don't get me started on public images when you're in bed with some other fae and I'm supposed to act like I'm okay with that? You're being a hypocritical ogre, Asher Thornleaf! And it's *Zia*, by the way. How many fucking times do I have to tell you?"

I ran a hand through my hair, fed up with Asher and petulant behavior, he was a fucking spoiled child and I wasn't having any of it.

He stepped closer.

"What did you just call me?"

"A fucking ogre, because that's what you are. Say one thing and act another!"

Asher stood in front of me now and I was vaguely aware of his broad chest, his bare feet, his loose shirt, and his dark green eyes that pinned me with an unreadable gaze.

I swallowed thickly, noticing our proximity. I didn't want to fidget or give myself away but Asher's presence was making me nervous, my heart raced and my skin heated.

"You *will* respect me, *Zinnia*." He emphasized my name and I knew he was playing with me, purposefully antagonizing me. And Gods, was it working, I was furious.

"You don't own me, Asher. I'm not a possession. We have a mutual deal, not ownership."

I stared defiantly up at him. Gods, he was gorgeous and I hated how I felt as we had some strange stare-off competition. For some reason, I itched to touch him, and run my fingers through his irresistible, dark hair. The tension was thick, palpable, and I didn't dare blink nor breathe for fear of breaking it. I wanted it all, I wanted him to press his hot mouth to mine, I wanted to feel his hands on me, all over me. I wanted the ease the friction I so desperately craved from him.

Asher broke it off first, and I heaved a sigh as he stepped away, running a hand through his dark curls, doing the exact thing I'd been fantasizing about seconds ago.

I shook myself, trying to get rid of that yearning feeling. Asher had made it more than clear that he wasn't interested in me. The fae in his bed this morning proved that, so why couldn't my heart just stay out of it?

"What did you want?"

"What?" I cocked an eyebrow, confused by his question.

"When you barged into my room unannounced earlier, what did you want? It must have been important considering your lack of clothing." He smirked as my skin flushed bright pink at the memory of me in nothing but my towel, of his smoldering gaze.

Now was *not* the time to be thinking about being nearly naked in Asher's room.

A fire lit under my skin, simmering and making my stomach twist deliciously. His dark eyes watched me intently, teasing, testing me.

I thought about my reply, I wanted to be honest but I was scared of his ridicule. He'd made it plainly obvious that he didn't care for anyone but himself, so why would he help my sister?

But I had to try, I owed it to Flora and I needed to help my parents. None of them deserved what was happening to them and if I could do *anything* to fix it I would. Even if it meant swallowing my pride and stomping down my ego for a second.

"My sister, she's not well. I wanted to ask if I could visit her." I said quietly, afraid of Asher's rebuttal. I glanced up at him, holding my breath, awaiting his reply.

He studied my face for a moment, eyes running over my features, and I wondered what he thought about me. Not that I cared about his opinion, but strangely, I wanted to see what he saw.

He nodded briefly and I smiled- just a small one- but enough to show I was grateful that he wasn't keeping me prisoner inside the palace.

"Be careful."

I almost snorted out loud, Asher was worried for my safety? That was a new one.

"Wouldn't it be convenient for you if I wasn't careful? If I disappeared, then you could pretend I ran away and all would be solved."

Asher frowned, much to my surprise, but he didn't answer my question.

"The rebels know your face, so you need to have your wits about you." He stepped closer again and I held my breath as he cupped my cheek.

My heart raced, my skin warmed at the contact of his soft, large hand over my cheek. I resisted leaning into his touch. No, I wouldn't give him the satisfaction. *He doesn't care about me!* I had to keep reminding myself or else I'd never survive this game.

"I'm going to give you a small glamor, nothing big, just something to keep you safe."

Asher's concern for my safety made me even more nervous. Since when did he really care what happened to me? I had been the one to save his ass yesterday after all.

The warm heat flowed from his palm on my cheek and I stared at his chest to avoid looking into his eyes. Sharing magic felt way too intimate and I was feeling all kinds of mixed up in my heart.

Asher didn't care, I needed not to care but instead my heart was feeling weird in my chest and my skin was warm and my fucking stomach wouldn't stop twisting around like there were too many butterflies inside me.

The heat stopped and Asher dropped his hand, relief and disappointed coursed through me, and I frowned internally at the stupid battle inside me. Why was it all so complicated?

I nodded as a thank you and he slipped a ring off his finger.

"Take this." It was a plain gold band with a simple rose, with a leaf on a stem, dotted with thorns engraved on the inside of the band. It was subtle and I actually loved it, although I was confused about why he was giving it to me.

"It's a little too soon for marriage proposals, don't you think?" I teased and he just watched me, like he was figuring me out, I didn't like it. I squirmed under his intense gaze, my skin feeling all prickly.

"Wear this and use your magic if you're in danger. I'll be there."

He slipped it onto my pointer finger and I nodded, admiring how delicate the design was and how it looked on my finger. It gently resized to the right size around my finger and I gasped. Asher turned away and walked to his desk.

"Be back at sundown, Zinnia."

And with that, I flew out of the door, determined not to waste another precious minute in the palace walls.

CHAPTER FIVE

ALL IS NOT AS IT SEEMS

Dashing out of the palace at lighting speed, I flapped my bigger wings, thanks to Asher's glamor, and made haste to get to the healer's homes on the opposite side of the city.

I was offered a carriage before I left, but I opted to fly, mainly because I really didn't want to be a spectacle. Plus the carriage was probably slower at this time of day with the busy streets.

I zig-zagged in between the faes who were on the streets, going about their day. I dodged them as I tried to make up extra time. Asher had said sundown, which gave me approximately three hours to get to the healers, help Flora, and make it back before the Brat Prince got himself in a twist about my punctuality. Only the Gods knew how I could help, but I'd assess the situation and then assist in some way and then get back to the palace.

My stomach growled and my wings began to ache as I sped through the city. I was running on no sleep and lots of magic- the walk with Finn in the gardens had replenished my magic and energy. I knew I'd be exhausted by tomorrow, but at least I could rest easy knowing I was doing all I possibly could for Flora.

As I flew downwards, three faes hovered in front of me. I slowed down, aware that I was wasting precious minutes by stalling. They were in a semicircle, blocking my direct path. I could have flown around them, but it felt unkind. They were dirty, their drab clothes ripped and hanging off their stick-thin bodies. I felt sympathy for them because who knew, with Flora's health costs, perhaps that would be my family one day. The thought sent a shudder down my spine.

"Any food?" One of them asked me, eyes wide. She was young, not much older than me and my heart went out to her. Her face was sunken in and her skin was dull, almost grey-toned. She was malnourished and her stringy hair made her look much older than she probably was.

I'd left the palace in such a hurry that I hadn't brought anything aside from the clothes on my back. I should have packed provisions, been more prepared for beggars looking for food. I was dressed in expensive clothes, with higher fae wings, of course, they'd stop me and ask for help.

"I'm sorry, I don't have anything." I apologized, trying to placate them.

"What about that?" The tall male in the middle pointed to Asher's ring on my finger. I tucked my hand into my cloak pocket and glanced at them.

"That'd fetch a pretty penny." He was almost salivating at the idea. My heart began to pump quickly in my chest as he flew closer.

"We'd have meals for weeks." His female counterpart grinned.

"It's not mine-"

"Then you won't mind parting with it." The fae on the far right countered, staring at me with dark eyes. The way he watched me made my stomach churn.

"I- I'm in a hurry," I said desperately, trying to escape the three faes closing in on me.

"It'll only take a second, just give us the ring."

I shook my head, despite my pounding heart. I couldn't give them the ring, it was Asher's and too beautiful to be bargained off for a hot meal.

"It's not mine to give," I said, my eyes darting between the three.

The fae on the right lunged at me. "Then we'll just take it."

I snapped my wings to the left, ducking under the female fae, and flew as fast as I could. I'd have to take a detour to lose them, but I couldn't part with Asher's ring so if I had less time with Flora, then so be it.

I heard their wings flapping behind me. My larger wings meant I was faster and I darted in between houses in an attempt to shake them off.

Checking behind me, I slowed down, as I realized I'd lost them. I was in a different area of the city, so

I looped back around, making sure to keep my eyes peeled for them.

My breath came out in short pants and I tried to calm my racing heart. I needed to be more careful.

Rounding the corner in a quiet street, I landed on my feet and heaved a breath. Sweat trickled down my brow from the race and I untied my cloak, feeling the cool, afternoon breeze kiss my hot skin.

Suddenly, a hand grabbed my mouth and my scream was muffled as two more hands dragged me back into a dark building. I kicked out, trying to escape, arms and legs flailing helplessly but the hands only gripped me tighter.

I cried out, knowing their fingers would leave bruises as I struggled to free myself. My blood thundered in my ears, tears blurred my vision and a heavy thump on the back of my head rendered me unconscious.

~

When I came to, I was aware of three things:

1. My wrists were bound in iron cuffs, but Asher's ring was still on my finger by some miracle. I guessed the beggars didn't want it after all.

2. My head throbbed like crazy, I could feel the painful lump at the base of my skull- again.

3. I was in some damp, dark cell by the looks of it and I shivered, my mind racing, contemplating why I was there.

I surveyed my surroundings, trying to figure out how I got here. The room was completely dark, a faint dripping sound came from somewhere to my left. The ground was solid beneath me and I ran my fingers across it, it felt like stone.

I remembered the chase, then landing and being abducted. Oh fuck, was I going to be held for ransom? How long had I been out?

There were no windows in the cell, so I couldn't judge any timings. From the ache in my arms from the weight of the cuffs, I guessed maybe an hour or two. But I couldn't be sure.

I shifted on the floor, drawing myself up to my knees, and squinted in the darkness. The room was damp and cold, it smelled moldy and I shivered, my dress was sticking to my skin from the moisture on the floor and my cloak was nowhere to be seen.

Making out a large dark shape that I assumed was a door, I slowly crawled over, aware of how loud the iron cuffs were as they clanged and scraped along the stone floor. I hesitated, straining my ears to hear if anyone was coming but only the sound of my own breathing greeted me.

I squinted in the darkness, desperately hoping that the shape was an actual door and not just a figment of my imagination.

If someone heard me, no one made an effort to check on me as I made my way to the door, my dress was probably grubby and scuffed up. I knew my knees were grazed from the stinging sensation and I sat up, reaching out to feel the door.

It was solid metal, my numb fingers fumbled around for a lock, even a keyhole but there was nothing. I ran my hands down the length of the cold door and I let out a cry of despair.

"Let me out! Please! Somebody!" I yelled, banging my cuffs against the door, their clanging echoed in the stone room, but I was met with silence.

I slumped against the door, my back pressed to the hard surface as tears welled in my eyes. I considered why I was there; was it because they'd seen me at the party last night? Was it because I'd saved Asher? Or was this a random kidnapping of someone who they thought was high fae and could pay their way out? Or- and the thought sent a sour feeling to my stomach- was this something much darker?

I dared not to think about the vast possibilities and tried to focus. But I was tired, my magic was being cut off by the iron, and so my body was feeling exhausted from zero sleep. I sniffed as a tear slipped down my nose and I leaned my head against the door. The large bump in the back of my head sent a shock of pain through me and I cried out.

Sleep must have come to claim me at some point because I faded in and out of consciousness, unaware of time or anything around me. The cold had seeped into my bones and I honestly considered the thought that I might die there.

I'd heard nothing, no footsteps, no one else around and I wondered if I'd be abandoned. Nothing made sense and I fell back into a state of semi-consciousness as I pondered my existence.

Perhaps it would be better if I died here. Then my parents wouldn't have to worry about paying for me too, my deal with Asher would be off and everything would be right again.

Only it wouldn't.

Flora would be alone, Dillon and Lilac would miss me terribly, and my parents would be so hurt.

No, I had to escape. I *had* to get out.

I shook off the sleepiness that threatened to pull me under again. Clearing the fog in my head, I blinked into the darkness.

As I heaved my exhausted body up from the floor, I heard footsteps. They got louder as they approached my room and I panicked, hastily stumbling over to the other side of the room with what little energy I had left. I tripped on the hem of my dress as the door flew open and I stumbled, my knee cracked against the stone floor painfully and I cried out again.

"Zia!"

The familiar voice was jarring and I spun around to see my supposed best friend standing over me. The light from the doorway hurt my eyes and I shied away from it, hiding in the corner. I glanced down at my knee and saw blood dripping from the open wound. It seeped into the fabric of my dress, painting it a horrific red color and I choked back the sob that threatened to break free. That was my breaking point.

Dillon crouched down next to me, reaching out and I cowered away.

"Don't touch me." I hissed.

"Zia, I-"

"Not another word, Dillon. I don't know what the fuck is going on here, but I want to go home."

"Home to the palace or home to your parents?" He said coldly and I clenched my teeth.

"Flora's sick, you said so yourself. I need to get to her."

"I had to say something that would lure you out of the palace. I knew you'd do anything for Flora."

My blood boiled in my veins. "So you used my sister's illness as bait?" I snapped at him, feeling so many mixed emotions. My best friend had tricked me, betrayed me, and that left an icy feeling in my chest.

"Just listen to me, Zia."

"Why should I?" I yelled. "You had me kidnapped and locked up in here for only the Gods know how long. I'm tired, fucking hungry, and I want to go home." I said the last sentence again, punctuating my words to emphasize just how pissed off I was.

"I needed to get you alone. But I wasn't sure it was you with the glamor, I had to wait until it wore off. We need to talk. There are things going on at the palace, the rebels-"

"The rebels?" I cut him off, turning to face him

as he crouched next to me. His face was remorseful, but I couldn't accept what he'd done. "The rebels put you up to this?"

"No, they asked me about you after they saw you at the party yesterday. They told me they needed to get to you."

"And you just listened, you obeyed? Dillon, they're crazy. They're extremists."

"They're not." He shuffled closer and I cringed, pushing myself away from him. His face fell, and he sat back on his knees, watching me. "Zia, there's dark magic at work in the palace. The faes going missing, the attacks on the crown, it's all connected."

His words swirled around my mind. How was any of it connected? It made no sense.

"The rebels told you this?" I said skeptically.

"Yes."

"And you believe them? You've known them for what, a day?"

He looked away, his features washed in shame. "I've been in touch with them for months." His voice was low, his tone guilty, and instant rage flooded my veins.

"You've been conspiring against the crown for *months*?! You fucking liar-" I launched myself forward to smack him but Dillon leaned back, out of my grasp. I flopped onto the floor and screamed frustratedly as I connected with the solid stone ground once again, only this time it was my elbows and palms that felt the impact.

The sharp pain only added to my anguish and I

screamed out.

"It's not like I could say no, Zia, you have to believe me, I didn't want to-"

Suddenly it clicked in my brain, it made sense.

"Is that why you didn't want us going to Cuckoo for my birthday? Because you knew something?" My tone was accusatory. Dillon's hesitancy at us wanting to go out, his constant hovering around us, that fact he didn't relax once on that whole night- it all came together like a puzzle piece slotting into place. I stared at the floor angrily, before heaving myself up again to a sitting position and pinning him with the darkest look I could muster.

He nodded and at least had the decency to look guilty. "I'd heard one of the princes might be there and the rebels wanted to attack. I wasn't sure if it was going ahead, but I wanted to keep you safe."

"And yesterday? At the party?"

"I didn't know you'd be there. Your parents told me you worked in the palace kitchens, I didn't know you'd be parading around with the princes, acting like you're one of them." This time it was his tone that was accusatory and I almost flinched. He wouldn't understand even if I explained my situation. "Guess I'm not the only liar."

"What do you want, Dillon?" I said tiredly, pinching the bridge of my nose. I desperately wanted a hot bath and a long sleep for my weary bones.

"I know you don't trust me, but there is dark

magic going on at the palace. I'm sure the princes are involved and I need you to see what you can find out."

My mouth fell agape at what Dillon was asking me to do.

"I'm not *spying* on the crown! It's treason, not to mention I'm there as a courtesy, I can't go around the palace like I own the place." Even though I did and no one stopped me. Dillon didn't need to know that though, I was trying to build up a plausible case.

"You don't need to 'spy' as in listening in on meetings, just peruse around and see if you find anything." He said it like it was the easiest thing in the world and not at all illegal.

"If I agree to this, will you let me go?" I asked, I didn't necessarily have to do any spying, just say 'yes' and get the fuck out of there.

"Yes, but we'll need to meet every week. I need you to take this seriously, Zia. Lives are at stake."

I was tempted to say something snarky back but I held my tongue. I just needed to get out of there and then I could figure out the rest later.

"Okay, but prepare to be disappointed."

Dillon watched me carefully before producing a key from his pocket and unlocking my cuffs. I looked away as he slid them off, knowing my wrists would be bruised and rubbed raw. How I'd explain this to Laurel, let alone Asher, I didn't know. Perhaps after some sleep, I'd be able to heal some of the wounds.

"I'll meet you every Tuesday then. Meet at the old

forge before sundown."

I nodded, knowing better than to argue and Dillon stood up, offering me his hand. I ignored it and pushed myself to my feet. I was beyond tired and I couldn't even think about the journey home, I hoped we weren't far out of the city.

Dillon led me out of the room and down a dark and empty corridor before flying up some stairs and appearing in a clearing in the woods. I glanced down in the moonlight and noticed we'd just come out of some kind of hidden prison in the ground. There was nothing but woodland for miles and I shivered, thinking about how prisoners would just be forgotten out here. No one around to hear their screams.

Two bigger faes stood guard and I didn't look at them as Dillon offered me an arm. I again ignored him, I wouldn't be taking anything from that traitor again and I launched myself into the air, pushing off the ground and flying upwards.

"Don't forget our deal, Zia." I heard him call after me but I ignored him, flying higher and higher. Everything in my body screamed in pain but I kept flying, escaping the whole nightmare.

I passed the tree tops and hovered in the air, above the kingdom. Surveying where I was, I spotted the palace to my left, more than a few miles back and I flew in its direction, ready to go home.

~

"Gods, where were you, Zinnia?"

Was the first thing Asher said to me when I arrived at my room way past sundown. I flew in the window, hoping it would be open because I couldn't face all the questions they'd have at the palace gates when I looked like shit.

Unfortunately for me, the questions were waiting for me in my room instead.

I'd been panicking the whole journey back to the palace, trying to think up a good story. In the end, I decided I couldn't rat out Dillon, he was my best friend after all, even if he'd betrayed me. I couldn't face him being put on trial for treason.

"I got lynched by some beggars. It was nothing." I tried to brush it off but Asher blocked my path. I sighed, looking up at him.

He gently picked up my wrists in his own warm hands and studied the marks that were obvious on my fair skin. The skin had been rubbed raw, it was angry and red, and bruises were starting to form in rings around my wrists.

"Beggars don't do this." His thumb ran over the torn skin and I sucked a breath through my teeth. It stung and I desperately wanted a healing bath.

"What happened?" He prompted quietly, glancing down at my wrists again, then looking back into my eyes. I turned my head away, completely exhausted from today. Asher's hand tilted my chin back to face him.

His dark eyes were soft and concerned and I

so very nearly spilled every detail of my horrific afternoon. It was tempting to confide in someone, even if just for a moment. But then I remembered he was the Brat Prince and no better than Dillon.

"As I said, beggars jumped me."

"And yet you still have my ring. Why didn't you use it?"

I pulled my hands from his grasp. I shook my head. Too many questions for now.

"Leave it be, Asher. I'm tired."

"I nearly had the whole Royal Guard looking for you and you're lying to me?"

"I said leave it be. I don't want to talk about it."

Asher's hard stare made my heart break a little. I wanted to tell him, but the words wouldn't come out. My loyalty in Dillon ran too deep, not that he deserved it.

"You don't trust me." He said quietly, his tone accusatory.

"Trust is earned," I replied coldly, I wanted him to leave and if I had to be harsh, that was fine by me.

Without another word, he turned on his heel and left, flying out of the room.

I'd got what I wanted, so why did I feel like shit then?

I couldn't even think about analyzing my crazy emotions, I slowly flew into the bathroom, turned the tap, and began to run my desperately needed bath.

~

Sweat beaded on my brow as I aggressively rolled out the dough for the batch of pastries I was making. Yep, I was stress-baking, hiding in the lower kitchen so no one could find or pester me, and I was taking out all my anger and frustrations on the pastries.

I'd been mulling over what Dillon said in my mind. He was a good person, through and through, and even though I knew he was making a mistake with the rebels, I couldn't help but feel like I needed to provide him with actual information. My gut instinct told me something else was going on in the palace.

A chilling scream broke my thoughts as I braided the pastry dough and turned to the doorway that led down to the dungeons. I stood-stock still, knowing what I should do but at the same time, I was terrified. Laurel had warned me about the dungeons but if what Dillon said had a shred of truth, then I needed to see for myself.

Brushing my hands off on my apron- thanks to Elsa- I hung it up on a peg and slowly flew over to the doorway. I inhaled a deep breath, steadying my frayed nerves and I entered the dark corridor.

Following the stairwell down, I flew further and further into the bowels of the palace. The air temperature dropped and the stench of death flooded my senses. From my limited experience with dungeons (a.k.a none) I knew the smell probably wasn't unusual. Another strangled cry raised the hairs on my arms and the skin at the back of my neck prickled in fear.

So the faes who end up in dungeons are usually despicable creatures anyway, but did they deserve to be tortured for their crimes? I wasn't so sure. Those screams weren't from rotting in a cell for months, maybe even years. They were cries of pain and anguish.

Two guards stood at the bottom of the stairwell in front of a large door. It was hard to see anything in the darkness but as I approached, I could make out the large swords on their belts. It made me nervous. The other guards around the palace only carried small weapons like daggers, whatever was down here meant that these guards needed extra protection. I swallowed thickly.

Landing a few feet away, I tentatively made my way toward them. The one on the left spotted me first and frowned.

"You shouldn't be down here." His voice was monosyllabic. I couldn't see anything beneath his dark armor but he looked stiff, unnaturally so.

I ignored his remark, staring at the large door ahead and wondering what horror lay behind it.

"I heard a scream-"

"It's none of your business, go back to your kitchen, maid." He spoke harshly and I took a step back, slightly worried for my safety. Whatever was going on down here, they were guarding it with their lives. It peaked my suspicions. What if

Dillon was right? And something else, something more sinister was going on here?

Before I could enquire more, footsteps interrupted me.

"Out of the way." A voice ordered from behind me and I spun around, seeing two more guards dragging a male fae between their arms. He was unconscious, blood seeped from a large wound on his forehead, and his legs were dragging behind him, my heart went out to him.

"What did he do?" I asked.

"Treason." The other replied flatly, and I plastered myself to the wall as they dragged him up the door, unlocked it, and slammed it shut behind them. The fae's small wings were lying limply on his back and my own flapped in pity.

Was that fae a rebel? He didn't look particularly rebellious in his plain brown pants and white shirt. If anything, he looked like a regular fae, a farmer perhaps, a hard worker, someone who didn't have time to get caught up in treason.

"Little fae, what a surprise." Cain's overly sweet voice was laced with danger and I curled my hands into fists as he flew into view.

"Couldn't keep your curious nose out of it?" He grinned and the skin at the back of my neck prickled unpleasantly. Something about Cain really gave me the creeps.

He stepped forward, crowding my space, and his scent, dark and sickly sweet, almost rotten, clogged my nose, making me feel nauseous. "I know what

Asher's doing, so run along now and tell him there's nothing to here. Don't come back, or he may not see his precious little pet ever again."

My heart stopped in my chest, Cain's threat was very obvious and I found myself nodding before watching the guards unlock the door for Cain and zooming off back to the safety of my kitchen.

CHAPTER SIX

A TASTE OF THE OUTSIDE WORLD

I'd wrung my hands about a hundred and fifty times by the time Asher flew through my door to collect me for dinner.

Laurel had asked me multiple times what was wrong, but I'd brushed her off, pretending I was nervous about dinner. And I was- partly, at least.

I'd used some magic to heal the marks on my body from Dillon's kidnapping, just so no one asked any more questions because Asher's interrogation had been more than enough. So once I'd bathed, slept, and eaten, I'd healed them quickly, making sure to add an extra rosy hue to my skin, so I didn't look so pale and permanently worried. It had exhausted me but was worth it, even though I really needed a healer to do a better job. It would suffice for the time being.

But now I had to face all the Royals again at

dinner, knowing I was unworthy in the King's
eyes. Plus, I had to see Cain The Pain again,
but the thought that he was doing something
less-than-nice in the dungeons had my stomach
churning in a way that ruined any appetite I may
have worked up using all that magic.

Asher landed in front of me and his eyes ran
down the length of my body leisurely. I'd chosen
a mossy green dress, which matched his eyes
almost perfectly. It wasn't as elaborate as any
of the other dresses I'd worn, with lacing or
embellishment, but the thick velvet fabric looked
luxurious, if not a little suffocating.

His eyes were unreadable and not for the first
time, I wondered what he saw when he looked
at me. His jaw clenched and I internally rolled
my eyes. Was nothing I did for the prince good
enough? He was probably mad at my choice
of dress, or how I was standing, or the color of
fucking my hair at this point.

I sighed as he wordlessly offered me his elbow. I
knew he was mad at me for not telling the truth
about Dillon and for the fiftieth time today,
I considered spilling my guts because Gods,
I needed to tell someone about this fucking
hurricane of thoughts inside my head.

We flew in silence and the closer we got to the
dining hall, the more agitated I got. My nerves
were frayed by the time we landed and I was a
bundle of fidgeting energy.

"Breathe." He whispered, his breath tickling

my ear. My skin broke out in goosebumps and I swallowed thickly, my heart skipping a beat.

That was all Asher said as the doors creaked open in front of us. He didn't even look at me, just flew in and nearly dragged me along behind him, if my wings hadn't jumped into action before my brain.

"Asher, good of you to join us. And Ms. Greenstem." The King's disapproval was evident in his tone and I could have sworn I saw Asher's jaw clench at his father's words. Perhaps it was just wishful thinking.

We were seated and I kept my wings pinned tightly to my back as a guard tucked my chair in, I wasn't sure if it was the same guard as last time, but I didn't trust anyone anymore. Asher's glamor on my wings had worn off, but I think he only wanted it used for public appearances since pretty much everyone inside the palace walls knew who I was by now.

Asher sat to my right and Cain to my left again. He grinned, his eyes glinting with his earlier threat. I didn't know what Cain was doing in the dungeons but I was pretty sure Asher didn't know where his brother was spending his days. He seemed clueless so far, but then again, Asher was a mystery himself.

I just needed to get into the dungeons and figure out what was going on. Because there *was* something going on, you didn't have a heavily guarded dungeon for just common thieves.

"Finn, tell us more of what you've found about the attack yesterday." The King ordered his eldest son while the food was brought to the table.

I glanced around the hall, noting there were fewer present than at the last disastrous dinner. Only the Royal family were dining tonight and that definitely made me feel less insignificant.

"Well, Father, we've found three of the rebels so far and they are being questioned in the dungeons as we speak. They refuse to talk, but I'm going down there every day. I'm sure we'll break through soon."

My skin felt clammy as I stared at Finn, wondering if I'd got the kind prince all wrong. Were the screams I'd heard ricocheting off the dungeon walls his doing? What was he inflicting on those faes? Was he involved with Cain in something sinister?

"Of course, they'll only remain tight-lipped for so long. Why not let Cain have a try at getting them to speak." The King gestured at his youngest son and the latter grinned in degraded glee at the suggestion.

"When you're done playing nice Finn, let me know and I'll get what you need."

I knew Cain was crazy, and from the way Finn's brow furrowed, I guessed he didn't agree with his brother's brutal and barbaric methods either.

Gods, why is it so hard to figure out what's going on here at the palace? My eyes sliced to the King for a second. He was watching his sons carefully, eyes roaming over each of them. Maybe he wasn't as he seemed either.

"I will not have my captives butchered. They're faes after all-"

"They're criminals." Cain interrupted Finn. "They signed a death warrant as soon as they made a move against the throne. They get what they deserve." Cain hissed and the King raised his hand, indicating to them to stop.

"Enough. We'll have no more talk of torture."

Silence settled around the room and I picked at my food, watching the fae servants cut up an array of colorful and delicious-looking fruits, and place slices on each plate. I spotted a platter of braided pastries further down the table that looked familiarly like my own and craned my neck to look closer.

"These really are delicious, Zia." Finn grinned, a pastry in hand and I grinned as he bit into the pastry, his greedy mouth full.

After Cain's threat in the dungeon, I'd hastily baked them, my mind wandering back to what was going on below me and I'd nearly burned the whole batch of pastries. After I'd rescued them from being totally charred and inedible, I'd dropped them off in the kitchens, intending them to be for the staff.

Obviously, someone had got confused and served them to us instead. Next time I'd add a note so the staff can have a treat once in a while.

The Queen turned to face me, holding a pastry in her delicate hand.

"You made these?" Her surprised expression caught me off guard. I wondered if she'd written me off as hopeless after our last dinner, even if I'd told them that I grew up in a bakery.

"Yes, Your Majesty." I smiled politely, taking a sip of water from my glass and she nodded appreciatively.

"They're divine, you must teach the staff the recipe so we can have more of these delights."

The joy of having an actual task overruled all of my worries about the dungeons for a moment and I grinned, excited to finally have a purpose here.

"Yes, Your Majesty. I'll start first thing tomorrow."

She nodded and I tucked into one of the pastries, savoring the light, flakey pastry and the sweet burst of flavor in my mouth. Yep, even if I was biased, they were pretty amazing.

"Is that a ring I see on your finger, little fae?"

And there goes my content mood.

I swallowed and glanced down at my hand, noticing that Asher's golden ring adorned my pointer finger. I hadn't taken it off since yesterday and he hadn't asked for it back.

"And none other than Asher's Royal ring. My, my Asher, You really are keen on your pet-"

"Enough, Cain." It was Asher who spoke, his voice firm and ice cold. A shiver involuntarily rolled up my spine at the way he spoke. It was commanding and … *hot*? Nope, I crushed that thought as quickly as it came. His face was closed off, his jaw clenched as he stared down at Cain. Thank the

Gods someone else was fed up with the youngest prince's behavior tonight.

"Why is she wearing your ring, Asher?" The Queen asked and before I could even think about making up a good lie, Asher cut in.

"I gave it as a gift. It represents my intentions with Zinnia."

My heart gave a strange, extra loud thump, but my stomach churned with Asher's blatant lie. I smiled weakly at the King and Queen who both wore different expressions.

The King, on one hand, looked mildly horrified that his son had chosen to be all but betrothed to such a commoner and the Queen, on the other, looked proud of her son. *I like to think that my delicious pastries have some sway in the matter.*

The room was silent once more and I wondered if every dinner was going to be as awkward as this. Didn't they just have normal dinners where they discussed mundane topics like the weather?

"That's fantastic news." It was Finn who spoke, his voice full of warmth and he raised his glass. "To Asher and Zia."

The rest of the table was hesitant to make a toast to us. Slowly the King raised his glass and in turn, the Queen did too. Only Cain ignored us and picked at his food.

A small grin tugged at Asher's lips and I considered that perhaps pissing his father off was just another part of his game. His game where I was a pawn.

The dinner moved by slowly after that awkward toast, the King excused himself, saying that he and the Queen had matters to discuss- probably us. Cain slinked off to Gods knew where and after Finn finished up eating, he said he'd be retiring to the library.

Asher and I sat in silence as he sipped his mead and I picked at a leftover pastry on my plate.

"Well, that went better than I expected."

"What *did* you expect?" I shifted in my chair to face him, he'd kicked up his feet on the chair opposite and lounged lazily, looking the whole part of the prince I'd pictured. Crown upon his head, rings adorning each one of his long fingers, and his dark eyes watching me intently as he held his golden goblet in his hand.

"A deliciously heated argument." He grinned wickedly and my stomach clenched. "I thought my father might explode when he saw the ring." He chuckled and took another sip.

"I forgot I kept it." I reached for the beautiful ring on my finger and slid it off. "Here." Somehow my finger felt empty without it.

"Keep it, no doubt you'll need it again, though I'd prefer if you actually used it."

I said nothing, not wanting to admit that the iron cuffs kept me from using *my* magic, let alone reaching out to Asher for help.

"Shall we retire?" He asked, sliding his feet off the chair with a thud and placing his goblet on the table.

I still held the ring between my fingers and he stared at me, refusing to take it. I didn't want to keep it though, it represented more than what I'd initially thought and I didn't like the weight of it on my finger. An unspoken promise. Even if it was all a lie, it made me uncomfortable just the same.

I clenched my jaw and thrust it at him, but he made no move to take the ring off me and actually crossed his arms in defiance.

Not taking no for an answer, I attempted to find a pocket on his shirt, scanning the loose, cream material and trying not to take note of how good it looked against his olive skin and sculpted torso. I swallowed thickly, Gods, it was taking a lot of self-restraint not to stare even more. I lowered my eyes and spied a pocket on his pants.

Without a second thought, I pushed my fingers into the pocket on his thigh and Asher stumbled forward from the force of my actions. The thick muscles of his legs rippled under my hand, my fingers dangerously close to his crotch, and I felt my heart thudding in my chest, a fierce blush crawling up my cheeks. He caught me by the shoulders, holding me at arm's length and frowning as I pretended to smile innocently.

"Take the ring, Zinnia. I won't ask again." His voice was low, almost predatory and the impulsive part of me wanted to push him, tease him, see how long it would take to break his walls down.

Why was I thinking like this? Asher just pushed me away, he'd made it very clear that he had no interest in me. So why couldn't I just see him platonically too?

He fished the ring out of his pocket and as I was about to protest, he grabbed my hand firmly and slid it slowly, inch by inch down my index finger. My eyes locked with his, the dark green swirling, and my heart thudded so loudly, I could hear it in my ears. A delicious shiver rolled down my spine, my thighs clenched as Asher's eyes bore into mine, he swallowed, his throat bobbing and my breath hitched. Gods, he was so attractive.

I barely breathed as he stepped closer, still gripping my hand. His breath tickled my face as he crowded me, pushing me back towards the table. My lower back bumped into it, my free hand gripping the wooden edge and the other, wrapped in Asher's large hand, holding my tightly as he towered over me and the tingles in my hand were back in full force.

"Don't disobey me again."

Asher's stern tone made me jerk back to life, my body suddenly functioning again, how dare he treat me like a child! The words rolled off my tongue before I could stop them.

"You don't have to act like such a possessive troll, you know."

I thought he'd lash out, tell me to watch my mouth and sharp tongue, but instead, his lips quirked up at the corner as he suppressed a smile. Butterflies erupted in my stomach and his eyes caught mine.

"I know." Was all he said as he took my hand and pulled me to the doors. They swung open of their own accord and his huge wings flapped, lifting him off the ground.

We flew in silence to our rooms, me slightly behind Asher. I stared at his broad back as I pondered this evening's events. His behavior confused me. He'd gone from closed off and telling me to watch my mouth every five seconds to something else entirely and I wasn't sure about it. The latter made me feel confused, made my stomach twist and my skin heat. He made me want him and that was something I really didn't want to consider.

When he landed outside my door, he turned around to face me.

"You've done well, Zinnia, despite everything and so I'm granting you whatever you'd like."

Minus the fact he just praised me like you would a child, my eyes widened, whatever I liked? The first thought that popped into my head was Dillon and how I needed to be granted leave to see him. I wanted to use that time for Flora too, perhaps I could do a two-in-one and visit them both in the time I was allotted.

"I'd like to request leave to see my family once a week."

Asher's eyebrows rose, perhaps he'd expected me to ask for expensive gowns and jewels. Maybe another fae would have taken advantage of his offer, requesting luxurious gifts and excessive wealth, but I was simple. My family came first or maybe spying on the palace, and reporting back to Dillon and the rebels came first. Gods, if I got caught, I'd be executed for treason. I needed to be extra careful.

"You can have two hours on a day of your choice. But wear that damn ring." The way he swore made something inside me jump to life and I nodded silently, my stupid heart making me feel weird.

"Goodnight." He said and with a slight bow, he left me in the corridor as he flew through his open door and it closed behind him.

What in the Abyss just happened?

~

I woke early the next morning, deciding to try and prize some information out of Asher since he was in good spirits. I just wanted to cross him off the list in my mind of people who could be involved in the dungeon situation. And I desperately didn't want Asher to be. Maybe my heart also had something to do with it, but I tucked that thought away for the moment.

The Royals weren't having breakfast together, which I was thankful for, but I knew I'd have to encounter a Royal breakfast at some point.

"How's that handsome friend of yours?" Laurel asked as she braided my hair. I glanced up from the stray thread I was picking on my dress and looked at her through the mirror. Her blue eyes gleamed with some cheeky curiosity and I grinned.

"He's well." I thought of Dillon and how much

he'd changed, what had caused him to become part of the rebels. My face fell and Laurel noticed, she stopped braiding my hair and rounded the chair, crouching down to face me. "He's different though. I think my time here has changed us."

"People change, sweet girl. You mustn't lose heart. Sometimes, change can be for the better too."

A solitary tear trickled down my cheek, surprising us both as it dripped off my chin and fell onto the fabric of my pale yellow dress, darkening it in a little circle. Her face was sympathetic as she gripped my hands in her soft, warm ones.

"He's not who I thought he was, who I grew up with." I whispered.

She watched me with kind eyes and for a second, I wished she was my mom, I wanted a hug so much.

"He'll come around, it's a big change for all of us."

I nodded, and she stood up, finishing up my hair and humming quietly as she did it. Her kind heart comforted me a little, but I worried about Dillon as much as I did Flora, if not for completely different reasons.

Once I was ready for the day, I flew out of my room on a mission. I needed to strike Asher from my list and the best way to do that was to interrogate him in the nicest way possible. If only I'd had time to bake some pastries to smooth it all over.

I knocked on the large oak door that led to Asher's study- I'd already learned my lesson from not knocking so I made sure to remember this time.

I felt a little anxious but for a new reason. The Asher I saw last night, the one that took a joke rather than reprimanding me, had kept me up half of the night, thinking about his full lips and delicious smile. And finally, when I'd got some shut-eye, he'd plagued my dreams with flashes of his gorgeous body, his lithe hands all over me, touching, exploring and his hot mouth exactly where I wanted it. I'd woken up more than a little frustrated.

"Enter." He called and I pushed open the door silently. The room was large, as were all the rooms in the palace, and again, it reflected Asher's demeanor. The dark paneled walls were cozy and a dark red velvet couch was to the left of the door. His back was to me, his head dipped down between his shoulder blades as he sat at his desk, writing something.

I stood awkwardly for a moment, unsure of what to do. As he continued to ignore my presence, I wondered if I'd made a bad decision coming in here, thinking Asher was different. Perhaps last night had been a simple fluke.

The silence was heavy and each passing second made me feel like an idiot for believing Asher could be anything other than the Brat Prince. *Why would he be different? He's a spoiled, selfish, entitled-*

Another knock made me jump out of my skin, interrupting my not-so-polite thoughts and I spun around, seeing Finn's blond hair poking through the door.

"Zia, how are you this morning?" He said politely as he stepped in, smiling. Gods, he was so polite and kind. How was Asher the complete opposite?

"I'm well, thank you and yourself?"

"I'm well too." He glanced at Asher's hunched back. "Is he busy?"

"*He* is busy and doesn't like being interrupted." Asher all but growled, I guessed he was still feeling sore about mine and Finn's stroll around the gardens.

"I'll only be a moment," I said and Asher sighed dramatically, spinning around in his chair.

He looked divine and my feelings were all mixed up. His midnight hair was loose again, curling around his shoulders and face, his crown glittered against the locks. He wore a sky blue shirt, tucked into black leather pants, and his feet were bare-again. I swallowed thickly, a blush warming my cheeks and I could have sworn I saw Asher smirk.

"Well?" He prompted. "Your moment is nearly up."

I frowned, realizing I'd been ogling for longer than acceptable. I licked my lips, ready to ask about this whole dungeon situation.

"I was at the dungeons the other day-"

"Zinnia, how many times do you have to be told not to wander down there?" He sounded exasperated and I reeled back. "Laurel told me you've been curious, but you have the whole run of the palace, why are you always going back there?"

"I saw something, Cain was there."

I'd expected Asher to perk up, perhaps sit and listen to me but instead, he got up, waving his hand at me and shooing me away.

"My brother has a sadistic personality, of course, he's spending his time in the dungeons."

"But-"

"Go and bake your pastries and stop trying to cause trouble." His patronizing tone was like a bucket of ice water over my head and I felt like an idiot for thinking he was anything more than a selfish prince.

"I'm not causing-"

"You're making things into more than they are. Cain likes to spend his time in the dungeons, we don't question it because he's always been like this. Now, be on your way. Go and sniff the flowers, and leave me in peace."

Asher turned around and all but threw me out of his study. I was beyond furious, he wouldn't even hear me out and worse, he treated me like a fucking child.

Before I knew it, my feet had me marching up to him and as he spun back to face me, I realized I was dangerously close to his chest. So close that I could smell the scent on his skin, like fresh grass and something else. Something so alluring that I almost forgot my anger. Almost.

"If you'd just listen to me, you're not taking me seriously-"

"Well, why don't you ask Cain yourself since you're so obsessed with him and the dungeons." He spat, his face full of anger. Obviously, he didn't like to be undermined, but I didn't like to be treated like an idiot. "Or better yet, why don't you court him and spend all your days in that rotting place with him, huh?"

He towered over me but my wings lifted me to his level, our eyes met and I felt the spark between us. His lips, his stupid mouth, his hurtful words. There was chemistry between us, anger, hatred even, mixed with lust. Yep, I was definitely attracted to him. I was torn between smacking him so hard that he'd never treat me like a child again and kissing him so hard that all those mean words tumbled back down his throat and never came back up again.

His hot breath brushed over my skin, our lips only inches apart. The feeling was heady, my mind hazy and the weight of Asher's stare made me suspect he felt the same.

"We better go, Father's waiting for us." Finn cleared his throat behind us and I clenched my teeth, trying to calm my heart and the anger that buzzed in my veins.

"This," I motioned between the two of us. "Isn't over," I warned Asher and I flew out of the room without another word.

～

I was tempted to go back to the dungeon, to prove to Asher that I was *not* making shit up and I was definitely not obsessed with Cain- it was the exact opposite. His presence repulsed me, like a snake, he slithered around the palace and wasn't to be trusted under any circumstances.

Instead, I seethed in my room for a while, pacing to burn off that excess energy. I decided to write another letter, even though I hadn't heard back from Flora yet. I wondered if my letter had even been delivered. Laurel had promised that Henrick would deliver it personally but perhaps it had got lost or forgotten.

I sighed, sliding down at the desk and beginning to write again. The words flowed out of me as I told Flora about me being a Bloom, about my pastries going down successfully, and how much I loved the palace gardens. I had no skill in drawing or else I'd have drawn the gardens, giving her something to picture, although even the best artist in the world wouldn't have done it justice.

The door flew open as I was sealing the envelope and I didn't even bother turning around to see who it was. I knew it was the Brat Prince; his lack of knocking had proven that.

"We're going to the city this afternoon, I need you to dress properly."

"Good afternoon Asher, I'm well thank you and I hope you are too," I said sarcastically. I spun in my seat and glared up at the prince.

He ignored my tone and eyed me carefully, standing a good distance from me. Perhaps he thought I'd blow up at him, yelling or crying after this morning. Maybe it would work on him. But I suspected not.

"My father has heard rumors that the people think

you're a plant, a spy from another kingdom because of the recent attack and the mixed information."

I frowned, confused about what he meant by "mixed information".

"It seems our noble friends have a hard time keeping their mouths shut when it comes to the affairs of the crown and lesser faes." He answered my questioning frown.

A quiet "oh" came out of my mouth as I realized the nobles were spreading vicious gossip about me being lesser and all the controversy around it. But then they were probably confused when I turned up with golden wings. Yeah, I'd be a bit thrown off too if I were them.

Asher strode towards me, his eyes watching me sharply.

"We're leaving at three. Laurel will be in to help you get ready." He looked down at me, his tone said business, and his stare made me want to squirm. "I need you to do better, Zinnia."

"I'm hearing a lot of 'needs', perhaps if you asked politely-"

"I don't have time for your sharp tongue today." Asher interrupted, obviously not enjoying my remarks. I swallowed my rebuttal and glared at him.

"Well, I had plans this afternoon."

"Consider them canceled." And with that he strode out of the room, leaving me gaping behind him.

His audacity never ceased to amaze me.

~

Emerging from my room some half-hour later, I saw Asher leaning against his door frame, ankles crossed, taking a bite out of an apple. The way his teeth sank into the fruit did strange things to my body, making me tingle all over, and my eyes tracked every single one of his movements as he chewed and swallowed. I really needed to focus on the task at hand and not be obsessed with the way he ate.

His eyes leisurely wandered down my body, I thought I'd have gotten used to it but it sent a fire in its wake. Recently, it had gotten harder to curb my feelings for Asher. It had been nearly a week since I'd arrived and I found myself appreciating Asher's looks more often than not.

Again, he offered me his elbow and I joined him, dressed in a light blue gown. Asher had gone for a white shirt with light blue trim, again I wondered why he was so keen on making us match all the time. Yet another thought to tuck away for later.

We flew out into the entrance hall again and I looked out of the open doors to see the carriage awaiting us at the bottom of the steps. Why we had to take such excessive modes of transport I'd never know.

Two guards flanked us as we approached the carriage and my heart warmed as I was met with a familiar face. Henrick winked at me as I landed on my feet at the bottom of the huge staircase.

"Ms. Greenstem." He bowed and offered me his arm and I climbed the steps into the carriage.

But just before I could take up his kind offer, another hand grabbed mine and I glanced back to see Asher, jaw clenched, aiding me into the carriage. His grip on my hand was so tight I wondered if it might bruise.

I tried to smother a laugh that threatened to bubble out of me at Asher's obvious jealousy. First with Finn and now with Henrick, Gods this prince was possessive and it was all for show too.

"I don't like you holding hands with other males." He whispered angrily behind me as I settled down in the coach, ripping my hand from his death grip. Asher sat next to me, his size meant our thighs pressed together and I bit my lip, feeling the warmth from him spreading into my already flushed skin.

"Well, you better think about that when you have little Miss Pixie in your bed at night." I smiled oh-so-sweetly but inside I was bitter about that stupid female fae. Calling her a 'pixie' was a low blow but as I glanced at Asher, I could have sworn I saw a hint of a smirk tugging at his lips.

"Are you not going to glamor my wings?" I asked, confused why we were going out in public without my usual disguise.

Asher ignored me, and I huffed as we settled into silence. The two guards sat opposite us, Henrick grinned and then turned his head to look out of the window. I did the same, thankful for the distraction of the rolling city and a familiar face among the Royal faes. It was no secret that I was disliked by some of the maids or guards, I didn't blame them though, it was hard to see them treat me differently when they didn't even know half of the story. They just assumed I was a stupid lesser fae who stumbled into Asher's arms and got to play dress up. And I'd let them believe it, for now.

The carriage rolled to a stop as I was lost in my thoughts, my mind elsewhere. The guards stepped out first, surveying the area and I peered out of the window, recognizing the buildings at once. It was market day, so the square was bustling, faes flapping their wings and bartering goods.

An all too familiar redhead was sitting on a chair overlooking one of the stalls and that was all it took for me to launch myself out of the carriage as fast as my wings would carry me and bolt over to my sister.

"Zinnia!" I heard Asher call but I was already gone, my heart thumping in my chest as I tackled her chair and nearly knocked Flora over.

"Little sister!" I gathered her up in my arms, holding her close and breathing in my sister's scent. I pressed my lips to the crown of her head, giving her a heartfelt kiss. She smelled like the bakery and flowers and Gods, I really had missed her.

"I missed you." I sighed and she softly punched my stomach, laughing as I let her go.

"You were suffocating me with your beautiful and ridiculously expensive dress." She grumbled but the sparkle in her eyes said that she was as happy to see me as I was her. "What are you doing here?"

Before I could answer, my mom's voice pierced my ears as I spotted her flapping her way over, my dad in tow with a bulging sack full of items thrown over his shoulder. It was cheaper to buy items at the market than from the shops and I knew my parents bartered to the very last moment to get a good deal. I hugged each of them, my mom basically barrelling into me and I was enveloped by the familiar scent of the bakery, warm bread, flour, and sweet smells. The familiarity made my heart ache.

The Brat Prince strode up behind me, as confident and cocky as ever and as I turned, I saw a smile playing on his full lips.

"You planned this?" I asked, confused by the situation.

"Prince Asher!" My mom fumbled a curtesy and my dad bowed as the townspeople stopped in their tracks, taking a pause from their busy lives to stare at one of the princes in all his glory.

"I decided to organize this trip so the people of the city can understand and see for themselves that Zinnia is not a plant or a spy in the palace, she's one of them."

The way Asher said "them", the way he separated himself from the rest of us made my blood boil. I was wrong to think there was anything between us when he saw us as "them and me." I wanted to smack his stupid face and then my own for being so foolish.

My second thought steamrolled my first, Asher used my family as leverage? I clenched my fists, annoyed that he was acting so sneakily and putting my family at risk to save his ass.

"- and I'm sure she loves her time at the palace. She's so lucky to be baking in the kitchens." My mom was rattling on to Asher and I felt his arm slip around my waist, my skin prickled and flushed as his hand rested on the small of my back. It felt heavy, comfortable even and that surprised me the most.

"Zinnia and I are courting."

And at that moment, I could have sworn my mom was torn between fainting in shock and clapping in glee.

But me? I was annoyed that Asher had brought my family into our web of lies. It was one thing to fool his parents, for his sake but it was another entirely to bring both our families into it. My family had much more to lose than his.

My parents smiled, their faces cracking into the biggest grins, so wide that I had a hysterical image of their skin splitting from smiling so much.

"Zinnia!" My mom all but squealed, clapping her hands together and then gripping my dad's arm so tightly I was sure it hurt even though he didn't let on if it did. "This is great news, why didn't you tell us-" She began her mini-rant about being out of the loop and I glanced at my sister, her knowing smile playing on her lips.

"That would be my fault Mrs. Greenstem, I wanted us to have a private courtship but some nobles thought she wasn't to be trusted, so I had to show the city that she is honest and true to the palace." Asher's smile was enough to win my mom over for eternity. She practically wilted at his sparkling grin and I saw Flora's cheeks tint a rosy pink. My skin flushed and suddenly I wanted to make Asher smile, to know that that smile was just for me.

"That's no problem, Your Highness." My mom basically stumbled over her words and glanced at me, her eyes shining with hope and excitement. *I'll be the talk of the bakery now, I guess they'll get more customers though.* I thought as I smiled back.

Asher looked down at me, his dark eyes making my stomach do that weird swirly thing. What was up with that? I bit my lip and his eyes darted down to my mouth. The chemistry between us was undeniable and as he leaned in, I panicked turning my head to face my parents and I smiled sweetly as his lips pressed to my cheek. His warm breath lingered longer than necessary and my cheek tingled as he pulled away, my skin hyper-aware of his soft lips. And Gods, did I want him to kiss me.

I tried to avoid his eye contact after that near-kiss, but Asher's fingers found mine, weaving them together and my heart thumped double-time in my chest.

"It was a pleasure to meet you, Mr. and Mrs. Greenstem."

Asher's eyes slid over to Flora and she stood up on her shaky legs, she stumbled as she curtseyed and my mom rushed forward, holding her arm gently.

"You must be Flora."

How Asher knew her name, I didn't know considering I'd never said her name to him, but he was a prince and they really had their wily ways.

My sister's pointed ears glowed bright red as she grinned at Asher.

"Yes, Your Highness." She smiled at me, and then kept her eyes on the ground, obviously feeling shy around the prince. He was her idol after all.

She sat back down in her chair, and my mom's hand glowed as she tried to help Flora. My heart ached again, knowing I was living a life of luxury in the palace and my parents were still struggling with Flora, it made me feel immensely guilty.

I watched Asher's expression, but he wasn't giving anything away as he studied the interaction between my family closely.

All too soon, we were back in the carriage after bidding my family farewell. Asher had charmed them of course, and so they were over the moons over the whole thing. The lies settled heavily in my stomach and left a bitter taste in my mouth.

I hated lying, I hated the fact that my family had been sucked into this poisonous web Asher and I had spun, I hated that I still didn't have any way to help Flora and I especially hated that something was going on in the palace and no one listened to me.

"We're having another dinner tonight, but we're hosting to officially announce our courtship."

Asher's voice cut through my whirlwind thoughts and I turned away from the window to face him, noticing the way the setting sun bathed his skin in a gorgeous golden tone. I wanted to preserve that memory forever and think back to it when all of it was over.

I was deep in thought and no longer sure of where I stood. If Asher was announcing us officially, this was getting out of hand. It was supposed to be a fake, mutual courtship but with the rebels and now Asher's determination to see this through to the end, I was beginning to panic.

Before I could even consider what I was doing, I threw open the carriage door and nearly tumbled out, watching the solid ground rush past us as we went at a steady speed toward the palace.

"Zinnia!" Asher yelled and tried to lunge for me but all I felt was his fingertip graze my wing as I took flight and left the Brat Prince behind.

~

My breath came out in pants and my wings desperately flapped, climbing higher and higher than I ever had been before. The air in my lungs felt constricted like I couldn't breathe, I needed a moment's reprieve.

The world had always seemed so big to a small fae like me. Growing up and living in the same place,

I'd forgotten other kingdoms existed, happy in our own. But as I flew higher above the sprawling city, my eyes roamed over the boundaries, past the line that separated Nissa and Eloch, and further into the neighboring kingdoms. My heart thudded in my chest as I considered life beyond Nissa, life without the troubles I had now.

It was tempting to fly away, leaving everyone behind and start afresh. I knew I'd be able to find somewhere within another kingdom to fit in, to bake, and pretend all my worries and problems didn't exist.

But they did.

Flying away wouldn't solve anything.

My wings ached as I hovered, so high above the city that the other faes looked like tiny little bugs, scurrying around. I knew Asher would be searching for me, if not flying around himself, worried I was bailing out on his grand plan.

The problem was that I didn't like his plan anymore, he'd said we'd have a fake courtship to convince his parents, perhaps even his entire family, but the whole kingdom too? When this eventually came to an end, would I even have a place in Nissa, after I'd fooled everyone? Or would I be shunned?

I glanced longingly at the boundary line, marked out by an outpost house. Life would be different, but by no means better.

I had Flora, Dillon, and Lilac to worry about, not even to mention my parents and sweet Laurel.

No matter how much I wanted to fly away and

escape, I needed to stay and face my problems.

With a heavy sigh, I began to spiral down back into the city.

CHAPTER SEVEN
THE ROYAL LIBRARY

I knew I was in Asher's bad books. He'd had to call off the engagement dinner, even though I'd got back in enough time to attend. He'd refused to speak to me or even hear my side of the story and eventually, I'd given up pleading at his closed door and retreated back to my room.

Sleep had evaded me, no matter how tired I was, my eyes stayed wide open, different thoughts threatening to drown me if I stayed awake too long.

In the end, I got up, watching the first rays of the sun breaking through the trees that surrounded the palace. I'd watched the sunrise before, remembering what it was like to see it from my parents' house. It was obviously more spectacular here, everything was.

I'd thought a lot about Finn's words about being a Bloom and I decided that I should be investigating what that meant, so I pushed everything else to the back of my mind for now. A trip to the famous Royal library was in order.

I loved to read, but my parents hadn't been able to afford many books, the ones they had were about baking and magic or specific ingredients that elevate a dish. It was safe to say I'd memorized those back to front and I was in dire need of new reading material. Ever so often I managed to get my hands on a book at the market for a cheap price, and I'd greedily read it until the spine was broken and the pages worn.

I donned a soft dress and peeked out into the silent hallway. As the sun had only just risen, I knew the palace would still be asleep as I crept down the corridor, taking care to flap my wings lightly and I flew down an elaborate, marble staircase.

Pushing open the large oak doors, I gasped at the beautiful room. The library was huge, with walls lined with books, full to the brim with brightly colored spines and covers. My eyes ran hastily over each book, fingers tracing over the words painted in gold onto the spines.

It was the library of my dreams and I almost forgot the reason I was there.

I found the magic section quickly, after practically tearing my eyes away from the fiction books. I'd always been a sucker for stories and fantasy about humans and how different their lives were from our own, like the fact that they didn't have wings or any magic. I so desperately wanted to dive into a book and forget everything for a few hours.

But I was here to learn, I could always take a book to read in bed after I'd found what I needed.

Of course, the magic section was huge, there were so many books that I had to blink a few times to focus my eyes and actually start reading the titles. The spines ranged from thick to such slim books that I had to check it was an actual book and not just one piece of paper slipped between two covers.

Flapping my wings lightly, I hovered as I scanned the shelves. I was looking for Blooms or any type of book that could help me understand my magic.

But before I could find a relevant book, my eye caught on a title that stood out, and my skin prickled at the words that ran down its spine.

The Art of Darkness: Necromancy and Black Magic

The book didn't have a listed author but as I reached for the spine, goosebumps raised on my arms. I knew I shouldn't, it was dangerous to meddle in things like that. I remember my mom warning me about the lure of black magic, but Dillon's voice nagged me at the back of my mind about dark magic and how the Royals could be involved. So, against my better judgment, I grabbed the book and flew to a soft-looking chair by the window, tucked away from everyone so no one could disturb me.

The room was silent, aside from the ticking clock and the crackling fire, and as I snuggled down, I took a breath and opened the book, half-loathing and half-intrigued to learn more about the dark side of magic.

Black magic can come in many forms, mostly guided by the negative feelings one portrays. No matter your breed: fae, ogre, witch, or otherwise, black magic will call to your soul, and without proper training, it can lead you down the darkest of paths. That is why this book exists, to teach you the dark ways of the arts.

Necromancy and The Magic of The Dead

Necromancy or Death Magic as it is commonly known feeds off the dead and dying beings. Many use the magic to resurrect the dead, but be warned, resurrection is an impossible task for even the most talented of Necromancers, and often the one being resurrected is not as they were before.
Side effects may vary but resurrected beings can become doll-like, losing their natural-like qualities and becoming monotonous and unfeeling. They have no soul and therefore no morals. You must keep a close eye on the resurrected as they can wreak as much havoc as they please, with no guilt on their conscience.

Beginning Necromancy

To begin your path to being a Necromancer, you will have to find yourself close to death, either in one's being or find death around you. Being close to the dead, and feeling the decay and the withered souls will help you develop your power to a larger magnitude.

My mind buzzed with the words on the page, imprinted inside my head. It was insane to even think that people would bring others back from the dead, and for what? Even if you loved someone so much, why would you risk bringing them back if they ended up like a vegetable anyway? Us faes have long lifespans, but we can be killed, perhaps the reason why someone would want to resurrect another?

I shook my head. Nope, still didn't make sense. I continued reading, my eyes were drawn back to the pages in morbid curiosity.

When you have begun to feel the withering life forces around you, you must learn this incantation-

"Are you sure this is a good idea?" A loud whisper interrupted my reading and I glanced up, straining my ears to hear if anyone was around.

"It's fine Lily, everyone is still asleep, we're safe here." I recognized the voice and despite the lure of the black magic book, I crept forward, fluttering my wings delicately, so as not to make too much sound.

And between the shelves, huddled together, hands clasped in one another's were Finn and a female fae, dressed in maid's clothing. I'd seen her in the kitchens once or twice, but I couldn't recall ever speaking to her. She looked shy, her eyes looking at the floor as Finn whispered in her ear. A small smile tugged at her mouth.

I held my breath, knowing I was intruding on the moment when Finn gently pressed his lips to her cheek. She blushed, her dark skin glowing softly and he smiled gently.

Gods, they are too cute for words!

Not wanting to pry any longer, I stepped back, attempting to fly away quietly, and act as if I'd never been there, but my foot caught on a pile of books and I tumbled down, cursing the fae who left that pile there. My elbow hit the floor first and I bit back a yelp as the pain shot through my arm. *Fuck, that will need healing I'm sure.* The thud echoed in the empty library and I already knew I'd been found out. The loud thump of my heart beating was enough to give me away at this point.

A throat cleared behind me and I almost crawled away in an attempt to avoid the inevitable embarrassment of being caught ogling at a private moment.

I glanced up and when my eyes met two dark green ones, I groaned out loud.

"Asher, Zia, we didn't think you'd be up." Finn rushed past his female, leaving her still blushing by the shelves. "Are you alright?" He knelt down and grasped my elbow in his hands. They were soft and gentle, but there was no tingling sensation like with Asher. It surprised me.

I felt the all too familiar rush of warmth and looked down to see my arm glowing, Finn delicately put my arm back to my side.

"Best to take it easy on that arm for now, but it should be okay." I smiled at him.

"Thank you," I said quietly, grateful that he healed me otherwise I'd be attempting that myself back in my bedroom and failing miserably.

"Can you teach me that?"

Finn grinned and nodded enthusiastically. "Of course." He agreed, offering a hand to help me up.

But before he could even touch me again, Asher pushed him out of the way and grabbed my other arm, yanking me up roughly and gripping my upper arm firmly.

Gods, he's so damn pushy.

"Zinnia doesn't need your help." He spat. "What's the meaning of this?" He gestured his head towards Finn's fae and he winced at Asher's tone.

"I was going to explain-"

"Then get on with it," Asher growled, still holding me tightly. Not that I complained per se, but his grip wasn't exactly comfortable. I squirmed in his arms, trying to pull free.

His hard stare snapped to me and I nearly shrank away, my squirming ceased.

"Don't."

I swallowed as Finn led the female fae over, holding her hand gently, unlike Asher who gripped me like I was a leaf about to be blown away in the wind.

"Asher, Zia, this is Lily, the fae I was asking for advice about the other day." He glanced at her and she smiled shyly, not meeting either of our eyes. "We're courting."

I smiled widely, happy that Finn had finally mustered up the courage to pursue her.

"That's fantastic-"

"But she's a maid." Asher stated and I cringed at the way he said the word "maid". It was like he couldn't quite believe it.

"And Zia is a baker's daughter and here we all are." Finn smiled like Asher hadn't just greatly offended both of them. "We'll be taking our leave now, see you both at breakfast."

Finn and Lily left the room quickly, obviously eager to get away from the awkward situation. Asher spun to face me, eyes dark and I backed up a few steps.

"You knew? You knew all along and you didn't tell me? About my own brother?"

I held my hands up in surrender, realizing a pissed-off Asher was not easy to reason with.

"No, I didn't know. He told me he liked someone, so I told him to ask her for tea or something. He didn't say who." I rushed quickly, trying to explain my situation rationally to a prowling prince was not easy. "I'm telling the truth!" I pleaded and took another step back as he paced forward.

He stalked towards me like a predator, his dark eyes locked on mine. I felt the hard, wooden shelf dig into my back as he crowded my space, making me feel small and useless.

"I should punish you for keeping secrets. And for asking Finn for help like he's the one you're courting." He growled and I bit my lip, trying to tamper down the ridiculous giggle that was bubbling in my chest. He was jealous of Finn when there was literally nothing between me and his older brother.

"I don't owe you honesty Asher, you're one to talk with your string of lovers. Not to mention, we're in a fucking fake relationship which the whole kingdom now knows-"

"Shut up." He breathed as his dark eyes glared at me. My pulse quickened, the skin on my neck prickled and I knew I was playing with fire, but it felt so good.

"Make me." I breathed, repeating his words from a few nights ago. I could barely hear my own words over the loud thump of my heart. I knew I was testing him, but Gods did it feel good.

Before I could register anything else, Asher's lips were on mine. Hot, full, and demanding as he captured my mouth with his own. My heart beat a mile a minute in my chest and a sigh left my lips as I kissed him back, thinking about how many times I'd fantasized about this and how much *better* it was in real life.

A deep growl rumbled in his chest as he cupped my cheek, holding me tightly to him, his other arm wrapping around my waist. Asher hauled me up and my legs automatically spread, letting him guide them around his hips. My butt rested on the shelf behind and I knew I'd probably have a giant bruise tomorrow, but Asher's kiss was so worth it. His body felt strong, hot, and delicious against mine.

His tongue took no time in finding my own as I opened my lips and let him taste me. Gods, I was practically shaking as I ran my fingers through his midnight locks, feeling how soft there were. I was gasping for breath as he pulled me closer and trailed his lips down my neck, I sighed, closing my eyes and giving in to the feeling. I threw my head back, leaning against the shelves, eyes closed in utter bliss. His hot breath felt like fire against my flushed skin. He gently licked my neck and I moaned airly. Asher groaned softly in response and I clenched my thighs around his waist.

"Zinnia." He said my name like it was a prayer on his lips and I gripped his hair, pulling him closer. His sharp crown dug into my neck, but I didn't even care as his lips found the top of my chest, where my dress was pushing up my breasts into full mounds. He bit the soft flesh, my heart hammered beneath his mouth and I squeezed his bicep so hard that I was sure he'd have crescent moon-shaped marks indented into his skin permanently.

"Asher, more." I groaned and just as I was ready to hike up my dress and get this show on the road, he stood straight up and stormed out of the library, leaving me alone and panting.

And with that stupid, fucking love bite throbbing on my chest.

～

The dining hall was alive and bustling as I flew in. No one paid any attention to me as I sat down late. I'd waited in my room for Asher to come by and collect me, but he never arrived, so I'd resisted knocking on his door and decided to fly to dinner without him. Who cared if I was alone, he could be sick and I wouldn't care, he'd left me high and dry (well, wet if we're talking particulars) in the library and I was mad. I'd spent the whole day with the black magic book in my room, hiding out.

"Zia, good to see you." Finn smiled next to me and I nodded, forcing a fake smile. I scanned the table and realized Asher wasn't here. That fucking selfish prick was hiding out in his room. Was he embarrassed that we'd shared a kiss? Maybe he was with another fae. The thought sickened me. How had I gone from not caring about the Brat Prince at all to feeling a wave of jealousy when I thought about him in the arms of another?

I'd had to strategically choose a dress that had a high collar to cover that annoying and incredibly sexy love bite that was branded on my chest. The only one I could find was a dark purple color- one of my least favorite colors, but it had to do. The lace neckline was probably a little racy for meal times, but no one seemed to notice nor care.

The dinner went by uneventfully. No one spoke to me as we were served sweetmeats and rum. As it turned out, Cain wasn't present too- thankfully- so Finn and I made small talk for a short while, and I excused myself after the King and Queen had left.

I flew slowly back to my room, dreading the thought of being alone with my thoughts tonight.

Maybe I had to swallow my pride and actually talk to Asher. Ignoring him was easier and after hiding out in my room reading about black magic for the whole afternoon, I felt like I should probably suck it up and say something to him. Not that he was being very mature about the whole thing either.

I landed softly outside his door, mentally bracing myself for an argument, perhaps the cold shoulder but nothing, literally *nothing* could have braced me for the sounds I heard through his door.

Moans, grunts, and sounds that made my stomach churn sourly were coming from his room, I reeled back like I'd been punched.

Asher and I had shared a more than steamy kiss in the library less than twelve hours ago and now he was in bed with another fae. It may not have been his first kiss, but it certainly felt real enough for my first time.

My heart felt weird and heavy, almost like it ached, my stomach dropped and I swallowed back the horrific feeling in my chest. I hastily flew back to my room, not daring to be caught in the corridor listening at Asher's door. Tears filled my eyes and I flew straight to the bathroom, filling up a tub and stripped off before sinking into the hot water and crying my eyes out.

I should have known better than to trust the Brat Prince and his games.

∼

The kitchen was insanely warm as I rolled out the dough. I wiped the sweat beads from my brow with a little cloth from my pocket and glared angrily at Asher's fire like it was the cause of all my problems. Perhaps he could feel my anger through the flames, it was satisfying to believe that for a moment. My elbow twinged a little as I pushed the rolling pin back and forth, and I was reminded of yesterday's events. *Gods, I wish I'd never come to this stupid palace.*

The lack of communication from Asher meant that I'd spent the night alternating between cursing him and his stupid, gorgeous face and crying my heart out like I was some pathetic cretin. My face was puffy and red when I'd finally got out of bed and I had decided I'd done enough crying and moping around.

So I'd flown down to the kitchens and recruited Lily, who- I'd quickly found out- was an assistant cook, and told her to follow me to the lower kitchen. I thought I'd stay true to my word and teach someone else to bake the pastries. I felt a little protective of my recipe at first, but then I thought of a new one to try out later by myself; lavender and strawberries and I decided it would be okay to share my apricot and basil recipe with just one other for now.

"Okay so, Lily, you add the fresh basil and glaze like this." I showed her how to do so, spreading the shiny and sweet apricot glaze over the inside of the pastry and folding it down. She followed, unsure at first and hesitant in her actions.

"Mine looks nothing like yours though." She frowned and I glanced at the two. Yep, she was right, mine looked way nicer, the basil was a luscious green color and the pastry looked much fresher. Well, it was probably because I'd been doing this since I could talk.

"Practice makes perfect." I smiled cheerily, trying not to dishearten her, and we put them in the oven.

I looked back and turned to face her, watching her as she began to gather the utensils for washing.

"Tell me about you and Finn."

Lily turned away, smoothing down her dark hair before slowly looking back at me with her lime green eyes. They stood out against her beautiful skin and I wasn't surprised that she'd captured Finn's heart. She was gorgeous, right from the tips of her pointed ears, down to her round, sweet cheeks.

"It was just stolen glances at first." She brushed a lock of her hair behind her ear and glanced at the floor, fiddling with her apron as she spoke. "Then he'd purposefully touch my hand or catch my fingers. He'd say the occasional 'hello' or 'thank you'.

I thought he was just being polite or maybe it was a game for him. But he approached me a couple of days ago, asking if I'd like to go for a stroll around the grounds with him."

I smiled, thinking about how nervous Finn was to ask Lily out, how he wanted to do it right, and so he'd asked for my advice, some random fae who knew nothing of official courting. I believed his intentions to be pure, but I understood Lily's hesitation.

"I was unsure about his advances, you know how his other brothers are." She snapped her head up at me and bit her lip. I shrugged, not in the mood to defend Asher when he was treating me like shit anyway. "But he's been nothing but sweet and an absolute gentleman. Always asking if it's okay to hold my hand. And then yesterday in the library…"

She looked back down at her shoes again and I grinned knowingly.

"It's okay, you don't need to explain."

She nodded and glanced at me again.

"And you and Asher?"

I sighed, folding my arms across my chest and thinking about her question. Asher and I, Gods, even a full-length novel wouldn't be enough to cover all that was us. The layers of feelings between us, the anger, hatred, fire, and chemistry. It was confusing.

"It's complicated."

She nodded again, like she understood, and in a way, I guessed she did. Not that Finn would ever treat her the way Asher did me, but I guess like us, her and Finn's relationship would be frowned upon. Would they even have a chance? If the King's reaction to Asher's proposal to me was anything to go by, Finn would have to fight tooth and nail for approval. And even then, would it be enough?

Even if the King approved officially, there would always be the judgmental stares, the whispers, and the feeling of not fitting in or being enough for the Royals. Finn was heir to the throne, after all, it was expected of him to marry for politics and money, not for love.

A throat cleared behind us and Lily all but screamed at the sight of Asher leaning against the door frame, watching us. She excused herself quickly and scurried back to the upper kitchens, making herself the smallest size possible to squeeze past Asher's large frame and leaving me alone with the Brat Prince again.

"Sharing all your secrets I see?" He quirked a brow and I tried not to groan out loud at how delicious he looked. Dressed in all black, Asher's dark ensemble reflected my mood *and* made him look even more menacing and devious than I thought possible.

"Only the ones that matter." I bit back and turned to check on the pastries. I took one of mine out of the oven and practically threw it onto the counter, as it burned my fingers and I let it cool.

Stepping further into the kitchen, Asher's hand snaked out and grabbed it before I had a chance to get it myself and he took a bite.

All the annoyance I felt at him stealing my pastry was long forgotten as I watched him chew slowly, his lips moving in a way that made my belly go all twisty, and he swallowed, whilst maintaining eye contact, his throat bobbing as he did so.

Gods above, my lower stomach clenched and I subconsciously wet my lips with my tongue. His eyes narrowed on my mouth and I stepped back slightly, not realizing I'd got so close to him. He really had me flustered, practically fanning myself over the way he ate. I needed to remember the way I felt when I heard the moans from his room last night. I needed to maintain distance from him for the sake of my foolish heart.

"What's complicated?"

"What?" I asked, still sidetracked by the way he was eating, the way he licked each individual finger made my brain go into a tailspin. I pulled my stare away from his mouth and busied myself with getting the other pastries out of the oven before they burned to a crisp because I was busy ogling at a prince.

"You said 'it's complicated' to Lily, what's complicated?"

"You know very well what's complicated, and the kiss in the library didn't help the situation either." I hated how sharp I sounded, but if it meant nothing to Asher then I needed to act the same. He couldn't know how much it had affected me and how much

I wanted it to happen again.

But before I could say another thing, Cain The Pain strolled in through the door that led to the dungeons, a smug smile on his face and I refrained from scowling at him.

"Lovers' quarrel?" He practically grinned in delight and both Asher and I ignored him. Asher's were eyes on me and mine on the floor.

"You look good in the kitchen, little fae, almost like you belong here."

He ran his fingers along the countertop, crawling their way to me and he grabbed a pastry next to me and leaned back to look me in the eye. He reached out and tilted my head up with his index finger but I jerked my chin away, repulsed by his touch.

"You know your time here is ticking away," he leaned in close, his hot breath making my skin crawl. "Make sure you're making good use of it."

Cain leisurely made his way out of the kitchen and I caught sight of Asher's clenched fists before he spun around and followed his brother.

Gods, why are both of those princes so fucking weird?

I crept closer to the dungeons, convinced I could gather more intel now Cain was away. A loud scream broke the silence and my heart thudded in my chest as I scuttled away from the doorway.

Maybe today wasn't the day for brave adventures.

~

Considering I was supposed to be using my time well at the palace- *thanks for the creepy reminder Cain*, I thought I'd take another peek at the library.

Greeted by the smell of old pages and ink, I pushed open the heavy door, gently closing it behind me. Someone had lit a fire, the warmth seeping into my bones. It was raining outside and the cozy room lured me in like a spell.

Scouring the shelves again, I paid more attention to each cover this time and I found a few different books that might help me with my newly found magical skills. I placed them in a pile on the table next to me, making sure to keep them away from the fire. I flew higher up the shelves, searching for more books about Blooms, or different magic, or no magic at all in the case of Flora.

I probably spent a good half hour finely combing every shelf from the bottom up and I had a pounding headache by the time I got to the top shelf.

This is useless, I angrily thought. If anywhere was going to have a book to help Flora, it would be the Royal library. I was frustrated with the thought that she was unhelpable, that no one knew what was truly going on inside her body.

Just as I was about to give up, a book wedged right at the back of the very top shelf caught my eye. It was lying horizontally, on top of the other books but pushed into the corner, skulking in the dark as if it were forgotten or purposely hidden. Any passing eye wouldn't catch it, not unless they were actively looking for it. I had to double back to make sure I hadn't just made it up.

I gingerly eased it out, trying not to knock any of the other books out, all I needed was a library catastrophe involving old and rare books raining down from every shelf and I'd be banned for life. After a mini tug-of-war session, I managed to heave it out and I landed back on my feet, eager to see what the thick book was about.

The cover was simple, red and leather-bound, and the words in gold read:

The Hollow Ones

Okay, not freaky at all. I tried to find some information about it, but the pages seemed to be blank. Something in my gut, a small nudge, told me to hold onto it so I added it to my pile and settled down on a chair next to the fire. The warmth enveloped me like a hug and I sighed, closing my eyes briefly before remembering that I had work to do and there was no time to nap.

My hand drifted to the red-bound cover of *The Hollow Ones* again, and I picked it up, giving it another closer look. I flicked through the pages, noticing the lack of ink again. Every page was empty, like a new journal that had yet to be touched. I wondered why they'd be hiding a blank book on the shelves at the top? Maybe it was a mistake?

As I peered closer, I titled the book slightly, the light hitting it better at this new angle. Words shimmered on the pages like a mirage. Quickly, I brought the book to my face, examining the pages closely and as I held it up to the firelight, I realized it wasn't blank at all. Each page, held against the light, had words written in some sort of invisible ink.

Okay, now I'm interested. It was going to take ages to read, but it had to be something important to be written so secretly? My curiosity was officially at an all-time high.

Snuggling down further, I began to read the first page.

The Hollow One can also be referred to as the coming of the rare species of the fae. Although alike in look, stature, and physicality, the Hollow One has no magical abilities nor can hold magic in its being. It is magicless in its entirety, leading to the name the Hollow One.

I perked up, Flora couldn't hold magic in her being. And she didn't possess any magical abilities either. I read on, intrigued about this Hollow One.

The power that the Hollow One could harness, is a destroyer of kingdoms, their magic beyond any capabilities of a mere fae, sprite, gremlin, or any other being.

Their magic signs are not exhibited outwardly, they are concealed until they come of age on their eighteenth day of birth. Then their magic will ascend, revealing itself. It must be harnessed correctly within this time frame of thirty days or else the Hollow One's power will only destroy.

Okay, so, there was a small, very, very small but real chance Flora could be a Hollow One. She was seventeen, she had no magic, and she couldn't keep any of our magic in her body. But realistically, what were the chances of my little sister being one of these mighty magic wielders? Improbable but not impossible. I read on.

The Hollow One comes around every one thousand years, their power proving too great to manifest sooner. For a time, there were more of them, many being born on the same night but since the Great Hunt of Breestock, The Hollow Ones are seen less often, perhaps protected and concealed for good reason.
They are fated only by their birth and the alignment of the moons. On the day of their birth, the three moons are aligned in one, a rare phenomenon that only occurs every one thousand years. It is then that one fae, born on that blessed day will be the Hollow One for the centuries to come.

My heart began to beat fast as my eyes scanned the words on each page. The reading was slow, almost painful and my eyes stung from the heat of the fire.

No, wait, what are the actual chances? I thought back to Flora's birth. She was born on that exact day, my mom called it good fortune that the moons were aligned and later took that comment back when Flora showed no signs of magic.

I stared into the fire, my mind suddenly a blizzard of thoughts. *Could this really be it? The answer to all our questions? The answer to every healer's puzzled look?*

I swallowed the lump in my throat, feeling strangely emotional. *All those years we worried about Flora and we might have just found our answer?* I knew I needed back up though, someone else to talk to about this, so that I wasn't just placing all my faith in false hope and myths, and I knew exactly who to ask.

～

I knocked on the door and waited, praying to every God under the moons that he was in.

"Come in." His voice called and I pushed open Finn's study door to find him sitting under a lamp, reading a book. His blond hair was like a halo around his head, he was in a plain white shirt, looking ever regal in his golden crown, and with his shiny jewelry, his rings glinted on his fingers as he turned a page.

"Zia. So good to see you." At least he was polite, unlike Asher who acted as if it pained him to even say "hello".

"Finn, do you have a moment?" I stood in the doorway, clutching the book to my chest as he smiled.

"Of course." He closed his book, put it on the desk next to him, and gestured for me to sit opposite in an armchair.

"I wasn't sure who to ask," I began, I knew I trusted Finn, so why did I feel guilty about the book. I hadn't been snooping, just searching for something else, and stumbled across the book. "I found this book at the back of a shelf in the library."

I passed the book over to him and he studied the cover for a moment, face unreadable before turning it over and then flicking through the blank pages.

"At first, I thought it was blank," his eyebrows raised as if to question me, or maybe he thought I was insane, he wouldn't be the only one. "And then I put it up to the light." I leaned over, pushing his hand up to the lamp opposite him and letting the light shine through the pages. A soft gasp escaped his lips and his eyes ran over the invisible lines.

"Zia, where did you say you found this again?" His gaze was still glued to the book and I watched him, he was entranced. I was hoping that meant that he knew what it was.

"On the top shelf of the right-hand wall, above the Healer magic section."

Finn glanced at me, smiling as he folded the book shut gently.

"I believe you've just found the missing book from the Library of Nissa. From the Temple."

I blinked a few times, trying to understand that I'd found a missing artifact that shaped our kingdom's history. That had been missing for the past centuries, until now. What the fuck? *So I guess no one looks in the library nowadays.*

"Okay, so that leads me onto my next question." I brushed away that colossal thought because I didn't want it to distract me from my mission. "This might sound crazy so bear with me." I took a deep breath, sure that Finn would laugh at me when I explained about Flora. So I told him about her, everything, every detail from her birth until now.

He'd sat silently for my story, only nodding ever so often. But when I finished, he leaned forward in his chair, a grin on his lips. He flicked through a few of the pages again, fascination in his eyes.

"No, the book isn't a myth. My father remembers the last Hollow One, and his father was there, at the slaughter at Breestock. They exist, but because the book has been missing for the last six hundred years, everyone thought they'd gone extinct. Many died without passing the story on and so, now people don't even remember the Hollow Ones." He leaned forward in his chair, resting his forearms on his knees, and looked me dead in the eye. "I think you were right to come to me Zia, we need to look after Flora. She could very well be the next Hollow One and if others find that out, she could be in great danger."

My heart thumped in panic, *danger?* I hadn't even thought about what would happen if others discovered my sister and her potential.

"I'll finish studying this book, you fetch your sister, bring her back here where she'll be safe. Take whoever you need to." He reached forward and gripped my shaking hand, his lapis lazuli eyes sparkling with excitement. I'd never seen him this excited over anything. "She'll be okay, Zia, but we need to keep her safe."

~

I'd never pumped my wings harder than on that flight home. Of course, I was exhausted, but the thought of anyone else getting to my sister before me spurred me on and my wings flapped viciously.

The bakery door was still open as it was mid-afternoon. I'd brought Henrick and another guard with me, just in case we got overpowered by some demon, witch or otherwise. Not that any of them had been seen in our kingdom for a long time, but you never know.

I tried to settle my pounding heart before we went in, smoothing down my dress with my sweaty palms. A warm hand on my shoulder made me turn and Henrick's smile eased the tension in my body.

"Whatever you need, we're here." I nodded, smiling tightly at him and took a deep breath before stepping into the shop.

"Zinnia!" My mom's reaction was like I hadn't seen her for weeks, as opposed to a few days ago. I smiled softly as she came around the counter and enveloped me in a warm hug.

"Hi, Mom," I whispered and she cupped my cheeks in her hands.

"Are you eating enough? How about enough sleep? Your eyes look a little puffy-"

"I'm fine, Mom." I swatted her hands away, instantly annoyed at her mothering. It wasn't about me and it was none of her business why my eyes were puffy. It was a certain infuriating male in the palace's business.

"Is everything okay? With Prince Asher?" Her eyes screamed concern and I tried to smile brightly. Tried to pretend that Asher and I weren't in stalemate after our heated kiss.

"Of course, but I wanted to take Flora to the palace for a few days, I'm allowed a visitor and it's getting a bit lonely-"

"To the palace?" Flora's voice filtered through the shop front and her sweet face popped up from behind the counter. "I thought I heard your voice, sis." She grinned at me and I gently hugged her small frame.

"Only if you want to."

Flora's face lit up, her green eyes twinkling and she spun on her heel to face our mom.

"Oh please Mom, please, please, *pleeeease*." She dragged out the vowel in the last word to emphasize her excitement, but I could see the hesitation written on my mom's face.

"I don't know, sweetie, you've been so tired recently-"

"It'll only be for a few days." The lie fell off my tongue too quickly and I cringed at how much I'd lied to my parents. When the truth came out, which I was sure it would, I expected my parents to ignore me. Not that I blamed them really, I'd brought shame on myself and our family name by even spilling a drink on Asher in the first place. Gods, I should never have gone to that club, staying home would have been a much better option.

But then I'd have never met Asher, the most infuriating, entitled, and incredibly alluring prince. Half of the time, I didn't know if I wanted to kiss him or smack him so hard he spun in a full circle.

Yep, I was in a dilemma.

"I don't know…" My mom began, her eyes flicked between my sister and me, obvious worry etched into her gentle features.

"William!" She called and my dad flew into the room, a smudged handprint of white flour on his pants. He surveyed the room, assessing the situation before his eyes fell on me. A soft smile appeared on his face.

"Zia." He said and I stepped forward to hug him.

"Hi, Dad." I muffled into his cotton shirt. My mom was always the strict one in our family, while my dad had wanted me to pursue my dreams, my mom was the realist and kept us grounded, making me work in the bakery for extra money to pay off our debts.

My mom hastily explained the situation, pulling my dad by the arm so they could discuss it privately in a hearing spell. My dad nodded intermittently, replying back when there was a pause. The conversation made me nervous. Every moment here was a moment wasted. We needed to get Flora to safety, I couldn't protect her here. The walls of the bakery weren't enough to keep the dangerous ones that threatened her existence away.

They turned back to us after a moment and my dad spoke first.

"We're allowing this trip, but as long as you make sure she doesn't overexert herself and get tired."

Flora squealed in delight and jumped up to hug both our parents. I smiled knowingly at Henrick and he grinned back.

"Pack lightly Flora, there are loads of clothes at the palace," I called after my sister who was already quickly climbing the stairs. I hoped she wouldn't tire too soon. My dad followed her and I assumed it was to help her pack.

"You look after her, okay? Make sure she takes her healer's potion twice a day-"

"Yes, Mom, I'll take care of her, don't you worry." I smiled brightly.

My mom grabbed different bottles, small, big, filled with green and red liquids. They clinked together in her hands and she hurriedly wrapped each of them in cloth and slid them into a sack.

She passed it to me, my arms sank with the weight of all the glass bottles and I huffed. She then glanced at Henrick, a smile breaking out on her face.

"Let me get you another ambrosia cake for the

journey home." She said and he grinned at me, excitement in his eyes.

Flora appeared in the kitchen, wearing a dark green cape despite the warm weather. My dad carried a small bag stuffed with some of her items and gave it to the other guard whose name I didn't know.

My mom handed a cake to Henrick and one to the guard who juggled Flora's bag and a cake between his hands. They both thanked her and she gave me a nettle and blueberry cookie for the road. I kissed her cheek and thanked her as she rubbed my back softly.

"Take care." My dad stepped forward and pressed a kiss to my sister's forehead, then did the same to me. "You too, Zia."

I nodded and hugged him tightly before Henrick picked up Flora gently and we made our way back to the palace.

CHAPTER EIGHT
YOUR HIGHNESS

The next couple days with Flora provided a well-needed break from all princes and black magic problems.

My sister was keen to learn everything about the palace and meet all the princes, but Finn had been called away to another kingdom for negotiations by the time we got back. Asher was nowhere to be seen and Cain- thankfully- was elsewhere (probably sulking in the dungeons).

We weren't called to any dinners or breakfasts, Laurel brought us a tray of food when we needed it and for the most part, I was happy.

Flora marveled at the huge rooms, the painted ceilings, and the beautiful gardens. She'd been to the library, in awe of all the books. We'd spent hours browsing the shelves, collecting all the books we liked the look of, and taking them back to my room to read.

Then she'd wanted to see my kitchen so we'd baked some pastries together, falling back into a natural harmony. Flora organized ingredients as I rolled out the dough and created the glaze. Living with my sister in the palace was a dream, and it was easy to forget my worries.

All too soon, came the day I dreaded. I'd not managed to get word out to Dillon, so I hoped he had palace scouts who saw me leaving because I only had one trip a week, and I didn't want to waste it.

"But why can't Dillon come here?" Flora pouted, picking up a fresh grape from the bowl that lay on our bed and popping it into her mouth. She told me she hadn't seen Dillon as often since I'd left and I thought it was probably because of his rebel ties. He wanted to keep my family safe and I was grateful for that. I didn't want them to be a target just because of my foolish mistakes leading me to being associated with the crown.

"Because you have to be invited to the palace, and besides, he got escorted to the gates last time he tried to come here."

She giggled, probably imagining him being dragged out and lay back on my bed, sighing lightly. We'd been sharing a room, for extra safety and because we'd been up talking into the early hours of the morning. When we weren't in the library or my room, we were in the lower kitchen. I hadn't realized how much I'd missed my sister until I had her company again.

"Can I come with you then?" She asked, sitting

up and watching me as I pulled on my boots. The pathetic slippers Asher provided me with were fine for floating around the palace, but I needed shoes that were more robust, just in case I got kidnapped again or something.

"Not this time."

"But-"

I spun around to her, sighing as watched me with a pouty lip, pleading with her soft eyes.

"No buts, please just trust me on this, sis. When Finn gets back I'll explain everything but for now, I need to see Dillon on my own."

She stared at me for a moment, studying me before gesturing to the air around her. She mouthed "cast a hearing bubble".

Nodding, I cast the spell and my ears popped. Flora slid to the edge of the bed, leaning in despite the bubble.

"Is this because of your deal? With Prince Asher?" She whispered, eyes wide.

I sighed again, I wanted to tell her the truth, I desperately wanted to spill my guts about everything, about Dillon and the rebels, about Cain and the dungeons, about The Hollow Ones. But instead, I said:

"It is."

~

Flora let me go without another complaint. I hastily flew out of the palace and into the busy city.

I waited by the forge, watching the sun paint the

sky pink and bathe the world in a golden glow. It was nearly sundown and there was no sign of my best friend-turned-rebel.

I rubbed my face, wondering whether I was stupid to trust Dillon again. He *had* kidnapped me after all.

"Zia." A voice softly called from inside the forge and Dillon's face emerged from the darkness. The dark circles under his eyes didn't go unnoticed, nor the blade strapped to his hip. Panic rose in my chest and I took a deep breath, reminding myself that Dillon wouldn't hurt me. At least, not when I had potentially important information for him and the rebels.

"I thought you weren't going to show." My tone was slightly accusatory and I folded my arms across my chest.

"Sorry." He shrugged. "I had to wait to make sure you weren't followed." He said, offering me a hand, I ignored it and stepped into the darkness of the disused forge.

"Well?" He prompted.

"No time for pleasantries then?" I scoffed, looking him up and down as I stood on the other side of the room, closest to the exit- just in case.

"I know you're mad Zia, but lives could be at stake here so put away your ego and help me." His eyes looked sad. "Please." He added.

I bit back the sharp remark waiting on the tip of my tongue and instead, I turned away, examining the leftover tools behind me.

"Yes, there seems to be something going on in the

dungeons." Immediately, Dillon stepped to my side and pushed my shoulder slightly, to turn me to face him.

"What kind of 'something'?"

"The bad kind," I said, running my finger along a piece of rusted metal.

"Stop playing games, Zia."

I spun around, infuriated. "I don't know, okay, Dillon? All I know is that Prince Cain spends the majority of his time in that grimy, dank place. The guards are creepy and the screams are even creepier."

Dillon turned from me, contemplating what I'd told him.

"You're sure it's only Prince Cain, what about the others?" He looked back at me.

I so badly wanted to lie, to say that both Finn and Asher weren't involved but in all honesty, I couldn't tell if they were. My lack of worldly experience meant that I found it hard to judge liars and was too quick to trust. I felt that both Finn and Asher had too much good in their heart to be involved with the stuff in the dungeons, but was I just placing my blind faith in them?

"I don't know. I can't be sure," I murmured, looking at the ground and Dillon nodded.

"You need to get out of there."

"I can't."

"Why not? You can go home, no one would treat you differently. We all know how Prince Asher likes his many playthings."

Offended that Dillon thought I was just a body

to warm Asher's bed, I gritted my teeth and willed myself to count to ten in my head before replying.

"It's not like that," I said simply.

"Then what is it like? Because he surely can't be courting you."

Okay, I'll just pretend Dillon isn't throwing blows on my ego like a hammer to a nail. I felt my hand curl into fists and I breathed roughly through my nose. Keeping a lid on my anger was not my strong suit, but the Gods knew I was trying.

"It's all fake!" I burst out. "Everything. I fucked up and ended up in a deal with Asher at Cuckoo after spilling a drink on him. He told me he wanted a fake courtship to convince his parents, I guess to prove he's a serious contender for the throne. I didn't want to be indebted to him and you know how my parents struggled to feed all four mouths, I just thought it was easier than…" I trailed off, wondering how Dillon looked at me now. He probably thought I was pathetic and the truth was that he wasn't far off. I'd been naive to believe Asher actually liked me. He was always stalking off or yelling at me. It was obvious he couldn't tolerate me.

Dillon was quiet for a moment.

"I don't understand, but you still can't trust them. You're not safe there."

"No less safe than at home," I spoke quietly and Dillon said nothing.

A throat cleared behind me and my heart jumped. I spun around, peering into the shadows.

"Zia, this is Elijah, he's head of the movement."

A fae appeared out of the darkness and patted Dillon's shoulder.

I eyed the fae warily. Dressed in simple clothes, he was tall and broad, definitely a laborer by the way his hands were worn and scarred. Probably not particularly wealthy or well-read if his scars and marks hadn't been fixed by a healer.

"Sorry for the interruption, Zia. I was listening to see whether you could be trusted."

I nodded, unsure what to make of this whole situation. He was the leader of the rebels? I was really in deep water.

"My wife, River, used to work in the palace upper kitchens, alongside Elsa as assistant cook, she went missing two months ago." Well, that made sense considering Lily's pastry skills left something to be desired. A big something. I guessed she'd only just been promoted if River had disappeared. I also guessed he wasn't lying to gain my favor when he said Elsa's name. Then again, I wasn't sure what was common knowledge to people who lived closer to the palace.

"No one knows where she's gone, she was last seen at the palace but not a single fae would speak to me when I got there. The guards said they never saw her that day, but River never missed a day of work. She went to investigate one of her friends, who'd also gone missing. I told her not to." He smiled wistfully, his eyes were full of sadness. "But, she never listened. She never returned that night. She's inside that palace, I know it."

I swallowed thickly, suddenly realizing the gravity of the situation, faes were going missing in the palace, lesser faes, faes like me and no one was doing a thing about it. I needed to find someone and get some damn answers.

"How can I help?"

~

It was long after dark when I returned to the palace. I knew if Asher was in the palace, he'd have had every spare hand searching for me like last time. Maybe he did care? Or maybe it was because me going missing would really mess up his plans.

I pushed open my door and blinked a few times, not believing the sight before me.

Asher and Flora lay on the bed, a wooden chess board in between them. They looked like old pals, lying opposite each other, enjoying each other's company, and wow, that *hurt*.

He glanced up at the sound of the door closing and his lips pressed into a hard line for a moment before he looked back to the board.

"You're back." He said simply. "You didn't tell me your sister was such a good chess player."

I couldn't help the grin that stretched across my face. With no other duties, Flora had taught herself just about every other board game that existed and had mastered every move. I stepped closer and ran my eyes over the board, calculating the positions of each piece. Yep, one more move, and Asher was toast. Good, it would teach him how losing felt, something I was sure he wasn't accustomed to.

"How are your parents?" He asked and hesitated, confused before Flora threw me a "play along" look and I nodded.

"They're well, busy as ever at the bakery. They asked after Flora too." She nodded as she stared very seriously at Asher's pieces on the board, a smug smile on her face.

"Checkmate." She whispered and Asher laughed-*actually laughed!* Where was this good-natured attitude coming from and why wasn't I a part of it?

"Well, I think a dinner is in order, my father and Finn are away, and Cain is indisposed, but how about we eat with my mother?" He watched me expectantly and I balked, staring at this weirdly friendly Asher in a daze.

"Um-"

"Sure, Zia would love that," Flora answered for me and Asher began to make his way to the door.

"Great, I'll tell Laurel to come by in an hour."

I shook myself out of my trance and followed him out, the door closing behind me.

"Are you crazy? You can't invite my sister to dinner with-"

Asher spun to face me, bending down low to look into my eyes.

"Are you keeping secrets from me, Zinnia?"

I shook my head, not trusting my voice.

"Then why were you out so late when I gave you

two hours?" Okay, so he *was* mad and just decided to play nice in front of my sister.

"My parents wanted to speak to me," I said, keeping my tone level even though my treacherous heart was beating loudly. I hated lying and recently, I'd been doing far too much of it for my liking.

"You saw them last week."

"I helped out at the bakery."

His eyes narrowed and my heart skipped a beat, he was onto me and I was *this* close to cracking.

"Your lies are worse than your clothes." His scathing eyes glanced down at my shapeless beige dress and boots. My cheeks flamed in humiliation, I hadn't cared about what I wore to see Dillon because he'd never openly insult me about my appearance. Just another thing Asher did to tear me down.

I spun around, storming back into my room and slamming the door shut for good measure.

"I'll see you at dinner," Asher yelled through the door and I screamed.

"You and Prince Asher have some hot chemistry," Flora said, fanning herself and I rolled my eyes.

"Stop it." I snapped, not amused by her teasing and she laughed.

"Why did you lie for me?" I sat down on the chair for a moment before getting up and pacing again. I was agitated, full of useless energy.

"Because I didn't think Prince Asher would be Dillon's biggest fan." She shrugged like it was really that obvious.

I snorted in response, agreeing with her, and made

my way to the bathroom. Perhaps a good bathe in hot, scented water would calm me down.

"You're welcome, by the way!" Flora called after me and I shook my head. Gods, everyone was pissing me off today.

~

As usual, Asher barged into our room a few hours later. Luckily I was only slipping on my shoes and not in the nude. Flora was in the bathroom where Laurel was brushing her hair. Laurel was like a second mom for us, she worried and cared about both of us a lot, and it was very endearing.

"Yes, Your Highness?" I mock curtseyed and turned to the mirror, making sure I looked presentable for dinner.

Asher said nothing, but his eyes caught mine in our reflections and I watched him as his gaze wandered leisurely down my body and back up again. I'd gone for a more sheer dress- call me daring- just to test the waters with Asher. I didn't want to openly admit that I was aching for another hot session like the one in the library, but I hoped the dress would encourage round two.

Asher wore an all-black outfit, the color of midnight and befitting for him. Embroidered golden thorns were around the cuffs of his jacket and on his collar. With a flick of his hand, my golden dress had roses stitched around the hem. Why was he so obsessed with us matching? Just another thing about Asher that I couldn't explain.

His eyes burned into mine as I gulped, the air in the room suddenly feeling too hot. My skin prickled and a shiver rolled down my spine as his dark eyes stared into mine. My mouth felt dry, Asher stepped closer, his chest mere inches from me. My heart hammered, my chest rose and fell rapidly. If I just pushed up on my toes and angled my head a little-

"Zia," I heard my sister call from the bathroom, breaking the tension between us as I looked away. "This dress is-"

She stepped into the bedroom, tugging at the corset and I watched Asher's face break into a gorgeous smile. I stamped down the jealousy that flared in my chest at the thought that he'd never smiled at me like that. Putting on smile, I turned back to my sister.

"Beautiful." He said and she blushed bright pink from the tips of her pointed ears right to her toes. He was right, the dress was more than beautiful, in a midnight blue that brought out her flaming hair, Flora no longer looked like the seventeen-year-old little sister I had and looked more like an adult fae. I felt a weird wave of fear flush over me at the realization. She was growing up too fast. I wanted to keep her safe, keep her locked away and not let anyone hurt her.

And then another thought smashed the first out of my head. So how come Asher complimented her and never me? Yet another angry thought to add to the angry box stuffed full to the brim inside my head.

Asher took Flora's arm and I trailed behind, not jealous of my sister because of the attention Asher gave her, but jealous that she got to see the good side of him. Not the angry, cold, dismissive side I'd seen.

He began to tell a story and I analyzed him from the back, trying to find flaws in his huge wings attached to his broad shoulders that tapered down to a slim waist, his tight butt, and his long, lean legs. Gods, he really was gorgeous. Another wave of anger made me clench my fists.

"- and then my brothers and I were caught outside the grounds…"

Asher's voice faded into the background as I wondered why he really disliked me so much. He was happy to make polite talk to my sister but unwilling to spend a second more than necessary with me. I sighed deeply, ready for another awful meal.

The room felt empty without the others and the Queen sat at the end of the table, gazing out of the window. She smiled softly as we approached. Asher led Flora to a chair next to him, while I took the one opposite, knowing I'd have to face him for the duration of dinner. *Gods, help me.*

"It's so good of you to join me." The Queen said and Asher kissed his mother's hand before taking his seat.

～

The dinner went by uneventfully, we talked about small stuff like the bakery and the annual ball that was coming up. The Queen was more interested in Flora than me so I sat quietly, picking at my food. Thinking about how much Asher was pissing me off and mulling Dillon's words over in my mind. *Could Asher really be involved with Cain and black magic?*

We flew back to the rooms together, Asher walking with Flora chatting away about something that I didn't care about, and Laurel and I walked in silence behind them. My mood was officially at an all-time low. I just wanted to curl up in bed and forget this whole evening.

"Laurel, would you like to go for a wander around the grounds?" Flora's voice interrupted my reverie and I glanced up to see her taking the older fae's arm and heading towards the double doors at the end of the corridor.

Poor Laurel had barely any time to agree as Flora started walking and didn't wait for her to catch up.

That left Asher and me. Standing in silence, watching them go.

Yep, it was awkward.

I stalked into my room, pretending I didn't realize he was standing in the corridor alone. He crept in behind me and shut the door, the sound made me jump but I stood still, jaw locked, facing away.

"You're hiding something, Zinnia." He said, prowling towards me. I spun around and faced him.

"So what if I am? We all have secrets, Asher Thornleaf!" I yelled, angry about this evening and fed up with how he was treating me.

"Pray, tell Ms. Greenstem, what do you think mine

are?" He stepped closer, crowding my space but I refused to back down as I glared at his perfectly symmetrical face.

"You tell me, I'm not a mind reader," I rolled my eyes and he raised an eyebrow, testing me. He leaned in, close to my face, so close that I felt his hot breath on my skin, felt the piercing gaze of his forest-green eyes, felt my heart thump loudly in my chest.

Without a second thought, I grabbed the back of his neck and pressed his lips to mine. A rushed breath escaped his lips and I molded mine to his, pleasure coursed through my veins as his warm lips caressed my own. My heart beat wildly and I eagerly wrapped both of my hands around his neck, dragging him closer. His fingers roughly grabbed my waist and he walked us backward. I felt the edge of the bed against my calves and fell back on the soft blankets. Asher leaned over me, eyes full of fire as he rested his hands by my head.

It was what I'd wanted, what I'd been craving but the small voice in the back of my mind told me to push him off, not to give in so easily. So, I surrendered the pleasure I craved and pushed his shoulders.

His green eyes stared back, confused as he complied and stood up. I ran a hand through my messy hair. I just knew my cheeks were flushed and my skin prickled with longing.

"We can't do this again," I whispered, releasing a deep breath. Asher's brow pinched and I itched to smooth out the hard lines that marred his perfect face.

"You started it."

"You're always doing that. Blaming me, acting like I'm a nuisance, a pain to be around. Like you can't stand my existence!" I heaved a breath, shooting up from my place on the bed and poking him in the chest with every point I made.

"You worship the ground my sister walks upon," another poke in the chest, "and yet, you can't stand to spend more than a mere second with me." I snarled and with lightning speed, Asher grabbed my finger as I went in for a final poke on his rock-solid chest. He needn't know that he saved my finger from being bruised at this point.

"You." He closed his eyes briefly as if to compose himself. He held onto my finger tightly. "You're infuriating, hot-headed, you swear like a troll and yet," Asher hesitated, his eyes opening and boring into mine. "I cannot seem to stay away from you. Our kisses light me from the inside out. I'm burning for you, Zia."

My mouth fell agape before I could stop it. He wanted me? *And* he said my nickname, my heart fluttered in my chest. His actions spoke differently, every move he made pushed me further away. I wanted him too, but the way he treated me hurt more than I could explain.

"You can't have everything. Your actions say different and you treat me terribly." I hung my head, flopping back down in the bed and staring up at the ceiling. "It'll all be over soon, anyway," I whispered the last part to myself, wondering how I'll be able to pick up the threads of my old life again when everything had changed. I had changed.

"It doesn't have to be over." He spoke softly and my heart skipped a beat before my mind kicked into gear. I sat up on the bed, glaring at him.

"You really think I'm fucking stupid enough to believe that you have actual feelings for me, Asher? I'm a shiny new toy for you, nothing more. And when you bore of me, when I'm no longer of use, you'll toss me out like the rest of the faes you've bed." I scoffed. "Leave me alone."

In a flash, Asher dove at me, rolling us onto the bed and pinning me down with his body. He ground his hips against mine and my skin flushed as I felt his hard length beneath my thighs. *Gods above.* My legs were spread wide, his body nestled between them. He really *felt* something for me, who knew what though. Yes, feelings, I was willing to admit that, but perhaps not the good kind. My heart raced in my chest as he ground harder, and he glared at me, his eyes hard and piercing.

"You think this is what "no feelings" feels like?" He growled in my ear, tracing the pointed shape of it with his lips before pressing a kiss just below it, right on my thrumming pulse. I gasped, my hips rising to meet his in desperation. He trailed his hot mouth lower, the feeling of his soft lips driving me crazy.

"Answer me." He growled and he reached above my face, tugging my loose hair. I wanted to yell, to tell him off for treating me like that, but I actually *liked* it. Gods, what was wrong with me? I liked the way he treated me! *I need help, and urgently.*

"No." I breathed out, barely above a whisper as thoughts clouded my mind, the feel of Asher's strong body on mine had me practically whimpering and he rolled his hips again, hitting that sweet spot between my thighs.

"'No', what?"

"N-no, Your Highness." I stumbled, mad that he was making me call him by his title but also loving every second of it.

He captured my lips with his own and I groaned into the kiss. His hand snaked up my dress, caressing my bare leg. His touch was electric, like thousands of lightning bolts dancing on my flushed skin. His deft fingers inched higher, teasing the soft skin of my thigh. His kiss was bruising, my body was begging to be touched. Running my fingers through his hair, I relished the feeling of his body on mine.

I ached with need and whimpered as Asher's fingers gripped my thigh, pressing into the soft flesh. I was sure I'd be bruised from his rough touch but I couldn't think of anything else apart from his hot hands on me.

His mouth wandered down my neck again as his hands got higher, brushing over the sensitive spot that made my body jolt with need.

"Touch me," I breathed, desperate for any kind of friction for the aching need inside me.

Asher groaned in response, exploring further and

his hand dipped under my cotton underthings, brushing against my wet skin, I almost wilted on the spot.

"So ready for me. Is this what 'no feelings' is?" He goaded, his fingers playing with me as my hips rose with need. My skin was flush and sticky as he brought his mouth to mine.

"Hmm?" He prompted and I tried to focus my mind, but his touch was too distracting. It was feather-light and teasing. I needed more.

"Use your words, Zinnia, I want an answer."

Gods, this commanding side of Asher had me all riled up and I kind of loved it.

"No, Your Highness." I breathed, my body practically shaking with need. His fingers teased me and he pulled down my underthings from beneath my skirt, exposing me. The cool air from the window hit my heated flesh and I wanted to cry out with need. The teasing was almost too much.

"Is this all for me?" He questioned, his finger lazily running up my seam and I refrained from rolling my eyes at the obvious question.

"Yes, Your Highness."

"Good."

And with that, he dipped his index finger into me. My hips rose off the bed as I moaned. Finally, something to help me reach that Gods damned satisfaction. But all too soon Asher pulled his finger out. I pouted before realizing that he was sliding down the bed, down towards... Oh, Gods.

His hot mouth between my legs had me writhing

on the bed, thrashing my head, and fisting the sheets as his wicked tongue licked between my folds. A breathy moan escaped my lips and my body rose off the bed as pleasure flushed through me. My body shook, legs tense before I relaxed, the waves of pleasure tailing off, and leaving me fully sated.

With shaking legs, I peeked over my body to see Asher standing at the foot of the bed, wiping his mouth crudely and Gods did that make me want to do that all over again. And from the look in his eyes, I knew he did too.

He leaned forward, pressing a kiss to my lips, my tongue greedily met his, and with one hand propping him up by my head, the other cupped my cheek.

A knock on the door broke the spell between us. My heart hammered and I pushed Asher's chest in an attempt to disperse the tension between us. Because right now, we were *this* close to tearing all our clothes off, and Gods, did I want it.

"Zia?" My sister's voice called from through the door.

"Just a minute," I yelled back, trying to calm my racing heart. I hastily pulled my dress back down my legs and Asher slid off the bed, leaning on the frame as he watched me scramble to look presentable and not like we were about to fully fuck each other.

But of course, Flora didn't give us a minute and the door creaked open.

"Oh." She whispered and I cringed, picturing the room from her point of view. I was very flushed, my hair a mess, my clothes crumpled and Asher's crown was askew on his head, his lips still slightly glossy. Yep, we looked guilty as the Abyss.

"I can just come back-" She gestured for the door, a small smile playing on her lips.

"No, no, Asher was just leaving." I rushed out too quickly, hating the pleading tone in my voice. I suddenly didn't want to be left alone with Asher anymore. He confused me. Love and hate, hot and cold, I couldn't figure him out.

Without a look back at me, the Brat Prince pushed off the bed frame and strolled towards the door. It clicked softly behind him.

I let out a sigh of relief and flopped back on the bed, my heart finally returning to its normal rhythm.

"I want to know *everything*." Flora squealed, jumping onto the bed. Her light weight meant that she didn't make a dent as she bounced off the mattress. It hadn't gone unnoticed by me that she was looking better somehow. Her skin glowed now and she'd put on some weight. She seemed to have more energy but that worried me, her eighteenth birthday was quickly approaching and Finn was nowhere to be seen. Just another problem to add to my list.

"There's nothing to tell."

"Your face says different and your lips are bruised." She grinned and I covered my face, burying my emotions.

"You know Zia, you need to check in with your feelings. It's obvious that Asher likes you and you like him. Stop acting like two kids tiptoeing around the situation and be honest. Maybe you'll surprise yourself."

When did my sister get so astute and wise?

～

The warmth of the fire in the library was comforting to my tired bones. I'd not slept a wink with too much on my mind, swirling around my head like a storm. I'd risen early and decided to see if my pile of books on being a Bloom was still there and whether I could pick up where I left off. Flora was visiting home today. I'd wanted to go with her but I had bigger problems and the idea of escaping the palace, although appealing, would not solve anything.

The sight of Asher in an armchair by the fire caught me off guard and I tripped over the corner of a rug in surprise. He lowered his book slightly and peered over the top of it, his face unimpressed.

"What brings you here at this hour of the morning?" He spoke quietly but his words were firm. Perhaps a trip to my parents was exactly what I should have been doing.

I was worried we'd be in limbo now, not sure where our feelings stood. I, for one, did not want to confess anything out of humiliation. Yes, there was frustration and lust, but I did not want to be another conquest for Asher. So until I figured it all out, I would not be letting him near me again. Or at least no touching, kissing, or anything. No matter how much I desired it. Lines were being blurred and I didn't like it.

"Looking for a book, Your Highness." I rolled my eyes and Asher pressed his lips together. Maybe he'd forgotten my sarcastic mouth as it was put to other uses yesterday. My skin flushed with the thought of last night and I was thankful for the stifling heat from the fire to disguise my pink skin. But Gods, did I want it again.

I hovered for a moment, before flying up the shelves and scanning them as I went. My pile of books had disappeared so I'd have to try and remember what I'd found last time.

After a few moments of looking at spines, the book below me snapped shut and Asher looked up, beckoning me with the curl of his finger.

I sighed and flew down, settling in the chair opposite the prince, and cocked my head, waiting for him to speak.

We watched each other for a moment and I analyzed his features; his strong cheekbones, illuminated by the firelight, made him look older, the shadows dancing across his face. His eyes were hidden by shadow too, he looked menacing.

"Would you play a game with me, Zinnia?"

The simple question caught me off guard, it was too mundane, too plain for someone like Asher.

"Haven't we been playing a game all along?"

He narrowed his eyes and I sensed I was treading on thin ice.

"What's the catch?"

His sudden burst of laughter surprised me. It was beautiful, a deep and rich sound that made my toes curl in pleasure. I realized that was the first time I'd heard him laugh and I ached to hear it again.

"No catch." He smiled. "Just two faes playing a game. Take it as a peace offering."

I was still suspicious, but I nodded and Asher magicked a board game in front of us.

Chess, of course. I refrained from rolling my eyes a second time and scooted closer in my chair.

We sat quietly at first, not fully comfortable in a presence that wasn't forced or fighting. I glanced up as Asher moved his pawn to the left and he caught my eye, winking before looking back at the board. My cheeks flamed, butterflies erupted in my stomach, and I focused on the game again, determined not to be caught staring again.

Once Asher checkmated me, I sat back in my chair, basking in the warmth of the fire but also in the enjoyment of our game. No mean words or jest were exchanged and I'd actually *enjoyed* his presence. Asher watched me from across the board and I smiled softly.

"Thank you for the game."

If Asher was surprised at my words, he didn't show it. He inclined his head and we sat in silence, just watching each other. The room temperature rocketed as his eyes wandered lazily down the length of my body. I'd abandoned my shoes mid-game, so my bare feet were tucked under me. My dress was a soft sage green with a low neckline and fell mid-thigh with a slight split in the hem that revealed a teasing sliver of my thigh.

Tension crackled between us, the room felt too small, my skin prickled with desire, my body ached.

"Fuck it."

Asher's words sent me over as he knocked the chess board aside and dove at me. I nearly shrieked in surprise as he lifted me up and pushed me against the wall, running his hands down the length of my legs and then trailing his fingers up my skirt.

My hands gripped the collar of his soft, burgundy shirt. The color was gorgeous on him and I could barely think straight with his hands on me.

His lips were inches from my own, his hot breath fanned my already flushed skin and I nearly wilted when he brushed his thumb over my neck again. Like he'd done the first time we were alone in my room. My stomach clenched in anticipation.

The pad of his thumb slowly stroked the column of my throat and I swallowed thickly, his eyes narrowing before he leaned in, his lips barely a breath away from my own.

"Thought I'd find you two here."

Asher growled and I suppressed an untimely giggle as he spun around to face his brother.

"Little fae, up to no good with my brother I see." Cain's sing-song tone made my skin crawl. Asher spun around to face his younger brother.

"What do you want?" Asher gritted out, even though he had turned around, his hand snaked out to find mine and he linked our fingers together. My heart gave an extra loud thump in my chest as his thumb- yes, the same thumb that had just been on my throat- now caressed the top of my thumb.

"Ah, you see, I was thinking about the annual ball. And," he paused for dramatic effect and I had to stop myself from rolling my eyes. I didn't want to be on the wrong side of Cain. "I thought we could invite the whole kingdom, you know, lesser faes and all those."

My mouth fell slack. Invite lesser faes? Was Cain out of his mind? Not that I didn't think the invite would go unappreciated but he *despised* us. Why would he want to spend an evening in our company?

Asher hesitated for a second before shrugging.

"Do whatever you please, brother."

Cain clapped his hands together, obviously elated that he'd got what he wanted.

"Perfect, I'll begin planning. Shall we say two weeks?"

Asher didn't answer, but Cain didn't care.

"Take care of your pet, Asher. You wouldn't want her to get caught wandering the palace alone, now would you?"

In the blink of an eye, Asher had Cain by the throat, pushed up against the door. He wheezed as Asher's hand tightened around his neck. This was the first time I'd seen Asher defend me when Cain spoke down to me and I was surprised. A wave of delicious pleasure rolled through my body at the thought of Asher being protective over me.

"Bite your tongue, Cain." He growled. But his brother simply laughed.

"Struck a nerve, have I? You don't actually expect our parents to accept a lesser fae into our family? We're Royals after all."

His eyes cut to me and even at the distance I was, I noticed the whites weren't as bright as before. They were tinged in black, like a dye that had run on white garments. It sent a shiver down my spine.

If he noticed, Asher said nothing, gripping his brother's neck for a moment longer than necessary.

Asher released his brother and threw open the door before storming out. Cain coughed, rubbing his throat before throwing me a sinister smile and following his brother out.

I glimpsed a guard outside and my blood ran cold. The eyes that stared back at me were the same ones I'd seen staring blankly up at the ceiling at the noble's house when the rebels had attacked. I'd seen the blood seeping from his wound, I'd seen the light disappear from his eyes. He'd been dead. And now, he wasn't.

Something sinister was going on and I needed to find out.

Before it was too late.

Chapter Nine
The Ball

Finn's return was music to my ears. It had been a week since he'd left and I'd been anxious about Flora. Her eighteenth birthday was only two weeks away and we needed to see if she was indeed the Hollow One and if so, we had to help her gain control of her powers.

I'd been watching her closely, checking for any signs of power, but there was nothing yet. The book hadn't specified an exact timeline so I had watched her like a hawk, making sure she wasn't hurting herself or Gods forbid, anyone else.

I donned a pale yellow dress with beautiful willowy sleeves and hurried to Finn's study, my sister hot on my heels. Her wings still didn't work, but we made do with walking.

Knocking lightly on the door, I heard him call for us to come in and I peeked around the door.

"Zia, come in, please." Finn's warm smile filled

me with a sense of safety and I took Flora's hand behind me.

"Finn, this is Flora, my sister."

He stood for a moment before stepping closer. Flora gripped my hand, out of nerves or fear, I wasn't sure, but I squeezed back reassuringly.

"Welcome to the palace, you're safe here." He smiled and she nodded, her face a mask of confusion..

"I trust Zia has brought you up to speed?"

Flora shook her head and I felt a little guilty for keeping her in the dark. It had been easier to pretend that she was just coming to visit and not because she could potentially be some famous and very powerful being.

"I see." Finn glanced at me, his expression unreadable and I bit my lip. "Perhaps you can let us catch up. I'll send Laurel for you when we're done."

I nodded and gave Flora's hand one final squeeze before leaving my sister to discover her true potential.

～

I'd flown exactly thirty-nine laps of the garden by the time Laurel found me. I was a ball of anxious energy, even the birds had avoided me when I'd accidentally grown a new tree on the west side of the garden. I hoped no one would notice the new sapling of an oak tree as a result of my excess energy.

"They're ready for you, sweet girl." She spoke softly and I sighed, relieved that Flora hadn't hightailed and left. That wasn't really her style but I wasn't sure how she'd react when she found out how much I'd kept from her.

I crept into Finn's study, poking my head around the door and seeing the back of my sister's head.

"Ah, Zia. Come in." Finn gestured to me and Flora didn't turn around. My heart sank, worry twisting in my gut.

"I'll leave you two to it, seems like you have much to discuss." He gave me a look and I twisted my hands together in front of me. Finn flew out of the room and silence took his place.

"Flora, I-"

My sister spun around, her face angry, red, and blotchy, her eyes accusing as she stood in front of me, her stance bold and firm.

"Why didn't you tell me?" She demanded.

I cringed under her gaze and harsh words.

"I wanted to keep you safe-"

"Safe?" She questioned. "You kept me in the dark on purpose, how many more lies have you told?"

"I thought I was doing what was best for you."
I was close to tears, I'd expected her to be mad, I understood why but it hurt that she spoke to me like a mother chastising her child. I'd been trying to keep her safe and in doing so, I'd broken her trust.

"I'm so sorry, Flora." My lip trembled and my sister's face softened as she hugged me tightly.

"I know." She whispered.

"But, I do have some other things to tell you." I

bit my lip and Flora's eyebrows shot up.

"You're not expecting a child, are you?"

"Gods, no, Flora!" I gasped. "Why is that the first thing you thought of?!"

She shrugged, leading us to the chairs by the fire and we sat down.

"Because you looked guilty and you were rolling around in the sheets with Asher a few days ago." She giggled and I joined in.

"No, I mean yes." I was flustered, still embarrassed that she nearly barged in on us. "But no, we didn't get that far."

"Did you want to?"

I pondered her question, would I have let Asher take all of me if he'd asked?

"I don't know. Perhaps in the heat of the moment." I sheepishly confessed and she fake-gasped.

"Zinnia Greenstem! You little pixie!" She laughed and I couldn't help but laugh along with her.

After a moment of silence, I glanced at Flora, bracing to tell her everything. About Dillon, being a Bloom, the dungeons.

"Okay, don't be mad at me, but I went to see Dillon about other stuff…"

"What stuff?"

I sucked in a deep breath, cast a hearing spell for safety, and began my story.

For the most part and to her credit, Flora sat still, barely breathing as I recounted my tale. Dillon's part in it, my kidnapping, the stuff in the dungeons, the Hollow Ones book I found.

There was a moment of silence between me finishing up my wild story and Flora staring at me. I began to fidget, worried she'd be so mad that I'd kept so much from her.

"I'm surprised your brain didn't explode from keeping all those secrets." She giggled and I breathed a sigh of relief. "I can't believe Dillon is part of the rebels and that you're a Bloom!" She grinned. "I guess that explains why your pastries always taste ten times better than Mom's or Dad's."

"What do you mean?" I frowned.

"Because all the ingredients come from the earth and nature, and if you're a Bloom, you have an affinity to nature, your magic makes the apricots sweeter and the ingredients taste better." She shrugged as if it was obvious and I balked for a second.

Why hadn't I thought of that? It made so much sense.

"And probably why you're so eager to spend so much of your time outside."

"Okay, little Miss Know-It-All." I leaned forward, pinching her knee gently and she yelped.

"I'm just saying," Flora shrugged again, rubbing her knee and pouting at me. "For someone so smart Zia, you're so stupid sometimes."

"Yeah, yeah, yeah." I waved her off and a knock on the door interrupted our banter.

Finn entered, followed by a short, withered, gray-haired fae who looked about a thousand years old.

"I hope I'm not interrupting anything." We both shook our heads. "Zia, Flora, this is Cardus, he's an Elder from the Temple."

We both quickly scrambled to our feet and curtseyed to Cardus. He smiled softly, the lines on his face stretching out and for a moment, giving us a glimpse of his once youthful face.

"Cardus has agreed to help train Flora if she is what we believe. First, he must do some tests." My brows shot up in alarm and Flora's hand snuck into my own. We gripped each other fiercely.

"Nothing painful." Cardus eyed our clasped hands, stepping forward and smiling again.

"Just to make sure what we believe is true. You can imagine how many hoaxes and shams we get coming to the Temple, acting like the Hollow Ones."

"There are faes who don't have abilities?" I queried, we'd never met one person in the whole city who'd heard of faes with no powers or working wings.

"No, we tend to get phonies as it were. People who suppress their power with hopes of being a Hollow One. Maiming their wings even." He shook his head. "It is not for the faint-hearted, what we encounter." He stepped closer and I noticed a gnarled wooden cane in his hand. "You'd be shocked what people will do for a taste of glory." He barely spoke above a whisper and a shiver rolled down my spine.

"Cardus will be staying with us for the next week if

all goes to plan, to help us wield Flora's potential."
We both nodded at Finn and he reached for Flora.
"Come now Flora, we'll test you right away." My
sister turned back to me, worry etched into her
beautiful features and my heart lurched in my
chest.

"Not without me, you won't."

Finn turned around, smiling at me. "Zia, Flora
needs to focus and you're a distraction. We'll come
and find you when we're done."

Flora sighed, shaking her head as I went to follow
the three of them out.

"No, sis, I'll be okay."

My gut told me differently and as I watched them
make their way down the corridor, I had to use all
of my strength not to follow them.

~

Flora didn't return until late in the night. Asher
hadn't come to me, hadn't sought me out as I
lay in my room, not ready to confess that I was
waiting for him. A part of my heart hurt because
of that. Was it foolish to want to be desired by
him? He said he had feelings but now I was sure
they were just lust, plain and simple. Perhaps he'd
sought out another fae for his needs. My heart
constricted. *No, don't think like that.*

Yep, I'd tortured myself with endless thoughts,
varying between me being a fucking idiot for
believing Asher had feelings for me and hoping

that there was something more than lust between us. It kept my mind off my sister and the worry gnawed away in my gut as the shadows grew longer and the sun dipped beneath the horizon.

The moons were crescent and as I gazed out into the moonlight bathed garden, I idly played with my magic, creating a vine that traveled all the way from my window to the ground of the castle, covering it with luscious green leaves and flowers with soft pink petals.

The door creaked open as I made another budding flower on my vine and soft arms wrapped around my waist. I spun around, running my eyes down my sister's face.

Was she hurt? Injured? No. She looked... fine, healthy actually. Her skin glowed softly in the moonlight, her cheeks a beautiful shade of pink. Her eyes were bright, full of excitement and part of me dreaded her actually being a Hollow One. She'd be at risk, she'd be sought after, paraded around like a show pony in the wrong hands.

I just wanted her to be okay, be healthy without all the baggage. *But you can't have everything.*

"Zia." She whispered and I wrapped my arms around her neck, pulling her close and a gentle tear slid down my cheek. Everything was changing and I hated it. I hated myself even more for feeling like that. It was selfish to not want Flora to get better, to be healthy, and to have a proper chance at life.

"Don't worry, being a Hollow One won't change me. I'm still your sister." As if she read my mind, she tried to comfort me, stroking my hair down as I cried but her words just confirmed my fears.

I pulled back, wiping my nose on my arm and sniffing, watching my sister through watery eyes.

"So it's true then? You're one of them."

She nodded slowly, unsure if she wanted to confirm or not. *She's afraid of how I'll react.*

Not wanting to put a downer on my sister's day, I sniffed again and smiled.

"This is fantastic news, you'll be training with Cardus then?"

I knew she saw through my lies, through my fake smile but she chose to ignore it- thankfully because I was holding on by a very thin thread.

"Yep, although Cardus smells like old chestnuts." She giggled, wrinkling her nose and I couldn't help but laugh with her, grateful for the comic relief.

"Perhaps you and Cardus have a little something going on." I wiggled my eyebrows suggestively and she playfully slapped my arm.

"Ew, Zia, that's gross! He's like a thousand years old."

"Never too old." I laughed and Flora joined in. It felt good, just laughing for a moment, not worrying about what was to come.

"When do you start training?"

"Tomorrow at dawn, Finn said you should come too. For your healing training."

I nodded, then looked away, back into the garden, and wondered what life would be like from here on.

~

The training was merciless. My body and mind ached and before lunch, my legs wobbled so much I thought I'd collapse, not even my wings could hold me up. And that was only healing and Bloom training.

I'd glanced over at Flora a few times and she looked even more exhausted than me.

Finn had insisted that training meant mind and body. *You can only wield as much magic as it takes you to get tired,* he'd said. *It's all about balance. If you train your mind and your body equally, you can use more magic without feeling the effects so strongly.*

And so after many laps through the garden and weights- yes, weights- for my wings, I practically crawled into my bedroom. Laurel carried Flora who was already asleep. She looked so sweet and innocent while she slept.

I knew we'd have to confess everything to my parents, I planned to next time we visited. It wasn't fair to keep them in the dark for so long. Not when there was hope for their mystery child.

As I lay my weary bones to rest in bed, Laurel placed Flora on the other side and she rolled over, snuggling up to me.

"I'll be back with lunch in an hour and then I'll run a healing bath for you both." She smiled and I didn't have the energy to tell her that healing properties would be wasted on Flora.

I fought to keep my eyes open and briefly saw

a mop of dark hair enter the room before I was wrapped in sleep's tight embrace.

When I came to, a hand gently grazed over my arm, its featherlight touch was initially soothing, helping ease the tension in my muscles, until I realized I wasn't at my childhood home.

I bolted upright and my magic sprang out of me, creating a vine that wrapped around the offending hand and pinned it back. Asher stumbled as the vine crawled around his hand and he tugged at it with the other.

"What the fuck, Asher? It's creepy stroking someone while they sleep!" I burst out, my sister was no longer next to me, but I heard the splash of water through the closed bathroom door.

"I was *trying* to be soothing." He gritted out. I stared at him, arms crossed for a moment longer before dismissing the vines. They unraveled from his wrist in an instant, obeying my command and he shook out his hand.

"Well, don't," I said simply.

Asher came to sit on the edge of the bed, still rubbing his wrist.

"I'm not saying sorry."

"What if I make you?" He leaned forward, eyes pinned on me and my heart leaped in my chest. *Gods, that escalated quickly.* Instead of making good on his promise- and trust me, I was tempted- I averted my eyes and ran my hand through my hair.

"Where were you?"

"Out, on business, contrary to what you may

think Zinnia, I actually have a job as prince which does require my time and focus."

I huffed, annoyed with his somewhat sassy answer. It was the exact same tone I used with him and I didn't like the taste of my own medicine.

"How's your training with Finn going? Which, by the way, I requested you didn't initiate. I told you *I'd* train you. Had I not made myself clear enough?"

My mind flew back to when Asher first kissed me in the library after being jealous. *Oh yes, he'd been loud and clear.*

"Yeah, well you were away "on business"." I used my hands in air quotes and rolled my eyes. "Finn was the only other viable option."

"I'm back now so I'm training you." He glared at me and I stuck out my tongue in response. Asher's eyes narrowed and my stomach somersaulted. "We need to talk."

"Fine, but let me have a bath first. I'm feeling bruised and tired."

Asher's nostrils flared and his eyes ran over the soft pants and shirt I'd worn for training. I could have sworn I saw his fist clench.

"Come and find me when you're done."

And with that, he stormed out of the room, slamming the door behind him.

"Is he gone?"

Flora's redhead poked out from the bathroom.

"Yep." I popped the 'p' and flopped back down on the bed. Gods, I was exhausted.

"The tension in here was," she fanned herself. "I thought I might catch fire if I came out."

"Don't be so dramatic."

"Sis, you and Asher have some serious tension." She patted my arm as she sat on the bed next to me. She smelled sweet and clean and I rolled over, lying on my stomach to face her.

"No, we don't."

"Yes, you do."

"Asher, he's a pain in the butt."

"But a hot one." She grinned and I rolled my eyes. "What? Don't deny it. He's drop-dead gorgeous and moody too."

I bit my lip and she laughed.

"Fine, he's… easy on the eye. There, happy?"

My sister laughed and shook her head. I pushed myself off the bed and strolled into the bathroom before closing the door on her laughter.

Slumping on the edge of the tub, I began to run the water and contemplate my life.

～

I admit that I spent way too long in that bath. I knew Asher would be mad. But the "we need to talk" line had put me off hurrying. I was loathing having to explain myself to him, he'd probably laugh in my face if I confessed that Flora was a Hollow One.

"Zinnia!" A thump came at the door that made me jump up, splashing water everywhere as my wings flapped rapidly. "Stop wasting my time," Asher yelled and I rolled my eyes.

"Yes, Your Highness," I called back and stood up, letting the water cascade off me and then grabbing a towel.

I cracked open the door and saw Asher pacing the room, arms crossed over his chest. He was in that burgundy shirt again and my stomach did weird things as I watched him, back to me, and admired his body.

"Yes?" I asked, pulling the bathroom door open and in a moment of bravery, decided to tempt the beast.

He spun around, only flapping his wings once to cross the space of my room. He landed in front of me, his eyes roaming down my body. The short towel covered everything that was essential but left a large expanse of bare skin exposed.

His intense gaze, the way his eyes wandered over each curve, each inch of my body made my skin heat up. A flush crawled up my neck and fire ignited in my belly.

"Zia." He breathed my name and Gods, it sounded like a prayer on his lips. He took a step closer. My pulse raced as his finger traced my collarbone then worked its way up and followed the outline of my jaw. His feather-light touch had my blood singing and as he tucked a stray hair behind my ear, my body practically wilted at his feet.

But all too soon, his hand dropped and he took a step back, closing his eyes briefly to regain his composure. The cold, distant mask slipped back onto his face.

"Meet me in my study in five minutes." He began to fly to the door but paused and said "clothed" over his shoulder before carrying on out of the room.

I sighed as the door closed behind him and flew to my drawer, picking up a pale pink gossamer gown that had a cute little tie at the cleavage. It was short-sleeved and floaty, perfect for my training. I assumed we wouldn't be doing more weights if Asher wanted to meet in his study. Or at least, I hoped, perhaps my attire would put him off making me do physical training. I slipped it on and found some matching slippers.

Wondering whether Flora was still training with Finn and Cardus this afternoon, I made a mental note to ask her how it went as soon as I saw her again. I didn't want them to overwork her, she was only just starting to get better.

I padded down the corridor and gently knocked on Asher's study door. There was no immediate response so I twisted the handle gently and pushed it open.

He was sitting at his desk, writing away as he always seemed to be. And he was barefoot. Again.

My eyes shot back up to the back of his head, cheeks heating involuntarily.

"Asher," I whispered and he spun around, eyes locked on me.

"Zinnia." Back to my full name again. This fae's

mood swings really gave me whiplash.

"You wanted to see me."

"About two hours ago, yes." He spoke sharply and I refrained from rolling my eyes. They'd be well-oiled at this rate.

"Well, I'm here now." I shrugged and he crossed the room before dropping down on the couch and beckoning me with a hooked finger.

"Tell me, when were you going to come clean about Flora?"

I walked to the couch slowly, deliberating his question. Did he know about the Hollow Ones?

"Let me clear it up for you, I can see the cogs working in your head. Before you make up a terrible lie, let me remind you that you live under my family's roof."

The threat was clear and for a moment, I saw red. *How dare he threaten me!*

"And let *me* remind *you* that I could go to your parents right now and tell them it was all fake!" I retorted.

"And what proof do you have?" He challenged me. "You'd ruin your reputation, Zinnia, not mine."

Fuck! I wanted to scream and yell. He was treating me like a child and I hated it.

"Flora, is she a Hollow One?"

My mouth fell agape.

"How do you-"

"The hows are not important, although you assume I'm more stupid than I am. Why did you go to Finn about it?" The hurt in his voice was evident. "Why didn't you come to me?"

I sighed, wondering whether to tell the truth.

"Because what's between us, it complicates things. With Finn, I know where I stand. But with you? It's like one minute we're about to tear each other's clothes off and then the next, we're yelling at each other."

Asher sat quietly for a moment and I still stood, hands in fists by my sides. I was riled up by his threats.

"Be my guest to the annual ball."

Okay, literally a non-sequitur. How random could Asher be?

I hesitated, not because I wasn't sure I'd agree. But because I wasn't sure I wanted to go. The last party hadn't gone well. I recalled dragging Asher's limp body to safety in my mind and shivered at the horrific memory.

Asher must have read my expression because his face softened and he stood, walking towards me. He took my hand in his own, the tingles ignited on my skin as he threaded his fingers through mine. He tilted my chin up to look at him and I almost got lost in those forest green eyes.

"You're safe here. I'm here." He whispered. I wanted to believe it so badly, but the stuff in the dungeons and Flora's new skills, everything made me feel so unsafe.

"Yes," I whispered. "Flora is a Hollow One, one of

the Temple Elders came to test her." I looked away, thinking about how Flora's true power will change everything. "I'm scared, Asher. She's my little sister and every day I'm worried for her safety, worried that some other Kingdom will get wind that we've found her, and they'll try and kidnap her."

Before I knew it, Asher's arms wrapped around me and he pulled me close, resting his chin on my head. His hug was warm and inviting, and I buried my face in the crook of his neck, breathing in his scent. Woody and like freshly cut grass. I inhaled deeply and Asher's arms tightened around me.

"I won't let that happen, Zia. You have my word."

"I know," I murmured, feeling safe in Asher's strong arms. I breathed in again, inhaling all that was the gorgeously, annoying fae in front of me.

But there was something on my mind, a thought that rolled off my tongue too quickly for me to stop it.

"What about the moans I heard from your room the other night?" I asked and Asher breathed a laugh, his hot breath fanning against my cheeks.

"A fae has needs, you know? And I had a considerable amount of leftover energy after our kiss."

I huffed, my cheeks blushing bright pink as I tried to think of a suitable reply that didn't involve asking why he hadn't come to me to sort out his *needs*.

He glanced down, his dark eyes burning into mine before dipping down to my mouth.

And that was all it took.

His mouth met mine, his lips molding so easily with my own. They felt almost familiar, now we'd shared more than one kiss together and I groaned as Asher's arms tightened around my waist, one hand coming up to grip the back of my neck. My eyes fluttered shut at the contact, my heart racing in my chest, threatening to jump out at any second.

Pulling him closer, I moaned, wanting to feel all of him, every inch of his delicious skin. He pushed me back and I felt the velvet couch against the back of my legs. He eased us down, never breaking the kiss as my hands wandered down to his waist. His fingers wove into my hair, nails slightly scratching my scalp as he tilted my head up gently, his tongue exploring my mouth. I tugged at the shirt he wore, indicating that I wanted it off.

He stepped back, breaking our contact and I almost whined at the loss of his touch on me. Eyes still on me, he pulled his shirt off, revealing the body that I was sure was sculpted by the Gods themselves. The hard planes of his torso led to his tapered waist where the delicious V led down to the waistband of his leather pants. More. I wanted more, I wanted to see all of him, taste all of him.

I reached for his pants, eager to make good on my mental promise but he stepped away, smirking as my lips dropped into a pout.

"Patience is a virtue." He teased as his deft fingers pulled the bow I'd tied at the bust of my dress. It fell loose easily at his command and it exposed the rounded flesh of my breasts. Asher inhaled a sharp breath, his throat bobbing as his eyes wandered down my body and I decided enough was enough.

"I never had time for virtues."

I shrugged out of my dress and kicked it to the floor next to Asher's shirt. I sat bare from the waist upwards, looking somewhat more confident than I was feeling. My nipples beaded in the cool air of the room and Asher's heated gaze made me feel like I was about to be set alight.

He knelt down so that he was eye level with my chest, and without hesitation, he took my nipple in his mouth. And Gods above, I thought I'd died and ascended right there and then. The feeling of his hot, warm, wet mouth on me was enough to send me over, but I refused, heart hammering in my chest and instead, I let out a moan, my head rolling back in bliss. Asher's hands snaked up and he massaged one breast while sucking the other.

Heat blossomed in my lower belly, causing me to moan and squirm. I wanted more, needed more, something to satisfy that friction that was burning between my legs.

"More." I breathed out, my voice husky and unrecognizable. Asher ignored me, switching to my other breast and my body shook, hips scooting to the edge of the couch, seeking out his body.

He let my nipple go with a pop and it glistened with his saliva in the fading afternoon light that shone through the window. Leaning forward, he wrapped his hands around my lower back and pulled me closer, close enough to feel how much he really wanted me. And wow, he really *did* want me.

I tried not to consider that it was just lust, all this tension built up between us. I wanted this, regardless if it was just that. I *needed* this. There was no going back now.

His hands trailed lower, toying with the waistband of my undergarments and I huffed, frustrated that he was stalling us. He chuckled quietly before his finger curled around the thin fabric and slowly slid them down my legs, his eyes on my body as he did so.

I was fully naked, laid bare before him and a fleeting thought told me to cover up, to not be so stupid. I squashed it down like a bug and focused on the gorgeous fae before me.

Asher's eyes took their time in memorizing every curve, every inch of me and I almost squirmed under his heated gaze.

"You're so beautiful." He breathed, almost to himself. His hands swiftly unbuttoned his pants and he slid them down his long legs before slipping them off and discarding them with the rest of the clothes.

I marveled at his body, and of course, my eyes automatically landed on his length. It was thick, hard, and before I knew it, I was reaching forward, taking him in my hand and rubbing him, wanting to feel every hard ridge of him.

Asher let out a pained breath and I glanced up, relishing in the fire in his eyes. He looked ravenous and I was the meal. My insides clenched and I repeated my actions, before leaning in and taking him in my mouth.

"Zia." His breath was ragged, his words rough, like he was showing much self restraint. Too much for my liking. He grabbed a handful of my hair and held on for dear life as I slid my mouth down his length, running my tongue along the underside of him and moaning around him.

"S-stop." He stuttered and I released him, momentarily worried that I'd done something wrong.

"Did I-"

"No." He said firmly, running a hand through his hair and I marveled at his bicep, the way the muscles flexed.

"I need to be inside you. Now." His command left no room for debate and my legs spread for him and he knelt down again before me.

I knew I should probably say something, about it being my first time otherwise it felt like another lie on top of the never-ending pile of lies that I'd created.

His hands slid up my milky thighs, fingers brushing over the center of me and my body jerked forward, craving the friction.

"Asher," I whispered and he looked up at me, eyes concerned. "This is my first... you know."

His face went from concerned to annoyed in an instant and he stood up.

"No, Zinnia, I can't." He rubbed his face, before running his hands through his dark hair again. "I cannot take all of you."

"I want you to." I urged, trying so hard to stop my eyes from running down the full length of him naked in all his glory. Because he was everything I wanted right now, and I was too weak to resist.

"You cannot know that."

"I do." I insisted, standing up and in a moment of bravery, I grabbed his hand and pushed it between my legs, where I knew I was practically dripping for him. My thighs were slick with my own desire. "Can you not feel that I do?"

Asher barely breathed, his finger gently teasing the most sensitive part of me and I bit my lip, my hips trying to create a rhythm against his hand, a breathy moan escaped my lips.

"Gods." He groaned and I knew I'd won.

In an instant, all his resolve disappeared and his hands wrapped around my thighs, lifting me up as he strode to the wall, pushing me back against it. The hardwood dug into my back deliciously. The fire in his eyes drove me wild. I wanted him, I needed him like I needed air to breathe.

"This is your last chance-" He began but I cut him off with my lips, confirming my intentions, and Asher's tongue dove into my mouth, claiming me. His hips rocked against mine, his length so close to my entrance. He was teasing me, his hot breath on my neck as he pressed a not-too-gentle kiss to my skin, his lips burning me.

His fingers reached out, gently caressing the thin membrane of my wings. A delicious shiver rolled down my spine at his soft touch. It was so *intimate*. I moaned lighty, eyes closed in pleasure. His deft hands wandered their way along the veins of my wings, teasing, caressing, stroking.

Asher grabbed his length, guiding it to my entrance and I spread my legs wider. His tip inched in, and I breathed a sigh as he pushed further. It burned, stretching me and my head fell into the crook of his neck, biting his skin as he sank all the way in. He groaned, hissing through his teeth as I licked the bite mark on his skin.

He heaved a breath, before pulling his hips out and thrusting in again. The pain was replaced with sweet, hot pleasure and the fire in my stomach reignited. My hips matched his rhythm, my arms wrapped around his neck and Asher's hands gripped the flesh of my ass, his touch bruising as he pushed back into me.

A moan tumbled off my lips as our sweat-covered bodies moved together, I felt the tight coil building in my stomach, Asher's thrusts became frantic, his stomach taut as he kissed my neck, my collarbone, my breasts, anywhere his mouth could find.

The sound of our skin against each other filled the room with breathy moans and the coil snapped as Asher's teeth met my skin. I moaned as I unraveled around him, waves upon waves of pleasure washing through me. My eyes fluttered shut, absorbing every morsel of the ecstasy that I felt.

Asher came soon after me, his breath labored as he groaned, filling me up. We stayed connected, chests heaving together, and he pressed a gentle kiss to my shoulder.

I didn't know whether to laugh or cry at what we had just done, what I'd sworn not to do.

Would this change everything?

~

Cain The Pain's ball was in full swing by the time Asher took my arm and led me into the ballroom. Anxiety riddled my body, my hands shaking as the noise overwhelmed me. Memories flashed in my brain of the chaos of the last ball. I willed myself to forget.

He'd spared no expense, dancers, a full band and a whole wall's length table of food lay in front of us as we descended down the spiral steps.

The array of beautiful dresses each fae wore beneath us made the room burst full of color. A fae in a pink dress bumped me, momentarily knocking me out of my daze. She apologized profusely, her bright turquoise hair was like the sea in waves around her face. I smiled and she returned it with a bright one.

I hadn't forgotten that Cain had invited lesser faes, more common folk. He was up to something so I needed to try and keep an eye on him tonight. I scoured the crowd for my parents and spotted my sister's bright red hair, tied up in an elaborate style with iridescent pearls threaded through her locks. They matched her shimmering ivory-colored gown which made her look even more luminescent.

Our training had been going well. Mine no longer required weights, although Asher tended to prefer testing out how far my powers would go rather than show me how to hone in on them. I guessed he didn't want to admit that he was out of his league on Blooms and healing powers. I read a lot in the library and we often discussed notes in books, we both were learning a lot together.

And it didn't go unnoticed by me that we were enjoying our time together, less yelling, less arguments and more talking, listening to each other. Our night together didn't change us the way I had expected it to. I thought he'd ignore me, treat me like a conquest. Instead he'd begun to respect me, not talk across me or cut me off and treat me like a child. There were still times where he ordered me around, so it was still baby steps on improvement. In return, we'd played more chess games, read books in the library and enjoyed our time together. I didn't dare say it outloud, but I thought perhaps I was falling for him.

It was a big perhaps.

Flora's training was different. She didn't speak about it much, often coming back late and so tired that she passed out with her clothes on. I was concerned but Asher said Finn and Cardus knew what they were doing. She was getting stronger though, no longer the weak, small fae I once knew.

Her limbs had muscle definition, her skin glowed, and her cheeks had a healthy hue. I was equally excited as I was worried, her secretive training made me nervous. What were they actually teaching her to do? I hadn't managed to catch up with Finn yet, but I planned on squeezing answers out of him.

I followed my sister's path with my eye and spotted my Mom's head by the food table. *Of course, she'll be judging all the food, I'm sure.*

"Zinnia," Asher whispered beside me and I brought my focus back to him.

He looked delectable in his fine forest-green jacket, with golden embroidered vines. His golden shirt was unbuttoned dangerously low, showing me his toned and sculpted torso. I'd had to actively try to reduce my salivation when he'd knocked on my door. The fire in his eyes said he'd felt the same as his searing gaze had roamed over my golden gown, which in turn had green roses embroidered into the V-shaped neckline. It dipped low, exposing an almost indecent amount of cleavage. I knew Asher had made it as a tease, to tempt others but flaunt what was his.

But it wasn't real.

None of this was.

I had to remind myself every day that at the end of this, *I'll have paid off my deal with Asher and we'll go back to our old lives as we were before we met.*

But I wasn't sure if I'd fit back into my life so well. Would I be shunned by the community? By my family? I doubted Asher would come clean about it with his family so he'd live happily knowing he'd fooled everyone while I'd have to tell my family, and explain why it didn't work out between us. And no, I would not tell one more lie.

Asher spun me out as we descended the steps, my thoughts disappearing and I gasped as he reeled me back in, our chests flush, the gold buttons of his jacket felt cool against my heated skin.

"Dance with me."

It wasn't a question and my blood raced as I placed a hand in his, the tingles igniting and lighting up my skin like the fireflies that glow in the night. His other hand gripped my waist and we followed the rhythm of the song, dipping, and weaving as we went. The crowd parted for us as we floated to the dancefloor. The room rotated, my heart throbbed in my chest and Asher's dark eyes remained on me, watching me as our bodies moved to the beat together.

Dipping back and tilting my head back to expose my neck, Asher leaned down, his lips grazing my collarbone as he pressed a gentle kiss to my skin. I gasped, looking around us and seeing the faes whispering, pointing at my wings, and calling me out. The golden diadem on my forehead grew hot from my flushed skin. I saw the King's disapproving look as he watched on from his throne at the end of the room.

It was too much, too real when it was all fake. I wanted to scream it out loud so the whole Kingdom would know it was a sham.

I quickly stood back up and excused myself before

dashing off to the drinks table. Asher didn't call after me like I'd expected him to. I glanced back and saw him already speaking with some lesser faes surrounding him, all female of course. A surge of jealousy peaked inside me and I squashed it down.

I had no reason to be jealous of his female attention when I was the one who'd bailed out from our dance. I had to remind myself again that what we had wasn't real. He'd find a real bride someday, a higher fae who'd share the crown, the dances, his bed with him. Not me.

My thoughts made my mood sour and I threw back two drinks before sighing and turning around to face the party.

"Zia!"

A familiar scent of lavender and violet greeted me and I grinned as I hugged my best friend.

"Look at you! This is where you've been hiding!" She gestured to the palace and I laughed.

"How have you been?"

She shrugged. "Not rubbing shoulders with princes."

The jealousy in her tone took me back. I guessed it made sense though, Lilac had always had her sights set on a prince. I bet she wondered why Asher had picked me. Little did she know.

"You could always introduce me," her eyes sparkled with mischief. "I'm sure Prince Cain would remember me from the last dance."

"I don't think that's a good idea, Lilac…" I tried but she waved me off before I had a chance to explain exactly why I thought introducing Cain to Lilac was a bad idea.

"I see, you're with Asher but you don't think I'm good enough, do you?"

"Not at all-" I was shocked she'd think like that. Lilac was always the confident one of us, she never put herself down.

"I see you in your expensive gown Zia, exchanging looks with Prince Asher. You think you're above us, don't you?" Her face was angry, eyes wild and I shook my head, raising my hands in defense.

"No, I'd never-"

"Whatever, you've always been like this."

And with that, my purple-haired friend disappeared into the crowd, leaving me standing there, mouth gaping.

Before I could even have a second to consider what was going on, why Lilac was acting that, Lily was at my side. She was dressed in her uniform, carrying a tray under her arm.

"Prince Asher's looking for you." She whispered and I sighed, following her to the end of the room.

As we approached the throne, I curtseyed to the King and Queen, then my eyes found the three Princes. Finn smiled softly and I mustered as much of a smile as I could back, Cain The Pain was grinning ear to ear, and not for the first time, I wondered what his ulterior motive was. He was too smug to just be organizing an event of this scale for fun. I needed to keep a closer eye on him.

And finally, my gaze fell on Asher. I expected him to be mad that I ran away from him but instead, he extended his hand, and before my brain was thinking about it, I took it, savoring the tingles that ignited on my skin again.

"You got what you wanted then," I whispered as he pulled me to his side, wrapping an arm around my waist. I watched the heads turn around the room, all eyes on us. Eyes on who had captured the heart of one of the most desired princes in Nissa.

"Not quite yet." He replied, his lips dangerously close to my neck as he whispered in my ear. His hot breath made me want to shiver with pleasure. *No, Zia, not now, we're in public.* His fingers traced the skin of my back, the dress had a lace-up style at the back that left a lot of bare skin and Asher wasted no time in caressing my sensitive skin.

My knees buckled slightly as he deftly ran his fingertips over my heated flesh. He left a trail of fire in his wake and I wanted nothing more than to grab his lapels and smash my mouth into his. Gods, I had to reign in the feelings swirling around in my chest.

I peeked at Asher out of the corner of my eye and cursed softly when a smug smile painted his lips. He was so pleased with himself, it was infuriating.

Someone rang a bell and the crowd quietened, a hush fell on the eager audience. The King rose, his navy suit fitted his broad body and as he reached out his hand, the Queen, in a lovely peach-colored dress, stood up next to him grasping his outstretched hand.

"We welcome you, residents of Nissa, to our palace." Applause and cheers filled the air before someone hushed them down again.

I scanned the faces in the crowd, wondering if I recognized anyone. My parents' familiar faces stood further back and my mom jumped up and down, waving and grinning. I smiled softly, giving her a little wave. My dad chuckled next to her and grabbed her hand as she tried to raise it again, I smiled to myself. At least they looked happy. Flora stood next to them, her eyebrows raised as she glanced at Asher and then me again. I smothered a giggle that threatened to bubble up inside me.

"We encourage you to eat our food, drink our wine and be merry! For tonight, we celebrate!" More cheers threatened to deafen me. "But before we go back to our merriment, I believe one of my sons has something to say."

My heart dropped as the King gestured to Asher, his face unreadable.

No.

He stepped forward his arm behind me, urging me along and Asher stood on the step, facing the crowd. My knees trembled. Gods, what was he doing?

"You're probably wondering who this delicious female on my arm is. She's captured my heart, bewitched my mind, and holds my emotions prisoner." He glanced down at me, gripping my waist and his eyes searched mine for a moment. Panic flooded my veins as my mind made up a million different scenarios as Asher spoke. "And in truth, I don't want them back. So, I'm delighted to announce Zinnia Greenstem as my wife."

No.

Fuck.

What the fuck?

This was not part of the deal!

My stomach dropped, my palms began to sweat, the blood drained from my face. The cheers, the applause, the sheer sound hit me like a wave, threatening to drown me. What in the Abyss was happening?

"N-no, Asher-" I stumbled.

"Hush, Zia. Smile." He grinned out at the crowd, grabbing a flute off a passing server and he thrust it in the air. "To Zinnia."

The audience followed suit, all cheering and clapping happily as they envisioned a Royal wedding.

I, on the other hand, was sure I was about to puke in front of the Kingdom.

Turning around, Asher led me off the stage. If looks could kill, Cain's would have cut me clean in half as we passed him. He was close to me, his hot, sickly breath on my cheek. My eyes cut to him, and not for the first time, I noticed the whites in his eyes were a dark gray tone, tingled with small, spidery veins of black.

"Enjoy it now little fae, this could be the last time you see these hallowed halls."

I didn't give him another look, though his words settled within me like a rock in my stomach. I pondered the way his eyes looked and why it rang alarm bells in my mind. I couldn't focus enough to recall why I felt like it was something important.

We hurried into a back room. My hands shook with rage and I spun back to face Asher as he closed the door, the sounds of the ball muffled from in here.

"How dare you!" I stalked over to him, my blood boiling in my veins.

"And here I was thinking you'd be pleased."

"Pleased?! You just told the whole fucking Kingdom that we're getting married when our relationship is a sham, a fake!"

"I told you what I feel is real." He stepped closer, eyes narrowing on me. I threw my hands up in the air in frustration.

"Real perhaps, but only a phase, Asher." I turned away from him, angry and tired. "I'm a fleeting moment in a lifetime."

He didn't reply, only confirming my suspicions and I gritted my teeth, it dawned on me just how far this deception had gone. Too far.

"You've gone too far this time. Deceiving a few people is bad enough but this? This is catastrophic!"

"Zinnia-" He reached for my arm as I lunged for the door.

"Don't touch me." I hissed. Asher stepped back, surprised at my reaction. But what did he expect? Me to jump up and down with glee? He was foolish if he truly believed that I wanted to fake-marry him.

I threw open the door and stormed out, cutting my way through the faes who tried to congratulate me. I waved them off with a fake smile and a brief "thank you".

I needed out now.

I spotted Laurel walking out with an empty tray and had an idea. I caught up to the lovely fae and grasped her elbow lightly.

"Oh, Zia." She said sympathetically as she turned to hug me. My heart broke and a tear slid down my cheek.

"Can... Can I stay with you tonight?" I choked, not feeling brave enough to try and sort out the tangle of thoughts inside my head by myself.

"Of course, sweet girl." She bundled me into her arms and we made our way towards the lower quarters.

$\sim$

Armed with a cup of hot tea, I settled in front of the fire burning away in Laurel's room.

Her partner, Ivy, was a tall, willowy, white-haired fae who bundled me into her arms as soon as I arrived with my tear-stained cheeks. They'd buzzed around me, one boiling the water, the other finding a cup and leaves for the tea. They worked beautifully in sync and my heart wished for someone I could work so well with. They had a natural rhythm together and I briefly caught a sweet smile on her face as Ivy bent down and pressed a kiss to Laurel's lips.

They lived in a small place with a kitchen, bathroom, bedroom, and a little couch. It was humble but homey, and I smiled as they bumbled around making tea and biscuits.

I had changed into a soft long-sleeved dress, a thick blanket wrapped around my shoulders. I was sweating next to the fire but the heat was a comfort. I contemplated my thoughts. Fuck, Asher told the whole fucking kingdom we're getting married? *We're not even properly dating? He must have taken way too many magic mushrooms to believe that I'll happily go along with his charade when he's taken it to the next level.*

My mind was a mess, on the one hand, I wanted out now. We didn't agree to this and it was too far, I couldn't see it through any more simply because there was no end and I was not, under *any* circumstances, going to fake-marry Asher.

On the other hand, I knew I needed to investigate the palace further and the only way of doing that was by playing along with Asher's charade. I felt like I owed it to Elijah to find out what happened to River as no one else seemed to care.

Plus, I was feeling something more than just lust for him and the thought of leaving him and the palace forever made my heart clench and not in a good way.

Gods, I was a wreck.

"Zia, you can take the bed, we can sleep on the couch." Ivy smiled and I shook my head vehemently.

"No, I'll take the couch, there's only one of me and I'll be fine here."

"I really think you'd be more comfortable-"

"Ivy," Laurel patted her arm and Ivy nodded, blowing

me a kiss before going into their bedroom.

"Sweet girl, rest your head now. Sleep on it instead of driving yourself insane with worry, and look at the situation in the morning with fresh eyes." Laurel rubbed my back comfortingly as I stared at the dancing flames of the fire.

Yeah, I should sleep on it, then tomorrow I'll decide what to do.

Chapter Ten
Endless Darkness

The morning was gray and overcast, and it perfectly matched my mood. Everything sucked. Big time.

I crept up the stairs and found my paradise untouched since I'd last left it. The fire still burned red hot in the oven and the ingredients had been restocked.

With nimble hands, I quickly got to work, doing one of the only things that helped me think whilst in a dilemma. Which seemed to be more often than not recently. *I guess I'll be making enough pastries for the whole Kingdom at this rate.*

I kneaded the dough particularly viciously, imagining the Brat Prince's smug grin from last night and I sighed. Punching dough thinking it was Asher wasn't going to solve anything but it made me feel slightly better.

The palace was quiet, I imagined everyone was sleeping in after last night's celebrations. I wanted to talk to Flora, to my parents, and explain everything but then what would I say? *"Oh sorry Mom and Dad, I was fake-dating the prince the whole time in order to save us from more debt."* Yeah, coming clean didn't really sit well with me right now.

"Gods above," I grunted as I rolled the dough one last time before shaping it into the braids I liked to make and spreading the apricot glaze on top of it.

A loud bang, followed by shouting interrupted my thoughts and I glanced down the corridor that led back upstairs, wondering what was going on.

I brushed off my hands, leaving the pastries as they were, and crept forward, poking my head out into the stairwell.

More shouting came, but I couldn't make out what they were saying from this distance. I inched closer, hands gripping the doorframe. It sounded bad, the yelling was urgent, and my heart sped up in my chest. Something was wrong.

Suddenly a large hand grabbed my shoulder. I yelped, kicking back and throwing some magic at whoever the attacker was.

"Zinnia!"

The familiar voice made me stop in my tracks and I spun around to see Asher rubbing his leg, and with a flower crown nestled in his hair. *Oops?* Okay, so my magic still needed some work on the attacking front.

"What do you want?" I kept my voice cold as I

plodded back into the kitchen.

"The palace is under attack." Asher panted, ruffling his hair and the flowers fell loose, drooping sadly as they hit the floor. "I couldn't find you, I was worried-where did you go last night?"

He was worried? *Yeah, only because losing you would mess up his grand plan.* I decided to listen to the angry voice in my head.

"It's none of your concern where I was," I said sharply, turning around to face him. "Why do you even care?"

Asher's fists clenched at his sides and his chest rose and fell rapidly. A muscle in his jaw ticked as he stared at me.

He looked divine in his armor, it was made of leather with the Thornleaf emblem engraved into the breastplate. His pale blue shirt peeked out from underneath and he wore black leather pants. His long sword was sheathed, the fire reflected in its polished silver handle. I'd never seen him with a sword before and the irrational part of my brain appreciated how godly he looked. *No, stop it.*

His boots were so shiny, that I was sure I'd be able to see my reflection in them if I looked closer.

"We'll talk about this later." He gritted out. "Stay here, lock the door behind me, and don't come out until I come and find you." Another loud bang made me jump and Asher stepped forward, his fingers grazing my arm. Goosebumps rippled on my skin at his touch.

"I'll come back for you." He whispered and for a moment, I wanted to believe that he was choosing to come back to me because he wanted me. Not because of his stupid games.

"Who's attacking?" I whispered, suddenly afraid. The weight of the situation had finally hit me, my hands shook as I gripped the stone counter.

"Rebels."

More yelling, more bangs, and I assumed they had breached the gate. The sounds were closer now, almost on top of us.

Asher unsheathed his sword from his belt, the blade looking sharp and deadly. I caught a glimpse of the engraving on the hilt of the blade when the light hit it just right. It was a rose, with a single leaf on a stem with thorns, just like his ring. I twisted it on my forefinger absentmindedly.

He stepped forward, gently tracing my jawline with his finger. It was tender and an unfamiliar feeling fluttered in my chest. His dark eyes watched my lips and my mouth parted involuntarily.

Footsteps thumped overhead, and dust from the stone sprinkled down on us, covering us in a light layer of white. Asher snapped out of his daze and raised his sword, ready to go into battle.

"Hide," Asher growled and my heart raced in my chest as he flew out of the room and into the fray.

Gods above, can't a fae just catch a break?

Heeding Asher's warning, I darted behind the

fireplace and wedged myself between the storage cupboards and the brick wall of the open fire. It was hot and I'd probably wilt if stuck down in there for any length of time but I needed to stay hidden. I worried for my sister, hoping wherever she was, she was safe. I sent a silent prayer up to all the Gods in the sky.

The footsteps neared and my heart thumped, blood rushing past my ears, making my hearing muffled. I swallowed thickly, gripping my skirts with white knuckles as the footsteps entered the room.

"Where are we going, Prince Cain?" The voice was too well-known, too sweet and naive and my heart gave out.

Why had she got caught up in all this? Couldn't she just have stayed away?

Cain didn't reply but I peeked my head out and the familiar purple hair made my chest constrict.

Lilac.

He had her by the wrist and he not-too-kindly yanked her forward, heading in the direction of the dungeons.

"Are you sure about this?" The hesitation in Lilac's voice was obvious, she stumbled as Cain tugged harder. "Ow, you're hurting me."

Cain's grip only tightened and I knew I had to do something. I couldn't just let my best friend get dragged down to some Godsforsaken place without a fight.

I crawled out from my hiding space and stood tall.

"Cain." My voice was strong and firm, despite my quivering hands which I held tightly behind my back. "Let her go."

The prince's eyes sparkled in delight and he grinned sinisterly. The hairs on the back of my neck prickled as he stepped towards me, tugging Lilac behind him.

"Little fae, what a surprise. Where's your protector now?" He spoke too sweetly, full of falseness and my mouth went dry.

I stepped back, trying to create space between us. I stumbled slightly, not taking my eyes off Cain.

Lilac's lip quivered as she reached out to me.

"She's coming with us." He called. "Seize her." Two guards flanked me, grabbing my arms before I could react. I thrashed around, kicking out and screaming as they began to drag me towards the dungeons. I couldn't let myself be captured, be taken down to the dungeons. Only the Gods knew what was waiting for me down there.

"Zia!" Lilac screamed and I kicked out again, catching a guard on the leg. They didn't even stumble, despite my heavy kick to their shins. Were they even faes?!

She began to cry, tears streaming down her cheeks, her skin turning red and blotchy as she hiccuped, Cain yanked her forward, practically yanking her arm from the socket. She yelped and attempted to fight him off, a feeble punch to his chest earned her a slap to her face, which forced her head to the side and echoed around the stone room. Lilac ceased her attack, silent tears still dripping off her chin.

My fighting was to no avail as the guards barely reacted, their blank faces only watching what was ahead as we flew down the stairs. I struggled, trying to pull away from their iron grip. The air got colder, stagnant, and stale. The stench of death invaded my nostrils and I gagged, my body repulsed by the rancid air of the foul place.

As we made it to the bottom of the stairwell, Lilac's face was pasty-white, her tears had stopped but she sniffed quietly as Cain disposed of her and she crumpled to her knees. The guards pushed me forward roughly and I tripped on an uneven stone, landing on the unforgiving ground with a thump. My knee caught most of the impact and I sucked in a breath as a jolt of pain struck me. My leg throbbed and I felt a warm trickle down it, I knew the skin had been split open.

"Get up." Cain spat but before I could do so myself, the guards lifted me up and off my feet, leaving me dangling between them. The weight of my body made my arms ache terribly. The other set of guards standing to attention wordlessly unlocked the main door and Cain once more picked Lilac up by an arm and dragged her through. Her tear-stained face glanced back at me, pleading with her purple eyes as if there was something I could do.

The guards dragged me too, my legs suspended

in the air and though my wings flapped, they were useless as the guards practically yanked my arms out of the sockets. The smell was far worse now we were in the bowels of the palace and I forced myself to breathe through my mouth to avoid chucking up my guts.

As we passed through the main door, I glanced around me, somewhat morbidly eager to find out what was behind that door. But all too soon, I wished I hadn't.

My heart froze in my chest at the sight before me. In each cell were lesser faes, slumped against the walls or the floor, horrible black shadows that twisted and moved like living beings loomed over the unsuspecting faes. Their ashen faces and blank eyes stared up at the dripping ceiling and I gaped as we passed rows upon rows of the same image.

I'd read about this in the Necromancy book. I'd finished the whole thing one afternoon and I knew all too well what Cain was doing.

The faes in the cells were hosts to the black magic, their bodies being used to fuel the resurrected and the Necromancer himself.

And then, as Cain spun back to face me and the guards halted, I knew what had been plaguing me last night when I looked into his eyes at the ball.

Cain was a Necromancer. How had I not realized that before? The black eyes- it was a tell-tale sign. *Once the Necromancer reaches the point of no return, his soul is unredeemable and his eyes become like the*

night sky with no stars- endless darkness, tinged in
the shadows that now linger in his soul. Death will
be visible through the eyes, the windows showing his
stained and tainted soul.

I shivered at the thought. Gods, Cain had gone too far, so far that his soul was tainted. This was worse than I thought, *way* worse. He had no guilt, no morals, no conscience anymore, and that I feared, was far worse than death.

"Here's your new home. I'll enjoy using your magic, little fae. The taste of a sweet Bloom turned into black magic." He almost sighed in pleasure and my body shook in disgust.

"You'll never have me," I snarled and the guards roughly pushed me into the open cell at the far end of the long corridor. I stumbled but another heavy body crushed me to the floor, splitting open both of my knees no doubt. Lilac rolled off me and crawled to the gate.

"We'll see about that," Cain slammed the iron door and twisted the key in the lock, his evil eyes glittering in the half-light.

"Please." Lilac sobbed, on her knees, begging as she gripped the iron bars. "Please, let me go. I promise I won't say a word." She hiccuped. "N-not a word."

"Shut the fuck up." Cain snarled and dark shadows slithered out of his hands. Lilac fell back, shuffling backward on her palms and butt as she kept her eyes locked on the shadows that stalked her, silent tears burst out of her eyes and dribbled down her face.

Cain reeled them back in and Lilac slumped against the wall, all the breath exhaling from her body. She looked awful and my heart went out to her, she didn't deserve to be caught up in this despicable mess.

"Why?" I croaked, my voice barely above a whisper.

"Because that throne is mine." Cain sounded bored like he'd had to explain his plan a hundred times before. My heart squeezed tightly as I wondered whether Asher knew what his brother was up to. "Because." He came closer, his face almost pressed to the cold bars of the cell and I shuffled back a little. "Because long has my father's rule been weak and pathetic. Never has he tried to take back what was ours. Nissa and Eloch were both under our rule before our father became weak and chose to sell off the kingdom. I will take back what is rightfully ours and under my rule, there will be no time for peace. Only war."

His sinister smile had me wishing I'd never asked and I involuntarily shuffled back in the cell to the far wall.

"But, my father's army would never listen to me; the youngest prince. So I formed my own." He gestured around. "Use your imagination."

"I don't have to."

"Yes, Finn told me that you'd taken the Necromancer book. For a moment, I thought I'd got you all wrong, that I should have married you and we could take an interest in the dark arts together."

Bile rose in my throat at the thought of marrying

Cain. Nope, *never*.

"But then Asher's announcement last night squashed any hopes of swiping you from under his nose. It would have been satisfying, though. To have watched the delicious betrayal on his face if you'd chosen me over him."

"I would never." I spat and immediately regretted it. The shadows snaked their way towards me through the air.

"Bite your tongue, little fae."

I clamped my mouth shut as the shadows stroked my cheek, the wet, slimy sensation sent shivers down my spine, a cold sweat broke out on my forehead. I was fully, one hundred percent repulsed.

"We'll be back. Exhaust yourself with screams or rot here in silence for all I care." He tossed his words at me callously. "No one will hear you."

And with that, Cain and his guards left us alone in the cell, with nothing but the shallow breaths of the faes around us for company.

It was silent for a moment, both of us taking in what had just happened.

"What are we going to do, Zia?" Lilac whispered, her usual bright purple hair looking dull and dirty.

"Why did you get involved?" I didn't answer her question because I had no idea what to say. I leaned back and closed my eyes, I didn't want to play the blame game but Lilac had nothing to do with this, and yet somehow she was tangled up in this Godsforsaken mess.

I was desperately trying to hold back the tidal wave

of panic threatening to take me down, pinching the bridge of my nose, I let out a slow breath and counted to ten. *I will not panic, we'll find a way out.* I kept chanting in my head, over and over, trying to convince myself. We only had fifteen or so guards in here and a Necromancer to contend with. *Yeah, no biggie.*

Despair filled my body and a solitary tear slid down my cheek. I wiped it away quickly, not wanting Lilac to see how lost I was feeling.

"I don't know, okay? Prince Cain was interested and I'd felt so shit after seeing you and Asher announcing your engagement. I just wanted attention for one moment." Lilac sighed sadly, her voice cracking. "If I'd known, I'd have never gone to bed with him." She hung her head in shame, tucked her hair behind her ear, and wiped her eyes with the sleeve of her now filthy dress.

I felt bad for her, she'd been blinded by the wealth and status and hadn't considered for a second any of the consequences. In her defense, she wasn't to know Cain was a Necromancer nor that he was building a reanimated army using lesser faes' magic.

The thought of Lilac and Cain sleeping together was imprinted in my mind and I wanted to gag. Every part of me screamed to run away when Cain was close by. I would never, ever, in all my years willingly jump into a bed with him. *Ever.*

"It's all fake, you know."

Lilac's head popped up, watching me. I might

as well have come clean at this point, considering we were about to die in a dirty cell underneath the palace. It seemed like a good time to confess my crimes.

"Mine and Asher's relationship." I clarified, picking at the dirt caked under my nails. "It's fake. We struck a deal that night at Cuckoo. I messed up and spilled a drink on him and in return, I had to agree to fake-court him until the deal was done."

Lilac openly gaped at me, fear no longer present on her face.

"Zia Greenstem! You lied to the crown and the whole kingdom!"

"I'm well aware."

"Holy shit, that's insane." My friend shook her head in disbelief. "You were so convincing."

"Yay for me." I weakly pumped a fist into the air, pretending to cheer myself on. "Perhaps I should consider a career in the theater instead."

"And the proposal yesterday?"

"Yeah." I sighed. "That caught me unawares. We hadn't discussed marriage." *Although it doesn't matter now.* I didn't mention the last part, not wanting to squash the last tendril of hope in Lilac, it was bad enough that she'd got involved with Cain, but it would be worse to confess that our future didn't look bright for us.

She sat back, looking around the cell. "What else do I not know?"

I glanced over at her. "Dillon's a part of the

rebellion." *Might as well throw out all the secrets while we're at it.*

"I knew it!" I cocked a brow at her admission. "I mean, I didn't know," she corrected herself. "But I knew he was always hiding something, that slimy selkie."

I laughed, picturing Dillon as half-fae half-selkie with a seal tail.

"So what do we do now?" She asked quietly after our laughter had died down.

I shrugged, looking around the cell and I twisted Asher's ring on my finger absent-mindedly. *Of course, how could I have forgotten?*

I heaved myself up and willed some of my magic into the ring. Nothing happened, my hands glowed but the ring stayed as it was. I tried again, but nothing.

"Uh, Zia, what are you doing?" She eyed me suspiciously.

"This ring, Asher gave it to me. Said to use my magic on it and he'd find it."

"Oh, we're saved after all." Lilac held her hands in prayer and I didn't bother correcting her.

I tried three more times, trying to push my magic into the ring. I didn't know what I expected, but something, anything. An indication that Asher had heard me? A sign?

In frustration, I threw the ring on the floor. It bounced off the damp stone floor and rolled into the corner closest to the front of the cell.

"Perhaps it just takes some time to work?"

I nodded, unwilling to admit defeat but I'd also half-given up already. I slumped to the floor, watching the ring, staring at it. It looked out of place in the dungeons. It was shiny and beautiful, while everything else here was tainted by death.

"I'm sorry." She whispered and I turned to look at her. Her face was smeared with dirt and grime. "I'm sorry I didn't listen to you. Last night, I was just so jealous that you were living my dream and I so badly wanted a piece of it. But you were right. Cain wasn't a good idea." Regret laced her voice and my heart broke for her.

If only she'd followed her head and not her heart, perhaps she'd be snug in her bed in the outer city, waking up early to make dresses, and not trapped in a murky dungeon with impending death hanging over her head.

A low moan from a cell two doors down caused goosebumps to break out across my skin.

"Do you think we'll end up like that or will he kill us?" Lilac whispered, scooting over and gripping my hand tightly. Hers were shaking and I squeezed back, trying to instill some kind of courage in her. We huddled closely, listening to the horrible sounds of the dungeons.

I wished I had an answer for her. I wished I could assure her that she would be okay. But those would be lies. The outcome was not positive and I didn't want to fill her head with delusions.

"I don't know, Lilac."

~

The hours ticked by slowly. We had no way of telling the time from the tiny window in the cell, where I could see a sliver of the gray sky. It could have been any time of the day, not even the sun dared to show itself.

I knew it was some part of Cain's torment, to keep us awake, lucid, and guessing what our fate was. Surrounded by death and darkness. He was sadistic and I wanted him to burn in the Abyss for what he'd done to the innocent faes around us.

Lilac had cried herself into a fitful sleep and lay on the cell floor, curled up in her dirt-streaked dress. I watched her chest rise and fall and wished sleep would come, I wished for escape from this nightmare that was unfolding before my eyes.

I leaned back and pressed my head against the damp stone walls. As I stared at the dull sky, I only hoped that Flora was not suffering the same fate.

～

Eventually, I drifted off too, although it wasn't restful. My dreams were filled with nightmares of black eyes and magic rings. When I awoke, sweat covered my body, making my dress stick to me uncomfortably. I shivered in the chilly room, my sweat making me suddenly cold. Glancing out of the window, I noticed the sky was black, no stars were out and the moons were blood red, casting an eerie glow. A red moon only meant one thing;

blood was going to be spilled tonight.

The night was silent, aside from the moans and breathing in the dungeons and the rhythmic drip of a leak from the ceiling that splashed into a puddle on the floor. I crawled over to Asher's ring and against all false hopes, I snatched it up again, pushing whatever magic I had left in me into the ring.

I was a fool to hope for it to work, I knew that. I sighed, watching the ring do nothing yet again, and slid it into my bodice, a part of me hoped it had worked somehow, even secretly.

A door clanged down the corridor and fear twisted inside my gut as footsteps got louder. I hoped it was Asher coming to rescue us, but I wasn't placing all my faith in his seemingly useless magic ring.

"Lilac," I whispered. "Wake up." I gently nudged her sleeping form, not wanting to be alone when Cain came back. It was selfish to wake her up, to take her away from her only escape, but I did it anyway.

She groaned, rubbing her eyes with her fingers before blinking and sitting upright. Her sleep-encrusted eyes surveyed the room before her shoulders sank. She wrapped her arms around her body protectively, resting her chin on her knees.

"I'd hoped this was all a nightmare." She confessed quietly and I nodded. *Yeah, me too.*

"Oh good, you're awake. It's no fun when you can't hear the screams." Cain's deranged expression appeared through the bars and was only enhanced by the sliver of red moonlight that streamed in from the window.

"Get up." He hissed and Lilac began to stand but I pushed her back, blocking her path to Cain with my body.

"Use me, not her. She has nothing to do with this."

Cain pouted. "Well, that's not exactly true now, is it, Ms. Buddleia?"

I glanced at Lilac over my shoulder and she sniffed, a tear slid down her cheek. Gods, she was an fucking idiot for sleeping with Cain. I only hoped she wasn't expecting his spawn or else we'd all be doomed.

"But since you're so keen, little fae. You can go first."

Dread filled my veins with ice, my body became sluggish as I stepped backward, Cain began to unlock the door.

I threw out my magic in self-defense but all it did was create some weak thorns, wrapping around his wrist and he tore through them in no time. I was tired, my body exhausted from the lack of food or water.

"Is that all you've got? I'll be surprised if you last the night." He laughed as he stepped closer.

"I think after you, I'll go and find that little sister of yours. She'd taste so sweet, fear filling up her tiny body as I fed on her." He grinned sadistically. Picturing Flora down there, in the dark, cold,

death-filled room unleashed an unruly wave of
anger that I didn't know I had in me.

The magic swelled inside me and burst forth,
releasing thorny vines that wrapped around Cain's
ankles, wrists, and neck. They squeezed tightly, tiny
bubbles of blood prickling on his skin as the thorns
dug their way in. I encouraged them to dig further,
to squeeze the blood out of him completely.

"Don't you ever speak of my sister again," I
snarled, anger filling my veins and fueling my
magic. Cain's eyes widened for a moment before he
narrowed them and his shadows snagged my ankles
before I had a chance to evade them in the small
space.

I fell forward, yelping as my head connected with
the stone floor. Pain shot through my temple, it
felt like a lightning bolt in my brain and I squeezed
my eyes shut to try and block it out. Stars danced
in front of my eyes and I blinked them open to see
Cain ripping off my vine like string, the puncture
wounds healing over with the help of the dark
shadows. He stepped over me, black eyes trained on
Lilac.

I tried to roll over, my arms straining to lift my
weight, but a heavy boot on my back shoved me
back down. My teeth clattered together as they hit
the stone floor and I bit my tongue on impact, the
metallic taste of blood flooded my mouth and I
instinctively gagged.

With the guard pinning me down under his boot,

all I could do was watch as Cain stepped over Lilac, kneeling down, legs either side of her, and pinched her cheeks in his hand. His shadows slithered out and into Lilac's gaping mouth. Her eyes widened in fear, her face draining of color and she tried desperately to fight back, screaming, crying, gagging. Her weak hands not even reaching Cain as she feebly lashed out.

Her body convulsed, as the shadows made their way down her throat. Tears slid out of the corners of her eyes and onto her grubby dress as her body shook. Her skin turned a horrific blue then as black as the night sky, spidery veins webbed over her skin. To my horror, her eyes rolled back in her head, only the whites showing as the black veins crawled into them, tinging them the same black as Cain's.

He turned to me and grinned as I stretched out, trying to send magic over to Lilac. I needed to help her, save her, she'd be okay if I could just reach her... The boot on me pressed down even harder and I gasped as I felt a slight crack in one of my ribs. Tears sprang to my eyes and I took a few shallow breaths, desperately trying to reach for my best friend. I barely noticed the sharp and strangled scream that was coming out of my mouth as she slumped back like a rag doll. Her body hit the floor with a muffled thump.

No. She can't be.

Tears streamed down my cheeks and I sobbed as

my best friend lay unmoving on the cold, stone floor.

Her body twitched slightly before the shadows crawled their way back out of her body, slithering out of her mouth and her head lolled to the side, her lifeless eyes blankly staring straight at me.

Cain strolled out of the cell and the weight on my back disappeared with him. I scrambled over to my friend, my hands and feet uncoordinated and clumsy. I tripped slightly, my elbow catching the stone again.

"Lilac?" I sobbed, crawling over on my hands and knees to her lifeless body. I cradled her head in my arms. She felt cold and heavy. I felt the torrent burst out of me and my cries echoed off the empty walls.

I barely heard Cain's laughter and the clang of the cell door shutting again, barely noticed the pained groans around us.

Lilac, my best friend, the one who brought the fun, the laughter, and the mischief to my life. She was gone. A lifeless, empty vessel.

I sobbed for everything, for every mistake I'd made that led me to this point, for every moment I'd trusted someone who turned out just to have their own agenda. I sobbed for Flora, for what would happen to her when I was no longer around. I just hoped Finn would take good care of her, and Asher too.

Oh, Asher. Was I foolish for hoping for a rescue party? I had no energy left to try and muster up any help for myself. I wanted to be my own rescue party, somehow fight my own way out and warn the others, but the odds were against me.

My heart ached at the thought of Asher searching for me, how he'd probably have turned the palace upside down just for me and I realized that somehow, I'd developed feelings for him. Not fake ones. *Real* ones.

All the jealousy, all the times I'd felt the tingles when we touched, the way my heart had raced when we'd finally kissed.

Could this be *love*?

I wasn't sure yet, but it felt like a path to love. We had a long way to go, and I wasn't sure if he truly felt the same way or if it was still a game to him. If it was, then checkmate because I didn't want to get my heart involved anymore. If I ever escaped, I'd be out of the palace and back to my parents at the earliest convenience. I wouldn't be able to be around Asher if he didn't want me the way I wanted him.

A guard flew past, pulling me out of my thoughts. I assumed he was patrolling the cells but when I caught a glimpse of his face through the cell bars, my heart broke even more if that were possible.

It was Henrick, my first friend, my protector, my one friendly face when I was new at the palace.

As he turned away with his blank expression and unseeing eyes. I sobbed for his loss too, gripping Lilac's lifeless body, I let the grief consume me.

CHAPTER ELEVEN

THE SHADOWS THAT SLITHER

While in my new home a.k.a the cell, I'd figured out two things:

1. Cain was the reason behind the missing faes, that much was obvious. As I'd glanced around in the dim light of the dungeon, while contemplating my escape routes, I'd made out a body wearing the Royal kitchen maid's uniform two cells down. A young female fae was slumped against the stone wall, unmoving and I assumed that was probably Elijah's wife, River. My heart ached for his loss on top of my own.

2. The faes who were successfully drained of their magic were transported out of their cells and into a pit at the end of the dungeons- a mass grave. It stank of death and rotting flesh and I dreaded to think what else was down there.

The sun rose and fell without any surprise visits from Cain The Pain. The dungeons were still, aside from the occasional groan and the rhythmic breathing, I'd believe I was alone. Henrick patrolled twice and each time, I averted my eyes as he came past my cell. I didn't want to feel the fresh wave of pain when I saw his face, reminding me of my fate. I'd either end up like the faes in the cells next to me, drained of my magic then tossed into the mass grave, or I'd become a reanimated corpse. I wasn't sure which was worse.

I heard the main door click open as the sun set on what I guessed was the third day. By now, I was sure either Asher or Flora would be desperately searching for me, perhaps even scouring the city, but I was right under their noses, little did they know.

Flora might have had an inkling, after all, I told her about my suspicions about Cain. I just hoped and prayed she wasn't foolish enough to try and come down here on her own.

Footsteps approached my cell and I cringed back. I'd had to roll Lilac to the very edge of the cell as her body had already begun to decompose. I'd ripped part of my dress off to cover her face so I didn't have to see her blank expression staring at me, even though I'd closed her purple eyes.

I'd give her a proper burial once I was out of there.

I supposed Cain had done her a favor, though

I doubted her last moments had been painless, she wasn't being leached for magic like so many others. At least she had some peace.

An unconscious fae was being dragged in by the guards, she wore formal attire, a pink dress which I recognized immediately. *The fae who'd bumped me at the ball.* Her bright blue hair was hanging limply around her face as the guards dragged her to the cell opposite me. They threw her in carelessly like a child with a toy they no longer desired. Her body landed with a sickening thud and she didn't move.

Gods above. Another puzzle piece clicked in my head.

The ball had been an opportunity for Cain to pick off lesser faes for his sadistic fae factory. That had been his plan all along. Invite them all over, slowly pick them off and no one would be the wiser.

I swore to every God under the three moons that if I got out of here, Cain was going straight to the fiery Abyss and if by my hand, then all the better.

Time moved slowly. At first, I watched the other fae, wondering what would happen to me. I hadn't accepted my fate as such, but I needed to conserve my dwindling energy. I'd had no food or drink for three days and I was so very tired. So I sat and watched everything around me, trying to figure out an escape route.

When the thirst became unbearable, I crawled

to the small puddle on the floor and licked the ground, trying to absorb some water to quench the dryness on my tongue. My cracked lips bled and my chin scraped the rough ground as I lapped at it like a cat. The water was acrid and sour, and my stomach rolled as I tried to swallow it. Spitting it out hastily, I dry-heaved until my sides pinched and my throat burned. *Not doing that again in a hurry.*

I'd considered trying to heal myself again, but each time I tried, I'd only managed to heal a small cut or a bruise, and more just kept coming back when I rested on the solid, cold, and gritty ground beneath me.

As I lay on the stone floor, contemplating my fate, I barely heard the footsteps until they were at my cell door.

"Oh, Zia." His voice made my heart jerk in my chest. *He's here! Gods, he's going to save me!*

I sat bolt upright and with what little energy I had left, I crawled to the cell door and gripped the bars between my dirty fingers.

"Help me." I croaked, pleading with my eyes. "Please." But his reaction wasn't what I'd anticipated, what I'd hoped for. He sneered, his once kind face turning cold and hard.

"You know, I have to thank you, Zia, without you, I'd never be able to have the upper hand."

My brow crinkled in confusion, I peered up at him trying to read his face. The moonlight glinted off his crown, enhancing the shadows under his eyes and making him look menacing.

"What do you mean?" I croaked, my voice was weak and hoarse. It hurt to speak and I licked my cracked lips, wincing as I did so.

"Well, you brought Flora to me. So kind and unassuming. I thought you'd have run off to your little Asher, but instead, you chose to trust me, the first born and the first in line to the throne." He stepped closer, his blue eyes watching me from behind the bars of the cell. "She'll make a fine weapon when we wage our war." He grinned and my stomach sank. *No.* Flora wouldn't be used and wielded as a weapon, I couldn't let that happen.

"I'll let you in on a secret. Since you'll die here anyway, there's no harm done." Finn shrugged. "Although Asher is tearing up the city looking for you, he'll go mad when he realizes you were here all along, right under your very own room." He chuckled as he knelt down, getting to my level and suddenly I was grateful for the bars that separated us, the gleam in Finn's eye gave me chills, and *not* in a good way. I shuffled back, away from the bars as he peered in.

"I was planning on making an alliance with Cain, after I discovered the little army he was growing down here, we struck a deal. I'd help him overthrow our father in return for shared ownership of the throne. We had an agreement until you brought Flora to me, she's the key, you see." He leaned in closer, his eyes sparkling with dark excitement as he whispered. Eyes I'd once thought kind and sweet were now cold and menacing. "With her power, I can overthrow Cain, defeat his pathetic little army and keep the throne for myself." He stood up, brushing off his pants, and looked around.

"You bastard," I whispered, my voice so hoarse I was surprised he'd heard it. He laughed at me wickedly.

"You fell right into my arms and you brought me my weapon. Foolish really, you should know better than to trust anyone who gives you a smile, Zia. Though I suppose that is how you got into this mess in the first place, isn't it?" He grinned and I clenched my fists, holding back the tears that threatened to spill. "Oh, I know all about your little game with Asher. He was an idiot to believe he had a shot at the throne." He shook his head. "I should really thank you, considering you'll have a pitiful death here."

"Fuck you," I spat.

His face hardened and he glared down at me, his glacial eyes as cold as the stone floor beneath me.

"Sweet death, Zinnia."

That was all he said before he flew out of the dungeons and the heavy metal door slammed behind him.

I barely had a second to gather myself before the

sound of running footsteps made me shrink back and Cain came to a halt at the bars, gripping them between his fingers until his knuckles turned white.

"What did he tell you?" He screeched, his face was manic, his tone wild and I hesitated, blinking for a second. Cain's usually cool, cocky composure was gone and for a second I thought he looked... scared?

"Tell me!" He shrieked and I shook my head, pressing my lips into a hard line. Even on my deathbed, I'd protect my sister until my heart took its last beat in my chest.

Cain shook the bars viciously, the metal groaned under his touch and the shadows snaked towards me. Even if he tortured, maimed, even killed me, I'd never tell.

"You'll regret this, little fae. Tell me what my traitorous brother told you!"

I shook my head again, lips clamped tightly. Even if I wanted to tell, I doubted I had the voice to speak. The shadows slithered against my skin, like wet slime on my bare arms. I held still, not giving Cain the satisfaction of backing away or cringing. The feeling was repulsive and invasive, I wanted to scream out as they wrapped around my neck.

"This is your last chance," Cain warned, but I held still, staring defiantly at him. The shadow crawled up my bare leg, snaking under my skirt and I kicked out in vain, my foot sliding through the mist.

It slithered past my knee and up my thigh, crawling closer and closer to the one place I couldn't stand it to be. I crushed my thighs together, but it was useless as the shadow dispersed in two and then rejoined together, resuming its journey up my legs. Cain's sadistic grin from the other side of the bars made me want to scream out every curse word under the sun.

"Prince Cain." A guard spoke from the other side of the corridor and Cain spun around. His shadows still continued their assault and I writhed beneath them, trying to desperately fight them off. One tightened around my neck, blocking my airway, but the other slid away from my legs and instead crawled up past my bust and shoulder, landing on my right wing. Without a moment to fight it off, the shadow sliced into the thin membrane.

Intense, blinding pain overwhelmed all of my senses. I opened my mouth to cry out as the raging, hot pain scorched my sensitive wing, but no sound came out. A shadow hovered above my face, daring to enter my gaping mouth and I tried to clamp my lips shut to stop it from entering my body.

It came closer, I could feel its repulsive slime on my nose, my cheeks, my brow. I thrashed against the shadows, fighting with what little energy I had left.

Suddenly the shadows ceased, slithering back to their master. Relief coarse through me, followed by excruciating pain. I glanced back and saw the tip of my wing lying forlornly on the floor. It has been sliced clean off. Blood gushed from the now separated tip of my wing and I bit back the tears in my eyes, not wanting to waste any more body fluids than necessary.

I remembered a story I'd once heard about a criminal who broke into the palace to murder the king and his punishment was to have his wings cut off. It was a long time ago, but it was said that he'd died from the pain before his wings had even been fully severed from his body.

I now understood that pain.

"Have a think about your answer, little fae. I expect a different one when I come back."

Cain The Pain stalked off and my body sagged. The tears broke free, despite my best efforts and I glanced up at the window, wondering if this really was my fate. What a sad, short life it was if it was to end now.

As I gazed at the window, the pain making me float in and out of consciousness, Finn's words repeated in my mind. *He'll go mad when he realizes you were here all along, right under your very own room.* Half-delirious, I crawled to the window and heaved myself up, breaking my nails in the huge slabs of stone to gain purchase.

Once I was standing, I craned my neck and looked up, noticing a vine dangling just a few inches above the window. But not any vine, *my* vine. The ones I'd grown out of boredom last week.

Giddy happiness rushed through me, I flapped my wings to reach the vine only to be shot down by the intense, searing pain that knocked me flat onto my back. I sat for a moment, trying to breathe evenly before I dry-heaved again. My face was flushed, beads of sweat dripping off my nose and chin and my body was *oh so tired*. But I had to grasp on to this one piece of hope. I just had to. It was all I had left.

I jumped up slightly, fingers outstretched but missed the vine. Stumbling as I landed, weak from lack of energy and the pain. Resting my hands on my knees, I counted to ten, drawing in slow, long mouthfuls of stale air and breathing out again before standing up once more.

I can do this.

I gritted my teeth, focused in on the vine, and leaped up again, the very tip of my finger brushed it, but not enough to grab it.

Fuck! The frustration was starting to kick in. I leaped up again, missing the vine fully this time and I screamed out.

I paused a second, wondering if anyone
would come rushing in. After a full minute, no
one appeared and I took a deep breath, filling
my lungs with the foul air of the dungeons,
and jumped once more. My energy was
quickly running out and I knew this was my
last attempt. I sent a quick prayer up to all the
Gods and pushed myself off the ground.

My fingers wrapped around the tip of the vine
and I almost cried with joy as my magic coaxed
it to grow longer and it crawled into the cell
with me.

Now I had access to something I could
manipulate, I had to get word out, send a
message or something, *anything*. I thought
back to all the books I'd read about the powers
of the Blooms. My tired mind flicked back
over the pages, trying to recall the words
written on them, but suddenly I remembered
how Asher's hand had felt as it had brushed
against mine when he turned a page. The
blood rushed to my cheeks at the memory.

If Asher was out there searching every
building in the city for me then he deserved
the same energy back. I held onto the vine
and with the last reserve of my magic, I sent
a message up the vine, whispering urgent
words to the plant, telling it to find Asher and
Flora, letting it know where I was and to be
careful. It crept back up the wall and out of the

dungeon.

I leaned against the wall, my mind exhausted by the strenuous use of magic. My wing throbbed and my body gave out. I barely registered the hard stone floor as I collapsed.

~

"Get off me!"

My sister's screams jolted me awake from my dead sleep. My heart sang for joy then sank faster than a stone in the river as I crawled to the edge of the cell and saw two guards dragging her through the dungeons.

No, they couldn't have got her. Not Flora.

"Flora!" I croaked out then coughed from the dryness in my throat.

My sister's face turned to me, her eyes filling with tears. "Zia." She cried, extending her arm to me, her fingers splayed out as if she could reach me.

"We'll be okay," I whispered, my hands gripping the bars of my cell.

Two shiny boots appeared in front of my face and I saw my reflection in them. My face was dirty, cheeks hollow and hair matted, stringy as it hung around my face. My bony hands reached out to smooth it down, for some irrational reason I cared about my presentation, I glanced at my broken nails caked in dirt.

"Have you thought more about your answer?"
Cain kneeled down and I cringed away from his
horrifying black eyes. They really were the stuff
of nightmares. "Or do I need to take off your
other wing?"

I shook my head, unsure of whether I was
responding to the first or second question.
Another yell from my sister took my attention
away from the Necromancer that knelt in front
of me.

I heard yelling from the far end of the room, I
was torn between watching Flora being dragged
away from me and Cain's torment.

A shadow snaked out from his hand and
slithered along my arm, raising goosebumps
as it went. Not ready for another assault, I
whimpered, a tear escaped from my eye and
trailed down my cheek.

"Zia!" Her voice seemed distant now like she
was being taken further away, deeper into the
dungeons.

"Flora." I croaked in response, my body
shivering with repulsion as the shadow slid
along my shoulders and onto my left wing. A
sob broke out of me as I pictured half of my
other wing on the stone floor of my cell. I'd be
wingless, my sister would be used as a vessel
to leach power from and our fates were to end
up in the pit with all the other dead and used
faes. Despair crept up my veins like a living,

breathing thing, cold and icy, and a sob shook my body.

"Now!" My sister yelled and I barely had time to think as an explosion of light momentarily blinded me. Cain spun around but stumbled back against the cell bars and I instinctively crawled behind Lilac's decomposing body as the shadows around him began to rapidly dart around as if in a frenzy.

He roared in anger, seemingly losing control of his shadows in the bright light emanating off my sister. I shielded my eyes with my hand, trying to understand what I was seeing.

Cain stood slowly like he'd regained control again. I couldn't see his features from where I was lying down, but I knew his face was like thunder. He threw out shadows with one hand and turned his head away with the other, shielding himself from the blinding light.

His eyes caught mine as he fought off the light with his shadows and he snarled at me, his face unrecognizable. Not only were his eyes fully black, his whites nowhere to be seen, but his face was now covered in the same black spider veins that Lilac's had been, they crisscrossed over his cheeks, neck, and forehead. They almost pulsed under his skin like a living thing and my stomach soured in fear.

I heard my sister yelp, as what I presumed was, a shadow caught her by surprise. I hoped she was far enough away that the slimy things didn't do to her what they'd done to me.

"I knew he was hiding something from me!" Cain shrieked as another shadow made its way past the bright light emanating off my sister. "He'll pay for it!"

The guards next to Cain were trying to slash through the rays of light, but their jerky, reanimated movements were useless and they began to fall to their knees, swords still swinging as they flopped to the ground, depleted of magic.

Watching the scene unfold before me, I didn't notice Cain's snarl before it was too late. A shadow hit me straight in the chest, I stumbled backward, legs flailing and arms scrambling as it dug its way into my dress. I felt the cold, wet slime on the skin of my torso and I screamed with all my might. My body jerked, repulsed by the feeling as Cain laughed sadistically.

"Zia!" I heard Flora yell from somewhere in the fray, her voice echoed off the dungeon walls. The shadow slid out of my chest and back to Cain and I scrambled to safety, unsure of any of the magic being thrown around here and whether it would hurt me.

I ducked behind Lilac again as another shadow aimed at my head. It flew over the top, just grazing my scalp, and slithered behind me. I kicked out at it in fear of it trying to crawl up my leg. But instead of scuttling to attack, it lay down on the stone floor, almost like a wounded animal, before slowly disintegrating like ashes in the wind.

Spinning my head back to Cain, I noticed all of his shadows were crumbling, turning to ash before they got more than a foot away from their host.

I wasn't sure if I could trust my tired eyes, and the toxic odor from my friend's rotting body could have been putting things into my mind, but I could have sworn that I'd read that Necromancers were nearly impossible to kill. And yet, his body was visibly weakening. He sank to his knees, the shadows around him weren't as thick as before as he tried to push them towards the light. The darkness was thinning, his body was withering. Could this nightmare really be over?

Bright orange and red fire set him alight and Cain's scream pierced my ears, making me clamp my hands over them to muffle the awful sound. My body shook as I rocked back and forth, trying to block out the image of Cain's pale skin blistering in the inferno that burned him alive.

And I thought I caught a glimpse of that familiar dark hair. The one who I'd been missing, the one who I'd been fantasizing about.

No, it can't be. My tired mind is playing tricks on me.

How did he find me?

Those were my last thoughts before my mind succumbed to the darkness.

Chapter Twelve
Adjustment

The plush bed felt as soft as a fluffy cloud beneath me when I stretched out my aching body. My wings tried to flap involuntarily and I yelped as the pain shot down my right wing like it was on fire. *Gods above*!

"Easy."

His voice. Oh, how I'd missed that voice. My heart hammered in my chest as his fingers gently caressed my arm.

"Zinnia." He breathed and my body leaned into his touch. The events of the last few days came tumbling back to me in flashes and I opened my eyes, peeking through my lashes to see him.

His strong nose, his mass of dark hair, his silver crown. And those dark eyes that watched over me with concern. My heart swelled as I stared at him.

"Zia, I'm so sorry." My nickname. I realized he only ever said it when he wasn't guarding his emotions. His expression was pained and it occured to me that I'd never seen Asher express any emotion close to remorse and yet, there it was clear as day, painted on his perfect features. "I wanted to-"

"Shh." I pressed a finger to his lips and watched him swallow thickly.

I pointed at the glass on the bedside table and Asher reached to pick it up, bringing it to my sandpapery lips. The water was cool and tasted like bliss as it slid deliciously down my throat. I almost moaned in delight, it had been far too long since I'd had a fresh drink.

The memories resurfaced as I cleared the fog from my mind; Lilac's death, Cain's assault on me, my wing. And then Flora and the bright light, Cain's crumbling shadows, and his flaming silhouette.

"What happened to Cain?" I whispered, unsure of whether I *really* wanted to know the answer.

Asher's eyes closed for a brief second before he sat on the edge of the bed, still caressing my arm. The rhythm of his fingers soothed me and threatened to lull me back to sleep.

"He's gone and Finn, he's currently in the dungeons, stripped of his title and preparing to be put on trial." He shook his head in disbelief. I couldn't quite wrap my head around it either, out of three brothers, only one remained true. And yet, he was a liar too, just in a different way.

"My parents want to see you," Asher said, his eyes on my bruised arm. I guessed a healer had tried to fix the bigger damage and left the smaller stuff to heal on its own. "When you're well enough."

I nodded, wondering what his life would be like now, without his brothers, Asher was heir to the throne. And how I'd fit into it. *I don't think I fit in anymore.* The thought caused a sharp pain right in my heart.

"Where's Flora?" I changed the subject, desperate to get rid of the ache in my chest.

"She and your parents are in the library, they wanted to be with you when you woke up, but none of them have slept a wink since they arrived two days ago." He chuckled to himself. "I can see where you get your stubbornness from." A small smile played on his lips and I grinned. Yep, my mom was as stubborn as a dragon. I bet she'd been bossing Asher around and kept everyone awake all hours of the day.

"And Lilac?" I asked, barely above a whisper, this time I really didn't want to know the answer. I hoped and prayed that she was safe at her home in the outer city and that her biggest worry was what mischief she'd get into next with the local fae boys.

"I'm sorry." Asher shook his head, his fingers traced up to my elbow, their light touch soothed my aching heart. "She'll receive a formal burial as will the others who were found in the dungeons."

A tear slipped out of my eye and down my cheek, Asher's thumb caught it and brushed it away before I could. I'd cried too much recently, and yet, there was so much to mourn for.

We sat in silence, Asher's fingers tracing my arm as I watched the clouds passing by outside the window. My eyes began to feel heavy, sleep calling me back to her sweet embrace and Asher's touch was lulling me back to a safe place. A thought struck me before I fell back to sleep and I turned to see Asher already watching me, his eyes full of an emotion I couldn't quite place.

"How did you find me?"

Asher sighed, looking out of the window before he glanced at me. My heart gave an extra loud thump as his forest-green eyes locked on mine.

"When I realized you were missing, I thought the rebels had kidnapped you in their attack. We thought maybe it was a hostage situation so I scoured the city with your sister, she was on foot and I took to the skies. We searched endlessly for three days. I planned on hunting every single one of them down and tearing them limb from limb if they'd hurt a single hair on your head." I shuddered at the blatant violence but said nothing.

"I came back to the palace, distraught. I refused to believe that you were dead." He shook his head, fingers stilling on my arm. He gazed back out of the window, recounting his story. "Flora found me as soon as I got back, she wasn't making any sense, screaming about a message in the vines. I thought she was delirious with grief but I followed her into your room." He paused, watching his hands trace over my pale skin.

"I couldn't believe it, but the vines spoke to us, they told us what was going on and where you were, then once they'd delivered their message, they retracted out of the window and down to the ground, to that tiny window in the dungeons. I swear Zia, I saw red when I heard what my brother had done." His fingers stilled on my arm for a moment. "So Flora devised a plan, she would pretend to search for you, stumble upon the dungeons, get captured on purpose, and then release her powers once inside. I followed her in, she told me to trust her that her power was strong enough. But Gods, I was so worried that I'd lose you both." His voice cracked and he cleared his throat, looking up to face me.

"But she did it. She's amazing and strong." He smiled briefly. "We were fooled by Finn though, I'll admit I didn't see that coming at all."

I reached up, stroking the frown lines out of his face. My thumb brushed over his brow and my heart soared as his face leaned into my touch. He gently pressed a kiss to my palm and my stomach did that flip-flop thing.

"I'll always look after you." He whispered and I nodded, unsure of his words. I knew there was truth in there, but how much of what he felt was real, I didn't know.

"Zia!" My sister's voice broke our trace and Asher stood, his hand grasping mine softly. *It's just for show*, I told myself.

Flora's wings flapped as she launched herself onto my bed.

"Ouch!" I laughed, marveling at this person who looked like my sister, and then somehow nothing like her. She was taller, had gained weight, her large green wings stook proudly on her back and I couldn't believe she could fly now. "Look at you, you're flying."

"I know." She grinned and spun in a circle above the bed. "Isn't it great?"

"They're green?" I eyed her wings, they were the same size as Asher's, translucent but bright lime green.

"Yeah, it's a 'Hollow Ones thing,' Cardus said." She used her fingers to make air quotes. "You know he saw through Finn the whole time? He told me this morning as he left that he knew Finn was training me to be a weapon. Cardus just showed me how to wield my powers, how I use them is up to me." She smiled, full of energy and I nodded. This new Flora would definitely take some getting used to.

"I missed your birthday," I whispered sadly and

Flora shook her head.

"It doesn't matter."

"It does," I insisted.

"I'll have another birthday, sis." She shrugged and I nodded, although I was sad I'd missed so much. Being cooped up in that dungeon made me miss one of the most important days of my sister's life. I hoped Cain burned in the Abyss for eternity for what he'd done.

Some yelling in the hallway took my attention away from Flora as she landed on the floor next to me. Asher stepped away slightly, letting go of my hand and I tried to squash down that empty feeling in my chest. I watched through the open door as my Mom argued with a guard that I assumed had been placed on duty outside my room.

"That's my daughter in there and Gods be damned if you can stop me." She huffed and pushed some magic into the guard blocking her path. He stumbled a little and she flew in, followed by my Dad who mumbled an apology to the surprised guard.

"Oh, Zinnia." My mom busied herself with re-tucking in the bedsheets, refilling my water, and smoothing out the wrinkles in the blankets. "You gave us all such a worry and we have a firm talk about everything when you get home. I can't believe you kept all of this from us." She gestured to the room around her and I cringed, knowing she'd go through the roof when she found out about Asher and my fake relationship too.

"Poppy, give her a rest, she's been through enough." My dad scolded and my mom huffed again before stepping away and fussing over my sister instead.

"I'm fine, Dad. Just need some sleep." I smiled up at him, recognizing my eye color in his own.

"I know." He whispered, grasping my hand gently. "You're in safe hands."

He was right, I was in safe hands.

"We'll come back tomorrow, or whenever you'd like." He smiled and I nodded.

"I'd like that."

He tucked a lock of my hair behind my ear before gathering my mom up and pushing her through the door. She called out to me on the way out, telling me she'd bring fresh bread and soup tomorrow. I smiled, knowing everything would be right again.

~

"Zia."

The words were soft and cherished and I opened my eyes, blinking a few times to see the lovely fae who'd been my friend from day one.

"How are you feeling, sweet girl?"

I tested my wings, feeling sore, and groaned in response. Yep, everything hurt and it sucked.

"Not so delightful." I struggled to sit up in bed.

Laurel gently pulled me up by my elbow and fluffed up the cushions behind me. She brushed some hair from my face and smiled softly.

"A healer will be with you soon." She said and brought a steaming cup to my face. "I made you some tea."

I smiled gratefully and sipped the hot liquid. It felt so good, sweetened with honey, running down my throat and warming me from the inside out. Turning to face the window, I noticed a dent in the pillow next to me. A suspicious head-shaped dent.

"Was," I paused, wondering if I was just hoping for something. "Was he here?"

Laurel grinned and I flushed bright pink at the thought of Asher next to me.

"He was, and he hasn't left your side since he brought you up from the dungeons. He was a wreck, tearing his hair out while the healers came to tend to you." She chuckled. "We had to practically drag him out of the room when they'd said you'd needed a healing bath."

I flushed pink at the image of being naked in front of Asher again, then a flutter in my stomach made me think that maybe it wouldn't be so bad. Under different circumstances, of course. I sat quietly, sipping my tea and digesting the information Laurel had given me.

So those actions weren't put on, they weren't for show, put on for the whole kingdom to see. But did that mean he was feeling anything more than the simple lust he'd shown me?

"Don't doubt your heart, Zia. It's a powerful ally in decision making." Laurel watched me closely as she folded the blankets at the foot of my bed and refilled my water jug.

I nodded, what did my heart feel? I felt sad, perhaps hopeful but I didn't want to be heartbroken when I found out that Asher didn't reciprocate my feelings. He had to marry, become king and rule Nissa, and what business did I have in that? I was just a baker's daughter after all. I squashed down the nasty feeling in my chest when I thought about that.

Just as I was thinking of him, Asher strode in, followed by a middle-aged female fae in a dark cloak.

"This is healer Marigold, she's been tending to you for the last few days," Laurel explained and I watched as the fae unpack her large bag onto a table by the window and flit over to me.

"It's good to see you finally awake." Her voice was soft and gentle. Her cool hand lifted mine and I felt the familiar warmth of magic flow into me. I sighed, feeling the pain seep away and numbness replace it.

"It'll take you a few sessions to heal your other wounds. I'm afraid your wing won't ever fully heal, you'll carry that scar with you for your lifetime." She said and my stomach sank at the thought of having a living reminder of the damage Cain had inflicted. Asher's fist clenched as he stood at the edge of the bed, watching me.

"Will I be able to fly again?" I asked tentatively.

"In time, perhaps."

It felt like a cruel joke, Flora had just been gifted the beauty of flight and mine had been taken away. The world demanded balance, I supposed.

Marigold stayed for an hour, mixing different pastes to rub onto my wounds and periodically giving me top-ups of magic. Laurel fetched me some hot broth and fresh bread. I felt warm, tired, and full to the brim with food and magic by the time she left. I felt better in myself and managed to walk around my room a few times. Walking solely on my legs would take some getting used to.

Asher stayed the whole time, silently watching. Marigold asked me what I remembered and I told her bits, but not the whole story. Mainly because I didn't want to relive the memories, they were too fresh, too raw in my mind.

When she left, the room was silent. Laurel escorted her back to the palace gates and that just left Asher and me.

There were so many unspoken words between us. They wanted to burst free from my chest but I mentally crushed them down.

"When can I go home?" I asked quietly.

I knew I'd be going soon, Asher no longer had use for me and in my heart, I knew our time was over. Better to get it over with quickly than draw it out. I'd only miss the palace more if I was made to stay here longer.

Even if his feelings were genuine, he needed to marry for alliance, for wealth, and not marry a lesser fae who had nothing to her name. Not even two wings anymore.

Asher frowned, perching at the foot of the bed.

"Your parents can come back and visit any time-"

"No." I interrupted. "I mean, go home for good."

His face registered what I meant, emotions flickered across his face like firelight before he became closed off, unreadable. He looked away from me and my heart broke a little more.

"You don't have to go." He spoke quietly, and I thought I detected desperation in his voice. Or maybe it was just me being hopeful.

"I no longer have a place here, Asher. You got what you wanted- a chance at the throne. So we needn't play this game any longer."

"You can't give up on what we have." He pleaded.

"And what is it that we have?" I almost snapped but reigned it in. I was tired and talking used up my energy. "A relationship built on lies and deceit. It was never real, Asher. It was a mirage, we made everyone believe what you wanted them to see. But nothing was genuine, every touch, every kiss was a lie."

"Not every one."

"Just about." I retorted, it hurt to say, but I had

to let him go.

"Perhaps for you."

"Perhaps indeed." As soon as the words came out of my mouth, I regretted them. They tasted bitter on my tongue and my stomach churned but it was better this way. He needed a chance at a real relationship for the sake of Nissa, not for my selfish needs.

I had to let him go, I had to let him be free, and because I loved him, I had to do this for him.

His face became hard, cold, and closed off.

"I see."

I wasn't sure what he saw, what he wanted to see, but I needed to protect my heart and his. Not to mention, I was damaged now. I couldn't fly, I was broken, and who'd want damaged goods? I wanted to go home, be safe, and forget this whole thing happened. The palace was filled with darkness for me right now and I needed light, sunshine, and goodness again. The Necromancy had taken its toll on me.

"Well, then I call off our deal. You may leave whenever you like, as you no longer have use here."

If words could kill, that would have been the fatal blow. A stab to my heart. My chest physically ached, my eyes prickled and I turned away, not wanting Asher to see the tears that threatened to spill. His words wounded me, they tore apart my insides, and let me bleed out, leaving me for dead.

He rose, not bothering to look back, and flew out of the room, slamming the door behind him.

Once it was closed, I let the tears flow, let the hurt out and I sobbed into my pillow. Mourning for everything I had lost.

~

I left the same evening. I found Laurel and she told me Marigold could visit my parents' home instead.

So we packed my bags, I left all the dresses, all the shoes, and jewelry that I wore, including Asher's ring that had miraculously survived. I placed it gently on the vanity in my room and with one more fleeting glance, I surveyed the space, taking note of every characteristic of the room that had been my home for the last few weeks. It was insane to think it had only been just over two months since that fateful night at Cuckoo and yet, I felt older, hardened by what I'd endured in my time here.

Walking to the entrance hall, a guard greeted me politely and Laurel looked close to tears as she hugged me tightly.

"Come and visit please, when the hurt has healed." She whispered. "I'll miss you, sweet girl."

"Thank you." I squeezed her back, inhaling her floral scent and knowing I wouldn't be back for a while, if ever. But she didn't need to know that right now.

The guard took my bag off Laurel and she waved me farewell as I descended the steps and slipped into the carriage.

The memories of the last time I'd been in here surfaced and my chest felt tight. I gulped in the fresh air from the open window and poked my head out.

I waved goodbye to Laurel as the carriage lurched forward and I could have sworn I saw a mop of dark hair lurking in one of the palace windows. My smile slid off my face as he disappeared from view and I slumped back in the carriage.

Everything would be different now.

∼

"I swear you're sleeping more than I used to." Flora's voice filtered through my restless dreams, dreams of forest-green eyes and shadows as black as night. Cain's dark magic often plagued my dreams, but usually, Asher stayed away. Last night was different. My dream had been unsettling and I'd watched the sunrise from my window, wondering how I'd fit back in here. Physically, I'd heal, but mentally? I wasn't so sure, only time would tell.

"I'm not sleeping," I mumbled, which was half true, I'd been in a sort of light daze, eyes closed but still aware of the world around me. Of the birdsong by my window, the bustling sounds in the kitchen, my mom preparing the bakery.

"Well, you look like you are. Mom says it's time to get up, you can't mope forever- her words, not mine." Flora sat on the edge of the bed and I cracked an eye open.

It still took some getting used to, seeing my sister so healthy, glowing, and strong with her big wings. She'd been the talk of the city when she'd arrived home two days before me. My mom had had to lie, pretending she'd been healed. It was safer that way. People questioned her large wings and my mom had swiftly changed the conversation. But with Flora's health improvement, we'd save money on the monthly potions we used to buy and we'd be able to pay off our debts.

At least something good had come of the whole situation.

Warmth caressed my arm and I turned to see my sister pushing her magic into me, healing me.

"Don't waste all your magic, you only just got it."

"I know, but you need it more than I do right now." And there she was, my selfless sister, always helping others before herself. My heart swelled and I managed the smallest of smiles.

I sat up, throwing back the sheets, and slipped on some shoes before making my way to the bathroom. I glanced in the mirror, my eyes catching the contrast of the stark white bandages that wrapped around my wing. My heart clenched, remembering the pain. It still hurt and Marigold was due to come this afternoon. I wasn't a fool to hope that I'd fly again, but a part of me still wished for it. Being robbed of my flight hurt more than I could have imagined.

"I'll save you some pastries!" Flora called as she swooped down the spiral stairwell and into the kitchen.

"Thanks," I whispered, more to myself than anyone else and I began to go about my new routine. Thanks to my broken wing, I was slower, still figuring out how to walk on my legs all the time.

At night, I cried myself to sleep, mourning for my lost ability, for Lilac, for all the other faes. And for Asher. I missed him so much, and I'd never thought I would. But I missed his face, his smug grin, the way he'd intensely watch me, his appreciation for my pastries. His kisses. I missed those the most.

I trudged into the kitchen, plastered on a small smile, and was greeted by my sister rolling out dough, my mom was testing out cakes in the oven and at the front of the bakery was my dad, selling the already cooked items and packaging them up.

Flora looked up, her smile wide and sparkling as she gestured for me to come over.

"I thought we could make some pastries together."

I didn't want to, the memories hurt and I wanted to go back to bed, stay in my room and drown in grief for another day. But instead, I nodded, pushing the tiniest bit of my magic into the apricots that had yet to be crushed into a glaze. They brightened to a gorgeous orange color and their skin smoothed out. Their scent brought back the memories I was trying so hard to keep locked away.

Silently, I began the process of making the pastries, a routine I knew so well that my hands mechanically reached for the pestle and mortar, crushing the apricots after I'd peeled the skin off them. My mind wandered, ignoring the chatter around me. I thought about what Asher was doing at this very moment; was he preparing to step into his future role as King? Was he reading a book in the library? Was he courting some beautiful princess and taking her for strolls around the walled gardens? Was he missing me as I was him?

No. Don't think like that, it'll only hurt even more.

A knock on the back door broke me out of my thoughts and for a moment, my heart leaped at the thought of either Lilac or Dillon at the door. But instead, it was a messenger, carrying a bunch of beautiful wildflowers. My heart sank when I remembered my best friend's fate. I hadn't heard from Dillon since the last time I'd seen him. I assumed he was involved in the attack on the palace. Part of me had mourned for our lost friendship, my mind considered it over. Our friendship was dead to me now.

"For Zinnia?" He asked and I wiped my hands on a towel next to me before making my way over.

"Thank you," I whispered, breathing in the beautiful scent of the bouquet. There was a scroll attached to the stems and I almost didn't want to look.

Please come back.

My heart hammered in my chest. I had no business going back to the palace, going back to a place where I didn't belong. But those three words written in Asher's hand made me second guess my decision. My finger traced over the ink and I sighed.

My family glanced at me and looked away silently, I knew what was on their mind, I knew why they looked at me with pitying eyes.

I put the flowers in a vase, filled it with water, and placed it on the counter next to my dad. It brightened the room even if it made my heart ache for Asher.

Suddenly I had this overwhelming feeling

of needing to escape. I had to get out, I realized I was no longer content in my old life. Perhaps I'd travel to a new city, a new kingdom even, and start a new life there. Now I knew Flora and my parents were safe, I could rest easy.

But I had to heal first, so I'd have to settle for a walk for now.

"Mom, I'm going to the market," I called one foot already out of the door.

"I'll come with you!" Flora yelled back, already washing her hands but I shook my head.

"It's okay, I'd rather be alone."

Her face fell and I instantly felt bad, knowing she thought I was escaping her. And in a way, I was. It was hard not to look at her and think about everything I'd lost versus what she'd gained.

"I'll be back soon," I said and she nodded.

The sun was high in the sky and I welcomed its glaring heat on my skin. After being in the dungeon for a few days with minimal light and warmth, I cherished every ray that shone down on me.

The market was bustling and I had to squash down the panic that flared in my chest. Seeing so many people again was strange. These faes had no idea what I'd been through, what had been at stake, and what kind of rule they'd be under if Cain had succeeded in taking down the King.

I watched a few different faces, wondering what their lives were like. Some smiled at me, a few watched, and others frowned as I walked, rather than flew, around the stalls.

Did they recognize me? As the girl who was on Prince Asher's arm in this very market only a few weeks ago? If they did, no one stepped forward or even registered my existence for more than a second.

I caught a glimpse of my reflection in a mirror on one of the vendor's stalls. My eyes looked dull, empty, and void of emotion. My skin was still slightly gray-toned, thanks to the shadows that Cain wielded. My hair was unwashed, tied back in a low bun at the nape of my neck. Days in the dungeons without food made my clothes hang off my skin and bones. I hadn't had much of an appetite since then, the healers told me to eat more often, to make up for my lack of nutrition whilst incarcerated but I couldn't muster the energy to eat more than a mouthful.

I guessed the townspeople wouldn't recognize me because I was so far from the fae they saw at the ball. She had been healthy, happy, and beautiful. Not at all like me now.

A familiar head caught my eye and I turned away from the mirror, Dillon strode towards me, his mouth set into a hard line. His grim expression caught me off guard and I subconsciously backed away from him.

"Finally free from the Prince then?" He spat and I flinched at his words.

"I was always free."

"I seem to remember you told me you'd been blackmailed into a fake relationship with Prince Asher." He spoke loudly, not caring who heard and a few heads turned our way at the sound of the Prince's name.

"Shh," I whispered. "Keep your voice down, that is not idle gossip and I wasn't a prisoner. Not technically, anyway." After all, I'd stayed with Asher and made use of the luxuries the palace had to offer, I had liberties and was only really a prisoner in the dungeons.

"So you're no longer pretending to court him then?" He arched an eyebrow. "And what about your engagement, I suppose that was fake too?" He said scathingly and I wondered where my best friend had gone and who had replaced him.

"What's going on, Dillon?"

"Your fake fling cost the rebels their only chance at taking down the crown. And instead of helping your people, you jumped into bed with the enemy."

I clenched my fist, anger boiling in my body. I knew people would believe that I'd only been Asher's bed warmer.

"You said you'd help the fae and what have you done? You're a coward and a liar, Zia Greenstem."

Perhaps it was the anger in his eyes or it was the fact that everyone assumed Asher had used me as a plaything, but I lost it, letting my temper get the better of me for a second.

"Have any more faes gone missing?" I asked,

stepping forward. "Those that were lost cannot be brought back, but no more have been taken. What do you think I was doing when you attacked the palace that morning? Rolling around with Asher? I'd been kidnapped, I was tortured for days, left without food or water." I watched his eyes widen, taking in my appearance.

"So, do not for one minute call me a coward when it is you, attacking the wrong Royals and slaying innocent faes in the name of the rebellion." I hoped he remembered how many people he'd killed in his attack on the noble's house a few weeks ago. My voice lowered at the end of the sentence and I began to spin on my heel, ready to leave this conversation and whatever was left out of friendship behind.

"His lies have made you weak. You'll believe anything. His words are like poison in your mind, Zia."

I spun back around, having had enough of the absolute bullshit Dillon was spewing.

"You're a traitor, and your lying tongue knows nothing of the poison I've endured, what Lilac endured. Do you know what her last moments were like? Did you see the light leave her eyes and then lie in a cell for days on end with nothing but her rotting corpse for company?" Dillon swallowed thickly. "You know nothing. You're fighting a battle blind, not using your senses. I will no longer listen to you."

By now, a sizable crowd had formed around us,

watching our verbal volley.

Many looked at me with disgust, obviously thinking I'd betrayed our people *and* slept with Prince Asher.

I couldn't care less what they thought, these were just strangers but Dillon, who'd known me for many years, I couldn't believe he'd think of me that way. His betrayal stung the most. I guessed his jealousy made him believe what he wanted to, made him believe that I'd screwed them all over for the sake of a hot moment with Asher.

They didn't know what I'd endured, what I'd had to suffer at the hands of the crown.

"You're a liar, Zia. You said you'd help and instead, you were having fun playing Prince Asher's wicked games."

I'd had enough, heard enough and I drew a line under our friendship. I strode away, pushing my way through the crowd as murmurs around me reached my ears.

Traitor.

Liar.

Whore.

It didn't matter if I explained, if I pleaded because the faes loved to label others with their own sins.

With tears blurring my vision, I ran back to my home, my heart heavy with the events of the day.

CHAPTER THIRTEEN

BEG

The next day, a small package arrived for me. We all gathered in the kitchen, my mom baking bread, my dad sorting the coins in the shop, and my sister mixing an apricot glaze. She no longer needed my help with making the pastries taste good as her powers trumped mine, so I was left taskless and again wondering where I belonged.

My parents and Flora had a life without me. I no longer fitted in and so I'd spent the rest of yesterday in bed, alternating between crying and falling into a dreamless sleep.

"Open it then." My mom urged as she peeked over her shoulder to make sure bread wasn't burning in the oven.

I ripped open the brown paper. A folded letter fell out and I scooped it up off the table. Emptying out the paper bag, a small item tumbled out onto the table- Asher's gold engraved ring.

My whole family let out a collective gasp.

"Oh my Gods, he still loves you!" Flora burst out and immediately clamped her mouth shut with her hands.

"Flora!" My mom scolded at her outburst but her hopeless romantic eyes said the same.

"What does the note say?" My dad asked, ignoring the other two lovesick fools and I unfolded the paper, recognizing Asher's script straight away.

Dearest Zia,

My heart skipped a beat as I realized that he was calling me by my nickname again.

I hope this letter finds you well and with it; my promise.

The ring is my promise to keep you safe. In the dungeons, it failed to do so and for that, I beg for your forgiveness. I realized after you sent us a message that Cain had created a shield against our bloodline in the dungeons, I presume to keep us out while he built his army. Flora had to weaken him in order for me to use my magic to help.

I couldn't send any magic in and you couldn't send any out using the ring. It breaks my heart to think about you using it with the hope that I'd rescue you and that's something I think about every waking minute, Zia.

So, I'm sending it to you now, to provide you with

protection, so I never have to worry about you. Even if you choose not to stay in Nissa, I'll always come to your aid.

Yours forever,

Asher

I read the letter over and over until the words blurred. My hands shook, gripping the flimsy paper and I slumped in the chair.

"Oh, Zinnia." My mom came over, wrapping an arm around my shoulder, and pressed a kiss to my temple.

"Why don't you go back?" Flora whispered but I shook my head fiercely.

"He told me he had no use for me now."

"What do you mean?" My mom asked and I hesitated, I hadn't yet told her or my dad about mine and Asher's deal. They thought I wanted to come home because of my capture and needing space from the palace, and that was half correct.

"Mom, Dad, please don't be mad. Asher and I… We had a deal where I pretended to court him and then I wouldn't have to owe him for ruining his shirt that night at Cuckoo." My mom gasped and my dad shook his head in disbelief. My shoulders sagged, I'd betrayed them and lied to them. The guilt weighed down on me. "But I didn't expect… I didn't think… I didn't mean to get my heart involved." I whispered and Flora rested her head on my shoulder.

"I don't think he did either, but you're both

hurting. Perhaps going back wouldn't be so bad?"

I sighed, she was probably right. I did like living there, I have a purpose in the palace, more so than I had now back home where I moped around most of the day.

"But he made himself clear," I said, my voice shaking. *Gods, keep it together.*

"It's your choice, we'll support you no matter what." My dad said, gripping my hand.

"Why didn't you tell us? We could have helped you." My mom looked appalled and rightfully so. I'd disgraced my family.

"I didn't want to add more debt, more worries on your mind. You worked so hard for us and you didn't need to be involved in my mistakes. You were so happy that I was leaving. I didn't want to ruin it." I glanced up at my mom and she shook her head, a hint of a smile on her lips.

"Well, I thought it was too good to be true, huh. Never trust something when it seems too good." She went to take the bread out of the oven, muttering to herself about dreams coming true.

"He needs to marry for alliance, not for love," I whispered and Flora sighed next to me.

"Obviously, we're not happy you deceived us, Zia. But you deserve to be happy."

My dad gave me a final pat on the back and went back to the shop.

"There's something on the back." Flora turned over the letter on the table.

P.S My mother misses your pastries. I do too.

I bit back a bitter laugh, *so he wants me back for my pastries? Fantastic.*

Flora sighed again, shaking her head and she went back to making her apricot glaze.

Everyone had a role.

Everyone except me.

~

I noticed the dwindling numbers of customers at the bakery. I noticed the shifty eyes, the subdued conversation, the craning necks to get a glimpse at Prince Asher's whore. The townspeople talked of me being used and disposed of, they looked at me with pity and some with jealousy.

I knew even though my family tried so hard to shield me from it. The more I noticed, the more I realized how little I fit in there anymore. Although it had been my home for my whole life, I'd never felt more like an intruder.

It broke my heart to see the usually bustling market day crowd whittled down to less than half, and I knew it was because of me.

And so, I knew I had to leave. The idea of starting a new life in Eloch was appealing, if not mildly terrifying. I knew that trolls and faes lived in harmony out there, or so they said. I'd never encountered a troll and I counted myself lucky. Many townspeople said that trolls ate faes and our wings were a delicacy. I'd not slept for weeks when

I was younger in fear of a troll snatching me from my bed and feasting on my flesh. Pretty horrific nightmare fuel.

And so, when the voice in the shop came in the next morning, while I was beginning to subtly pack, it was a surprise. Although it shouldn't have been, considering how close I'd been to this particular fae in my time at the palace.

"So this is where you've been hiding."

"Not hiding as such, just not going out much either." I shrugged and enveloped Laurel in a troll-sized hug, nearly knocking her fully over as I barreled into her.

"Gods, I've missed you," I said and she grinned.

"And I, you, sweet girl. But I'm strictly here on business."

My heart fluttered for a second, wondering what palace business she meant.

"Prince Asher is distraught without you. He made a mistake in letting you go, Zia."

Wow, she really went straight for the heart. I sighed, gesturing for her to sit down in the kitchen.

"Mom, Dad, this is Laurel. My mom away from home." She laughed and greeted my parents cheerfully, her pink cheeks glowing. My mom immediately placed a hot cup of tea and an ambrosia cake in front of Laurel.

"Now, enough distractions." She sat forward, sliding her fork into the sweet cake and watching me intently.

"Sweet girl, you've seen better days yet." Her eyes ran across my face, assessing each feature, each flaw. Her mouth munching mechanically as she studied me from across the table.

"Don't I know about it?" I huffed and consciously ran a hand through my hair, my fingers getting caught in the tangles. I had to practically yank them out. I smiled sheepishly as she watched the whole debacle.

"When are you coming back to the palace?"

"I'm not," I said simply.

"Do you not miss it?" She leaned forward and quirked an eyebrow. "Or someone in particular."

My cheeks involuntarily heated at her suggestion and I glanced away, sipping my tea and not meeting Laurel's eye. The damn fae could read me like a book.

"Okay fine, yes, I miss him but he needs to prove it. He needs to be the one to come here and take my hand and show me how he feels." I huffed, folding my arms across my chest for good measure. "Plus, he's the one who said that he didn't have use for me anymore," I said quietly and my heart ached in my chest when I remembered the way he said it, the look on his face, the icy tone of his voice. It'd been the fatal blow.

"Well then, perhaps he should explain himself."

And honestly, it felt like a stupid play because as Asher stepped in through the back door, I gasped like some over-the-top actor.

"Zinnia." He said quietly and I swore my mom nearly fainted at the sight of a prince in her home. She hastily began to tidy items away, shoving pots and spoons into random drawers then obviously panicked because she'd forgotten to curtsey and dropped to her knees in some sort of embarrassing bow/ curtsey. I would have laughed at the ridiculousness of it if I wasn't so absorbed in everything that was Asher.

His hair was tied back in a low ponytail, smoothed back to show off all his beautiful features, including those pointed ears adorned in jewels. He wore a dark green jacket, one that matched his eyes and I felt as if I was gasping for air as his gaze roamed down my attire.

Wearing a plain sleeveless, black dress, I looked like I was in mourning, which seemed appropriate considering everything. Asher scanned over my body and a hint of the fire I used to feel began to flicker in my chest. He was here. He was really here in my home.

"Glad to see some things never change." Were the first words to come out of his perfect mouth. Always commenting on my appearance, yep, some things didn't change.

"If you came all the way here to insult me, you'll be greatly disappointed because your words fall on deaf ears." I retorted and a hint of a smile played on his full lips.

"We'll let you two talk it out then." Laurel

ushered my mom out of the back door, the latter basically clung on by her fingernails to watch our conversation but my dad closed the door behind them and gave me a small wink.

It was silent and it seemed to stretch between us. So many unspoken words.

"You let me go-"

"Zia, I miss you-"

We both spoke at the same time and a small laugh escaped my lips.

"You go first." He said and I gestured to the seat opposite me at the kitchen table. He slid onto the chair, looking far too regal for our common kitchen.

"You let me go, Asher. You told me I was of no use to you anymore and then you send Laurel to do your dirty work?"

He cringed at my words. *Yep, I hope it hurts.*

"You left. And I knew you'd kick me out if I tried to come close and for good reason. But I promise, letting you go was the biggest mistake I've ever made."

My heart swelled in my chest, my body was set alight by his words.

"Apart from that fake proposal in front of the whole kingdom without asking me first. That ranks as one of your biggest mistakes too, you know."

He smiled softly. "I'm well aware I have many mistakes to make up for."

"But how do you know what you feel for me isn't just lust?" My cheeks tinted pink at the thought of when lust had overtaken our minds. The kisses, the touches, the way Asher set me on fire inside and out. I ached for that time again.

"Because, *Zia*," he emphasized my nickname and a small smile graced my lips, his eyes dropped to them for a second. "I have been with many females." I frowned but said nothing. *Okay, I don't need reminding.*

"And not once have I ever felt for them the way I do for you. You're infuriating, you're hot-tempered, foul-mouthed, and yet, I cannot stand to be away from you. You're the embers that light the fire inside my heart and when you left, when you got into the carriage, those embers smoldered and burned out, leaving me cold and empty."

Heart in my mouth, I had to try and calm the way my body felt after hearing those words, the words I'd longed for, the words I'd fantasized about, coming out of his mouth. Those words were for me only. No one else. No pretenses, no charade. Just us.

"I feel empty without you too," I whispered and Asher's hand covered mine across the table. His touch sent tingles, like little bolts of lightning down my arm. I felt that all too familiar warmth again, seeing the glow between us, and looked up, surprised.

"You can heal?" I asked. He smiled smugly,

obviously glad he'd caught me by surprise.

"When you left, I was so angry. Angry at myself for not being able to stop you. Angry at Cain for destroying what trust we'd built together. Angry at Finn for fooling you and with myself for that stupid deal we'd made over something as trivial as a shirt." He shook his head.

"But after a while, I realized my anger was fueled only by the destructive sides of my magic and I needed to work on it, just as you had done, in order to learn how to grow as well as destroy. I'll admit, my Bloom magic needs work, perhaps you can help with that." I giggled, picturing Asher trying to make flowers grow on a bush and accidentally setting it on fire. "But, I'm willing to learn to look after you."

Tears prickled in my eyes, this was his way of apologizing. He was learning new magic to make sure what happened in the dungeons never, ever happened again. My heart felt ten times as big as I gazed at this marvelous fae in front of me.

"Living in the palace gave me purpose," I confessed. "It made me happier and as much as I loathe to admit it. I missed you." I spoke quietly, almost unsure of my words.

"You loathe me, do you?" Asher stood, pulling me up by my hand and wrapping his arms around my waist, bringing me close to him. My breath hitched as our bodies came into contact.

"Absolutely. Loathe, despise, detest, hate. All the

words that exist in the whole fae language."

He grinned, gently dropping a kiss on my forehead.

"As long as you can loathe only me, no one else. Then we'll be okay."

He gently rubbed the length of his nose down mine before capturing my lips with his and kissing me tenderly. My blood sang as I wrapped my arms around his neck and kissed him back.

I pulled away as a thought crossed my mind and a particularly important thought at that.

"What about your parents? Do they know about us?"

Asher looked down at me, smiling and I bit my lip, anticipating his answer.

"They do. After you left, I told them everything. They weren't pleased." His thumb came up to my face and gently released my lip from my teeth, caressing the soft skin of my lower lip as he spoke. "But, soon they realized why I'd done it and my mother confessed that she liked your company. Especially your pastries and misses them dearly, Lily's just aren't the same."

I snorted, imagining the Queen upset about Lily's poor attempt at my recipe. Yep, I'd have to do something about that. *We couldn't have an upset queen, now could we?*

"My father is less-than-pleased about me courting a lesser fae," he continued. "But I told him it was my choice and my choice alone."

Asher pulled me closer.

"Do you still see me like that? A lesser fae?" I was scared to ask, Asher had such deep-rooted prejudices and it would always be a dividing factor. I'd come more to terms with mine, with my jealousy of the upper faes and their birthrights. I was okay with my less-than-okay wings.

Asher sighed, shaking his head.

"I know, I was prejudiced and it was simply because I'd been brought up that way. It's not an excuse, just a reason. But I've come to realize and I hope in time, many other higher faes will too, that we are all the same. And Zia, you're the bravest fae I've ever met, regardless of the size of your wings or the money in your pocket." He brushed his fingers over my face, my nose, and my cheekbones. "It's *you* I want."

My heart swelled, I was glad he was finally growing and learning. Perhaps he had changed but there was always room for more development, such prejudices were hard to change overnight.

"But no more freezing me out, storming off when we argue, or blocking me out," I told him firmly and he nodded.

"I know, I didn't know how to act around you." He confessed and I frowned, confused by his words.

"But you were so nice to Flora?"

"I know that too." He sighed, looking above my head for a second before letting his gaze fall on me. "With Flora, it was easy. I knew where I stood because I didn't ache to kiss her every moment I saw her." My breath hitched at his words.

"I didn't want to fight her on every little thing just to see the character in her eyes. I didn't want to drop to my knees and worship her body. I didn't know how to act around you."

His confession had me weak at the knees and I was glad his arms were still wrapped around me, or else I'd have collapsed onto the floor in a pile of mush. Gods above, I was a wreck.

"And I knew you hated me, you resented me for the deal we'd struck. It was an awful move on my part, I'd selfishly wanted you around from the moment I laid eyes on you at Cuckoo." His hand gently began to trace circles through the back of my dress as he spoke.

"At first, I thought we could fuck it out, this intense energy between us." I almost gasped at his crude words, my stomach clenching the curse word that sounded so sinful on his lips. "Once I realized that wasn't possible. I tried to be civil with you, but Gods, Zia you tested me every moment of every day. Your temper, your words, and your spirit brought out the very worst in me.

"But from when you stormed into my room in nothing but a towel to when you lay before me

on your bed, your body aching for me, when I
tasted you and when you gave me all of you…"
His eyes fluttered shut as if he was remembering
that moment and my skin flushed bright pink as
I thought back to that time. "I wrestled with my
feelings every day. And I will spend the rest of my
life making it up to you."

Gone was the spoiled brat who looked down
on me, mocked me, and belittled me. And in his
place was someone I could picture my life with.
Sure, we had hurdles we had to face, problems
to overcome but Gods, the way he gazed down
at me, the way his forest-green eyes locked with
mine, I knew I wouldn't have it any other way.

"Is that why you refused to call me by my
preferred name?" I asked, it was something that
had plagued me for a long time.

"It started as just another way for me to stay
closed off from you, keep my distance, but when
I saw how much it annoyed you, it became a fun
game to see the fire burning in your eyes."

I smiled, even though he had pissed me off by
constantly not obliging to my wishes of being
called 'Zia', I kind of liked the way my full name
sounded when it rolled off his tongue. *I guess I'd
got used to it after all.*

"So what changed?"

"I lost you." He admitted and I swallowed back
the tears that threatened to spill from the sheer
emotion in his voice. "When you left, I knew it

had been because I'd pushed you away. That wasn't the only reason, but I think it was the final one." I nodded. "I realized all the time I'd spent antagonizing you, I'd actually fallen in love with you."

My heart leaped at his words. *Love? Yes, this is love. It's the willingness to offer forgiveness and move on, even when the ache still lingers.*

"Somewhere between the hatred and sharp words, you'd captured my heart."

I wanted to cry, I wanted to scream, and I wanted to sing from the rooftops, announcing to all of Nissa that Prince Asher was in love with me. The feeling made me giddy, I felt light as if I'd float away from happiness.

And I did really want to forgive him. But forgiveness was something that would take time, as would the wounds that still linger on me and inside me, tainting my soul.

"But I'm damaged." I breathed out, my head dropping away from his gaze and I stared at our feet, my plain slippers, flanked by his shiny boots. Absolute opposites but somehow we matched.

His finger titled my chin up to face him and I held back the tears at the tender look in his eyes.

"Don't say that, what happened to you," he paused, his jaw clenched and he shook his head. "Doesn't make you any less perfect."

I stared into his eyes and wondered if that was really what he saw.

It didn't matter what he saw, it was what I believed when I looked in the mirror. It would take a long time before I could see myself as 'normal' and not 'damaged.'

"And the fake-engagement?"

He scratched the back of his neck and had the grace to look sheepish.

"That was my attempt at trying to keep you close because I didn't want to lose you once the deal was over. I realize now that trying to keep you close is what added to driving you away."

I nodded, wondering if he'd proposed to me in private, if I'd have accepted, knowing his words weren't fake.

"This doesn't mean you're forgiven, Asher Thornleaf."

He nodded, pulling me tightly against him again.

"I'm prepared to do anything."

"Beg for me," I whispered and Asher's surprised expression made me smirk.

He pulled away and dropped down onto his knees, clasping my hand.

"Please, Zinnia Greenstem, I beg for your forgiveness."

He looked up at me through his thick lashes, my stomach warmed, sending tingles down my spine and I swallowed thickly, mentally saving the image of Asher on his knees for me. Gods, the things I wanted to do to him right now, and by the look in his eyes, I knew he was thinking the same.

He needed to learn from his behavior though, as had I. My temper and stomping my foot to get my way weren't acceptable anymore, as Asher's hot and cold tempers weren't either. We needed to learn and grow and I was willing to open myself up to doing that together.

"I'll consider it."

To my surprise, he nodded, not fighting me on it.

"And that's all I ask for right now. I'm willing to beg for your forgiveness every day for the rest of my life if that's what it takes."

I knew it wouldn't take the whole of our lives to forgive Asher, I needed time, I needed to heal both mentally and physically from my wounds. But I also needed happiness and Asher brought that and more. I wasn't ready to forgive, but I was ready to start moving on with my life, a life that no longer existed at the bakery.

Sadness flooded my heart but somehow I'd found a home at the palace. I'd gone from someone without purpose there, to someone who preferred it there. Looking around our kitchen, I knew my parents and Flora would be okay.

Another thought crossed my mind, the one that added to my hasty exit from the palace last week.

"What about marrying for an alliance, marrying a princess?" I whispered and he shook his head firmly.

"No, I refuse to do that. I've nearly lost everything, my brothers, my friends, and you. I don't care who my father wants me to marry."

He cupped my cheek with his hand. "It's *you* I want." He repeated.

Asher stood again, and as he leaned in close, I watched his mouth speak the words I never expected to hear again.

"Marry me."

My heart beat wildly but I considered his words carefully, we were just starting afresh and I didn't want to be hasty, rushing into anything, but truthfully I knew I didn't want to spend my time with anyone else.

"Perhaps in time," I said, with no hint of sarcasm or sass in my voice.

Asher nodded, pulling me close and holding me tightly, resting his chin on my head.

We had a long way to go, but right there in his arms, I knew I'd made the right decision in taking him back.

We would be okay after all.

EPILOGUE

Life in the palace was remarkably easy to fall back into. Granted, I wasn't welcomed with a marching band or a parade, but Laurel for one was elated that I'd agreed to come back. She doted on me hand and foot in the beginning until I'd told her I needed some space and she'd reluctantly let me walk to breakfast on my own.

The King and Queen didn't exactly welcome me with open arms, especially with the rumors of me being Asher's whore circulating around the city, and I had no doubt they'd reached their ears.

However, they accepted me when Asher explained mine and Flora's role in saving the kingdom from Cain's destruction. The King still spoke to me with as few words as possible, he was reluctant to have me back after everything that had gone down, including mine and Asher's deceit. But the Queen had begun to request my company for afternoon tea or a stroll around the garden. It was a start and I was grateful.

Of course, the words still often reached my ears and a few days ago, I'd told Asher that I'd heard one of the kitchen maids call me a 'whore', the next day she'd been asked to leave. I felt bad for her because really she didn't know any better, so I'd stopped telling Asher anything like that incident after that. Perhaps she'd think about what she said next time.

Lily had left, taking a job in a noble's home not far from the palace. I guessed she was ashamed of her involvement with Finn, not that she knew. Asher had told me that they asked her to stay but she'd packed her bags the very same day I'd been found. I hoped to see her one day, even just to offer her a smile and let her know that it wasn't her fault.

I took my place somewhat covering her job, and whilst making pastries for the Royal family. It was a relaxed atmosphere, nothing was expected of me and I knew my healing would take time, I was glad everyone was offering it to me.

The Queen often looked at me with pity in her eyes, especially when her gaze landed on my half severed wing, and I wondered if she regretted not keeping a keener eye on her sons. I didn't hold it against her though, she was just another fae in the whole palace who'd overlooked Cain's obsession with the dungeons and Finn's greed.

The dreams were the worst, though. No matter how much I physically healed each day, the nights were awful, filled with dark shadows, pain, and Lilac's lifeless purple eyes. I often awoke in a cold sweat, screaming.

At first, Laurel had offered to sleep in the room with me, but I noticed the dark circles under her eyes and the stifled yawns. I told her I was fine, but of course, she mentioned it to Asher and now I had a constant companion at night. I wasn't complaining though, especially when his warm arms wrapped around me and his strong body held me tightly, trying to chase the nightmares away. The dreams still haunted me, but Asher's warm embrace began to make the shadows at the corner of the room less frightening.

Today was the memorial service for Lilac and all the faes who lost their lives in the dungeons. What the total number was, I didn't ask. Every day, I thank every God above that Flora and I weren't a part of that number.

"Are you ready?" Asher called from my bedroom. As I added the flower to my hair, I gave myself one more glance over and opened the bathroom door.

Asher spun around, running his eyes down my body with a heated gaze. We stood in silence for a moment, just absorbing each other's presence. He let out a slow breath, as if he was controlling himself. I rolled my eyes and smiled.

"A lilac." He said, softly touching the purple flower that was pinned behind my ear.

"For Lilac," I whispered and he nodded, offering me his elbow.

The service was short, although a lot of the kingdom had turned out to bid farewell to our loved ones who met such tragic ends. I wished them only peace in their afterlife.

"It's time." My sister whispered in my ear as the Royal Elder finished his speech about sending their souls to the arms of the Gods.

Flora and I stepped forward. I took a deep breath, centering myself. I'd been practicing this, trying to find the energy within me again. I'd locked it away subconsciously for a while after the trauma I'd endured and so it had taken time and a lot of coaching from Cardus to get my magic to resurface.

Asher and Cardus had each taken turns helping me, encouraging my magic in small ways.

"Listen, feel, breathe it in," Cardus said, his voice distant as my ears strained to be in tune with the world around me. The buzz of the insects, the chirping of the birds, the faint clatter of dishes coming from the open window in the kitchens. My body felt every inch of the grass, each blade tickled my bare skin, my hands, my legs, my neck. The sun warmed me, sinking into my soul and I let out a deep sigh as I tried to dig around in my body for my magic again. I felt the tether, the small string in my body

and I reached out for it, but it recoiled. As it did every time I tried. I let out a frustrated breath and sat up, opening my eyes to see Cardus sitting on a tree trunk a few feet away.

"Close, but not there yet." He commented and I shook my head.

"I can feel it, but it recoils every time I try to connect." I picked at the grass, head hung in defeat. It had been weeks since the attack but somehow my magic was retreating further way from me.

"You're holding back." He said and I groaned.

"I'm not." I argued.

"You are." He tapped his head. "Subconsiously."

Shaking my head, I went back to feeling the grass as I sat on it, trying to center myself again.

"What are you afraid of?" Cardus asked and I paused for a moment, thinking hard.

"Everything," I whispered and he rose, his bones cracking as he hobbled over with his gnarled stick. He stood beside me, looking down at me as I gazed up at my mentor.

Before we recruited Cardus's help, Asher had tried hard to help me find my magic again at first, but his patience had worn thin, not at me, just generally and we'd ended up having a yelling match before he'd stormed out. Nope, we still weren't perfect. He'd apologized the next day, but my magic still hadn't surfaced and that had been a week ago.

"Your memories are in the past, that's all they are, Zia. Memories. They can't hurt you."

He was wrong, they hurt me at night, they plagued me, they tortured me with images of those horrific days and nights in the dungeons. I had no escape, no reprieve from the darkness.

"Letting go and healing is part of the process. Acceptance that was is in the past, stays in the past is an important step."

Footsteps interrupted Cradus's words as Asher strode across the lawn and the Elder bowed.

"Try again." He encouraged and I flopped back onto the grass as Asher leaned against a tree opposite, legs crossed as he watched me.

Sighing, I closed my eyes again and centered myself. Digging deeper to feel the magic. There it was, the tiny slither. Instead of reaching for it instantly, I patiently watched it, we regarded each other for a moment, me and it, two separate entities in one body. I gently stepped closer and instead of retreating as it had done before, it came closer too. We inched slowly towards one another and I opened myself up as I gently reached for it. The gasp from Asher broke me from my trance and my eyes sprang open, seeing the bed of wildflowers that replaced the grass I'd been lying on.

A smile broke across my face, I'd done it! I'd reconnected finally with my magic. Tears sprang to my eyes as I jumped up, grinning with glee. Asher ran forward, grabbing me and spinning me in a circle as he kissed me.

"You did it." He breathed, holding me close.

*Cardus cleared his throat and Asher put me down,
still holding my hand as I stepped towards the Elder.*
*"Thank you," I whispered and I reached down,
growing a small poppy in the grass and gave it to him.*
"You're welcome." He smiled.

My heart warmed at the memory, it was a
beautiful day, just like today was.

The crowd waited in silence by the freshly dug
mound of grass on the edge of the forest. Flora
lifted off into the air, floating a few feet above us
and I stood at the side, I counted to three in my
head before bending down and pressing my palms
to the churned-up soil.

I centered myself, smelling the fresh soil, hearing
the chirping of the birds, feeling the sun on my
back. Connecting with nature again was hard, I'd
spent many days in the garden, connecting with
my magic again.

Suddenly, luscious green grass sprung from the
dark ground. Thick roots sprouted up and then
dug their way into the soil, creating anchors for the
beautiful bushes and trees. Flora grasped the rising
stem and pushed her magic into it. She shone
brightly and a quiet gasp came from the crowd
behind us. It was a risk we were willing to take,
exposing her for the sake of the burial. The weather
was sunny and bright, so we thought we could play
off her glow on the sun if we needed to.

Soon the dark plot of fresh, rich soil became a
beautiful garden, wildflowers sprouted from the

ground, Flora nurtured the trees' growth until they stood tall and proud, thick with leaves and vegetation. And, just at the end of the plot in a far corner, I gently grew one more plant, one that mattered to me more than the others; a lilac bush.

Applause rose from the crowd as Flora and I finished our work. It was beautiful, a tribute to the faes who lost their lives for no reason other than greed.

A wiped a stray tear from my cheek, Asher grasping my hand softly and I whispered a sweet farewell to my friend.

I hoped she was safe and wasn't suffering wherever she was.

～

The room was bursting full of faes, both upper and lesser alike, chatting, listening to the gentle music from the enchanted harp, or simply sitting and reflecting.

Asher held my hand from the far end of the room, where the throne sat as we watched the kingdom share this day together.

The class divide had always been an issue and would not be fixed overnight, but the losses on both sides brought them together, united in their grief.

Asher gave my hand a little squeeze, bringing me out of my trance and I noticed him gesture to the throne.

"These are delicious, Zia. Please pass on my compliments to your family." His mother complimented and I smiled.

"Thank you, Your Majesty."

My mom had got her wish; to bake for the Royals. She'd catered for every fae in the room and I'd heard from Flora that she'd worked tirelessly, so wound up about the food that she'd slept in the kitchen for a week.

I hoped it was everything she wanted and more. My eyes caught on my family in the crowd and I noticed the beaming smile on my mom's face. It could light up a whole room.

I stepped closer to Asher, tucking myself into his side and I peeked up at him, smiling contently.

"Marry me." He whispered. He'd been asking me nearly every day for the last month and every time, my answer had been the same; *perhaps in time*.

But today, as I watched the kingdom before us, watched the beauty and the pain, as I felt his caring touch around my body. I knew it was time for a different answer.

"Yes."

If you loved *His Wicked Games*, please don't forget to
te and/ or review it on Amazon and Goodreads.

You can find Violet E.C on Instagram, TikTok, Face-
ook and Twitter.

You can also contact her at violet.e.c.author@gmail.
m

Acknowledgements

Thank you, thank you, thank you for following Zia and Asher's story. It's been a long haul and not without heaps of writers' block, but they were such fun characters to write about.

There are so many people to thank, and usually I'd list them all but for this book, I'll just say you know who you are and my appreciation goes much further than just my words.

Lastly, thank you all for the constant support. Every purchase, every share, every review about my work is so kind and helpful.

Big love to you all and stay tuned for the next novel!

- **Instagram:** @violet.e.c.author
- **TikTok:** @violet.e.c.author
- **Twitter:** @Author_VioletEC
- **Facebook:** @violet.e.c.author

Or drop me an email at violet.e.c.author@gmail.com
Much love x

If you enjoyed *His Wicked Games*, check out the first
hapter of *Inferno*, the first in Violet's urban-fantasy
omance series *Hell On Earth*.

Chapter One:
Escape

Ten Years Ago

The hallways buzzed with a flurry of students, as the bell rang and the classes were dismissed for the day. Students flooded the corridor in a hurry to leave the dingy building that was Neverfield High School.

Mary sat on the closed toilet lid, staring at the graffi-tied door of the stall, clutching her bag strap as she lis-tened to the hubbub outside. She hated the crowds, the noisy students, and the slamming of the hollow, metal locker doors, but most of all, she *hated* Dante Enfer; her own personal bully who created her own personal Hell whenever he could... Which meant basically every waking moment at school.

Dante was an all-around bad boy; with his leather jackets, inky black hair, insanely sculpted torso, and his motorcycle, he made all the girls swoon and all the guys green with envy. He had everyone's attention, was good at pretty much anything he tried, plus he had looks to die for. Literally.

For some reason unknown to Mary, Dante loved to pick on her and only her. At first, she thought it was because she was quiet, worked hard, and didn't cause any trouble. Then she considered that maybe he was dumb and he was picking on her because she was smart. But when she saw his test scores in class, that debunked her theory. She couldn't understand why he had such a vendetta against her, but she'd stopped trying to understand a while ago. Dante was a mystery she wasn't willing to solve.

She mainly tried to avoid him like the plague. In the beginning, her grades had suffered because she flunked every class she shared with him, which she quickly realized was nearly all of them. How was it that they had almost the exact same schedule?!

So she settled for just laying low, getting to class on time so Dante couldn't tease her before the teacher arrived, and leaving exactly when the bell rang, so she could be out and into the next class before he could lay a finger on her. And if she had spare time? The girls' bathroom seemed like a safe place to go.

However, today, she needed to get home to her dad so she could help him cook dinner for the pastor and his wife from the neighboring town. Every month, her dad hosted a dinner, mainly for the local pastors, but sometimes for the Mayor or the Sheriff. Her dad was a social butterfly in the community, unlike Mary who tended to prefer her own company.

She couldn't be late this time, so she took a deep breath and darted out of the bathroom, into the throng of smelly, overexcited teenagers. Normally she'd have Ally, her trusted sidekick and best friend who was, if not a bit weird and experimental, her most loyal and truest friend.

Her extracurricular activities aside, she was a badass chick who'd kick some serious butt if Mary asked her to. All butt apart from Dante's however, because though she didn't like him, she believed it was better to be at the right hand of the Devil instead of his enemy, so she was civil with him. Plus she said he was "too hot" to be mean, whatever that meant.

But today Ally was with her boyfriend Mark, skipping classes. *They're probably somewhere getting high and having sex in the back of his crappy car.* Mary grumbled as she pushed in front of a tall boy who was blocking her path.

Mark was what Mary considered a bad influence, he was friends with Dante and his boy band gang so she didn't approve, but Ally was head over heels, so all Mary could do was smile and feign interest when her best friend rattled on about all the "cool" things Mark did.

It was February, so partway through the semester. The weather was cool, but not freezing cold, even so, Mary pulled her jacket tighter as she navigated the halls.

She'd heard along the grapevine that a party was happening at Jesse's-another of Dante's minions- on Saturday. She couldn't care less for him but she did like parties, so maybe she'd show face for a couple of hours for free food and good music.

Whilst contemplating the party and what she'd wear, Mary made a beeline for her locker, hastily pushing her way through the crowd. Boys were whooping, laughing and high-fiving. Girls were giggling and discussing their weekend plans. It was the usual high school scene.

Her locker was in sight and she breathed a sigh of relief at the blue metal door. She could be out of the school building in the next few minutes and on her way home for the weekend. Just as she squeezed past some skaters lounging around the lockers, a leather jacket, and t-shirt-clad, broad chest blocked her path. Mary internally groaned, steeling herself for more teasing and bullying from the Devil.

So close and yet so far away from freedom for the weekend, Mary swallowed thickly as she stared at the floor, refusing to make eye contact.

"Where you off to Mary Mary, quite contrary?" Dante always mocked her name, saying it with a distaste that made her clench her teeth in anger. She stayed silent, mentally thinking up ways to murder Dante; ballpoint pen to the eye, heavy chemistry book to the head...

"Got nothing to say?" He interrupted her murderous thoughts. "But Mary Mack, you always have an answer for everything."

Mary stared into his chest, she would *not* meet his cruel eyes.

All he ever did was mock her.

She never stood up to him though, telling herself not to stoop to his level and that he'd get bored of her if she gave him no reaction. It'd worked in the past, but recently, it was difficult to pretend like he wasn't bothering her. It was *every freaking day.*

Dante ran his eyes over Mary's small form, taking in her halo of white-blonde hair scrunched up into a messy bun on top of her head, her jacket and jeans, her white knuckles as she tightly gripped the books in her hands.

Her downcast eyes stared at the floor and he resisted the urge to pull her chin up to meet his. He wanted her attention, he wanted her eyes on him, he wanted to see sweet hurt in her honey gaze when he called her mean names. Yep, he was a dickhead.

Dante balled his fist, his nails digging into his palms. He'd resist touching her. *For now.*

"If you want to get to your locker, then you need to know the password." Jesse, Dante's right-hand man, had the personality of a middle schooler. His jokes were immature and dumb, but they made Mary feel like an idiot nonetheless.

She sighed and turned on her heel, deciding that she could forfeit her other books and catch up on homework early on Monday morning.

However, Dante was not letting her go without a fight, and he quickly stepped in front of her, blocking her other exit.

Dante's eyes were alight with cruel excitement, he loved to rile Mary up and by the sound of her quick-ened heartbeat, he knew she was starting to panic. A wicked smile stretched across his cheeks.

Mary ground down her teeth and turned around,

she quickly darted for the locker again, her shoes squeaking on the Lino floor. Dante was faster. *Always faster.*

Exasperated, Mary pushed against his arm which stuck out as he leaned against the wall. His arm was like solid metal, it had no give and Mary wanted to sink her nails into the sleeve of his leather jacket and tear it off. She wanted to make him bleed for all his mean jabs and bullying behavior. She wanted to scream in frustration as these idiot boys made her feel like shit. A crowd was forming around the two of them, high schoolers looking for any drama in their lives and hoping for a fight.

After burning a mental hole into Dante's t-shirt, Mary tilted her chin up and finally met his eyes for a brief second. Her heart beat a little too quickly as his dark, smug gaze burned into hers and she blamed it on the situation, rather than acknowledging his good looks.

Thick, dark curls brushed the collar of his jacket, framing his face. His angular jawline, perfectly straight nose and heavy brows accentuated his piercing eyes. He really was a work of art.

He's a bully and I'm his victim, she reminded herself. *It doesn't matter how hot he is. He's still a jackass.* Her gaze fell back to his chest as anger simmered in her blood.

A lazy smile covered Dante's full lips, his eyes glinting with enjoyment as he challenged her. A quick look at her silver eyes showed him a slight look of defiance mixed with fear. Exactly what he was looking for.

They stood in stalemate and Dante grinned at his friends, knowing they enjoyed teasing Mary as much as he did. They laughed back and the group of high school kids around them watched on.

"Just leave me alone," Mary mumbled quietly, tired of fighting. She just wanted to go home, curl up in her bed and never leave the house again.

"I didn't catch that. What did you say?" Dante's voice was obnoxious and loud, a few students snickered.

"Leave me alone," Mary said, her voice a bit louder this time. She didn't dare punctuate her words too much in case he decided taunting wasn't enough and started physical violence. She didn't know how far he would take his bullying and she wasn't planning on finding out any time soon.

Stooping down to her level, Dante got up close to Mary's face. She held her breath, heart thumping in her chest, terrified of what he might do. She could smell cigarettes on his breath, the musky aftershave he wore, the distinct scent of leather from his jacket. His hand snaked forward and he gripped her chin hard, hard enough to bruise. His skin felt hot and electric on her own and Mary tried not to think about how much his touch affected her.

It's fear, that's all. Nothing more, nothing less. She chanted over and over in her head in an attempt to calm her wild heart.

She was forced to look at his eyes again, and her heart thundered at his smoldering charcoal with a ring

of red around the iris- a color she'd never seen in anyone else. Dante's eyes were unique, only his, just like
her own silver ones. Her gaze accidentally dropped to
his full lips and she quickly looked away, jerking her
chin from his vice-like grip, pretending like he wasn't
bruising her milky skin.

Dante's eyes blazed, he was enjoying his little game.
Riling Mary up was his favorite pastime. Yeah, he
could get any girl in school, but it seemed that Mary
was immune to his good looks and bad-boy charm,
and that meant a challenge. Which he had yet to
conquer.

"Make me." He whispered in her ear, his hot
breath tickling her skin.

Mary blushed furiously, angry at herself for talking
back at him, challenging him in his stupid games.
She'd escalated it and that was stupid. This was the
first time she'd actually stood up to him and unlucki-
ly for her, he loved it.

"Whatcha gonna do, Mary Mack?"

She clenched her jaw at his nickname, silently
cursing the world for putting Dante on this Earth
at the exact same time as her. Her fists trembled and
she gripped her books so tightly that the hard edges
dug into her palms painfully. She felt her skin get hot
under her clothes like she was burning up. Glancing
down at herself, she noticed a faint glow on her skin.
No one else would've noticed, but she did.

This had been happening more often than not,
but she'd been keeping it quiet, perhaps it was the

fluorescents? *Best to blame it on the lights than end up in the nuthouse for saying you have glowing skin,* she willed herself to calm down. She needed to get out of there and fast. She didn't need anyone else noticing the weird glowing thing right now.

In a flash decision, with no hesitation, she shoved Dante's chest.

Hard.

Her push caught him by surprise and caused him to stumble backward into the lockers with a metallic thud. Without checking to see if she'd managed to cause any damage, Mary legged it in the opposite direction as fast as she could.

The crowd of students parted for her like the Red Sea and she sprinted out of the double doors that led to the car park, shoes skidding on the concrete. Her heart thudded, her breath coming out in short puffs as adrenaline spurred her on. Without looking back in fear of seeing Dante's face again, she spotted the yellow bus and leaped onto it, taking the steps two at a time, not stopping until she was all the way at the back.

Her chest heaved with adrenaline and fear. God, why had she done that? Why did she have to shove Dante? She mentally cursed herself for being so stupid.

She slid down in her cracked, vinyl seat, trying to remain inconspicuous and she opened a book in her hands, pretending to read, but also covering her face in case Dante decided to check the bus.

Her heart jackhammered in her chest as she watched the bus door around the edges of her biology book, anticipating Dante to appear at any moment and drag her off as she clawed at the sticky vinyl seats, leaving nail marks down the bus's interior. Exactly like a horror movie.

Luckily, the bus lurched forward and turned around, driving away from the school before her imagination could create any more cliché high school horror scenes.

Mary hesitantly glanced over her shoulder, back at the school entrance and her eyes caught Dante's. He was standing at the double doors, arms folded across his broad chest, eyes narrowed to slits, his mouth set in a hard line.

Do you know that saying "don't poke a bear"?

Well, Mary had just hit a very angry bear with a taste for payback and she was first on his hit list.

Inferno is available on Amazon in e-book and paperback.

Printed in Great Britain
by Amazon

15274664R00222